Also by Noire

G-Spot

Candy Licker

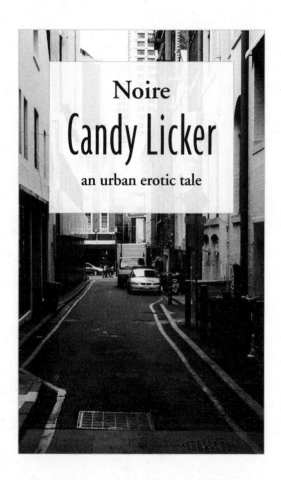

Noire
Candy Licker
an urban erotic tale

one world ballantine books
new york

Published in the United States by One World Books, an imprint of The Random House Publishing Group, a division of Random House, Inc., New York.

ONE WORLD is a registered trademark and the One World colophon is a trademark of Random House, Inc.

ISBN 0-7394-6237-7

Printed in the United States of America

Text design by Laurie Jewell

This book is dedicated to urban
scribes far and wide.

Shake the dirt off ya shoulders and
keep doin' the damn thing.

N O I R E

Acknowledgments

All props go to the Father above for blessing
me with the ink that flows from my pen.
Thanks to Missy, Jay, Man, and Tyrone for
having my back 24/7. To Reem Raw, keep
spittin those lyrics and don't forget about me
when you blow UP! And to Harlem's Nasty
Nisaa, keep laughing at the posers, ma.
We know they can't handle your flow!

STAY BLACK.

NOIRE

WARNING!

This here ain't no romance
It's an urban erotic tale
Real life, straight, unscripted
Which 4 some of us is hell

If truth and violence scares U
Then this story ain't 4 U
But someone's out there hurtin
Cuz they know these words are true

In this tale I give U
tribulations large and small
The streets are grimy, cash is king
And young girls take a fall

Folx chillin in the suburbs
Sucking on a silver spoon
Pretend this shyt don't happen?
Well yo azz is 'bout to swoon.

But 4 urban soldiers living on
The front lines every day
I speak your truth and sing your song
Cuz real's the only way

So this here ain't no romance
I'ma say it once again
It's an urban erotic tale
Not no bullshyt CNN

NOIRE

Candy Licker

In the beginning . . .

Have you ever laid down with a man and wasn't sure if you'd ever get back up? Tossed the sheets with a bone-knocking fear that only a cold-blooded hustler could produce? Sexed him like your life depended on it, because, in reality, it did? You still with me? Then let's roll over to my house. Harlem. 145th Street. Music and madness. Dollars and deals. Step inside the hottest recording studio on the East Coast while I put you up on what's real. Grab a seat and brace yourself as I show you the kind of pain that street life and so-called success can bring. My name is Candy Raye Montana. I lost my dreams in the House of Homicide. The house that Hurricane built.

Chapter 1
Money, Lust, Fame

It was a little after one on a Friday night and mics were on fire at the House of Homicide. Junius "Hurricane" Jackson was Homicide's CEO, producer, and all-around king niggah in charge. Hurricane commanded mad respect on the streets of New York City, and even the most thugged-out criminals feared him like the badass hustler that he was.

The House of Homicide was located smack in the middle of Harlem, on a block that stayed live twenty-four hours a day. It was originally built as a neighborhood movie theater, but when Hurricane started running things, he converted it into a hot nightclub/recording studio that attracted hundreds of ballers, rappers, and hopeful wannabe artists looking to get on a stage and get paid.

Every superhead in Harlem wanted to be down on Homicide's tip. The crack fiends, the teenage baby mamas. The video hoes who were lost and turned out.

"That Cane niggah is *hard*!" they'd laugh as they lined up half-naked outside the studio, posing and shivering in the cold, just dying to get a spot on his latest video shoot. "Let that rich motherfucka put the camera on me. I'll rock my ass so hard he'll forget his mama's name!"

Yeah, Hurricane was a living legend in Harlem, and he had his House on lock and under total control. He was a genius when it came to recognizing raw street talent, and he dominated the music industry so viciously it made those cats over at Crunk Cuts and Ruthless Rap look weak and broke-down.

Hurricane was in deep with the Mafia too, and they gave him a lot of rope. He strong-armed a bunch of small businesses and laundered Mob money through almost all of them, especially the corner liquor store he owned and his rib joint that was right next door. He played the role of a community leader and all that too. You know, giving out free turkeys during the holidays and sponsoring bookmobiles and things like that for the kids in the hood. He had fat knots in his pockets and was even known to organize street cleanups and pay people's bills when they got too far behind. But nothing went down in Harlem that Hurricane wasn't involved in. No deals got made, no pussy got sold, no dice got tossed. Nobody so much as rolled a blunt unless Hurricane got his cut.

Hurricane had mad pull from coast to coast. In the time that I'd known him he'd signed some of the hottest singers and rap artists from L.A. to Miami and snatched them into his camp. A few artists he straight stole from other labels, and some he actually got honest. But no matter how they got here, the minute they put their name on the dotted line their asses belonged to the House of Homicide, and Hurricane Jackson became their don, their daddy, and their dictator.

This Friday night was starting out just like any other. I was chilling downstairs in one of the recording rooms with two hopeful artists, Jazzy and Danita. Friday nights were fresh-talent night at the House of Homicide. The House was packed, and rappers and video hoes were lined up out the door and around the corner waiting for their chance to jump in the pit and impress Hurricane.

Jazzy had been here once before, but it was Danita's first night in the House. Since we were sitting around waiting for the pit to go live, we decided to kill some time listening to some bootleg mix tapes somebody had brought in off the streets. I'd watched both of these chicks rehearse the tracks they were gonna perform in the pit tonight, and they didn't sound half bad. The problem was they were regular. Didn't nothing stand out about them except they asses. I knew exactly which rooms they would end up in, and it damn sure wasn't gonna be no mic room like they were hoping.

Jazzy was the cutest of the two and she was rocking a pair of Donna Karan shorts that were so tight the V between her legs looked like a camel toe. Danita was just as hot. She sported a fly little Rocawear miniskirt that clung to her thighs and rode up her hips every time she moved. Upstairs, the music was banging and the party was in full charge. The way Danita and Jazzy were flossing I could tell they were ready to rush up the steps, grab a baller, and get crunk in the middle of the mix.

"Damn, Candy," Danita said, winding her hips and slurping from a cold bottle of beer. "I ain't into no bitches, but you one lucky heffah! Booming body, pretty red hair, blue eyes, light chocolate skin . . . I see why that niggah Hurricane got you laced up so lovely. Do you, boo! If I was laying up with Hurricane I'd be iced out and cutting hits left and right too. But just wait till your niggah hears some of *my* rhymes. I'ma press his ass *out*!"

I just nodded and thought about Dominica and Vonzelle, my girls from Scandalous! We was fresh and hot like Jazzy and Danita at one time too, so I understood what kinda cloud their heads were stuck in. Born singing, I'd had visions of being a superstar for as long as I could remember. But hard knocks and cold men had taught me a little somethin' about the music business that Jazzy and Danita must didn't know. These chicks couldn't see past the obvious. The bright lights, iced-out jewels, expensive cars . . . all this shit came with a price on it, a price that sexing Hurricane had taught me I couldn't afford to pay.

◇ ◇ ◇

I'd met some pretty mean niggahs during my travels, but Hurricane Jackson was the first one to show me what real pain was all about. Hurricane held a lease on my life. He'd paid the Mob cash money for my ass, and his word and his protection were the only things keeping me alive.

I got my first taste of Hurricane's cruelty while I was laid up naked in his bed, and the minute I saw what he was working with I knew my shit was fried. The niggah was a bonecrusher. He had a body like Mr. Universe. Mike Tyson didn't have shit on him. Swole chest, twelve-pack stomach. Muscles everywhere. But it was mainly for show. Sex with Hurricane was all about Hurricane, and he got his pleasure by seeing other people in pain. No tonguing me down or licking my neck. That was the last thing on his mind. He didn't even stroke the poon-poon or worry whether or not it was wet. Nope, fucking Hurricane was unlike anything I'd ever known, and I would find out the hard way that his foreplay was even more destructive than his name.

Don't get me wrong. Ain't nobody out here perfect, but there are some brothers who been blessed with gifts that can make a sistah climb the walls. Hurricane, too, had been blessed in a lot of ways. He was powerful, he was rich, he was fine, and everybody knew he had crazy musical talent. But none of that shit made up for what Hurricane was lacking, and a deficiency like the one he had, especially in a such a big, strong, buff-ass man, was enough to turn even the most mellow niggah into a raging maniac. Yeah, Hurricane Jackson had a whole lot of things the average brothah could only dream of, but what he was missing was the one thing all his money and his power couldn't buy him.

A dick.

◊ ◊ ◊

The first time Hurricane took me home to the banging mansion he kept on Long Island, nothing in my life had ever impressed me more. About a thousand niggahs lived up in there with him, but I didn't care.

He was rich.

His place was a palace compared to the holes I'd lived in. The windows were paneless and made of flat dark glass, the ceilings were twenty feet high, and the floors were smoked Italian marble bordered with gold trim. Everything about his crib screamed quality and cash, and as much grief and drama as I had just been through, I figured I was due to lay back and enjoy a few luxuries in my life.

Hurricane took me inside and made sure I met the other wifeys who stayed there, and then later on that night he let me bathe in his $30,000 onyx tub. I damn near melted when I saw his huge custom-built, oversize Hypnos bed. It was sitting up on a raised platform that was down in a sunken area in the middle of the room. The top of the bed had a canopy of black and white silk curtains that were tied back with tiny silver chains. Six carpeted steps led down into the sleeping area, and six more made of smoked black glass led back up to the bed on all four sides. I felt like a queen as he kissed my neck, then held my hand and escorted me all the way up to the top.

"Sweet Candy," Hurricane whispered as he pulled back the thick towel and stared at my naked body. "Soft brown skin and"—he tangled his fingers in my hair—"sexy blue eyes. I've run through some jawns up in here, but you's a keeper."

My nature was always running hot and I couldn't wait to feel him inside of me. My nipples were aching to be kissed, and thick juices were percolating between my legs. I laid there like a fool, grinning and posing all up in those sheets, ready to go all out for the man who was gonna make me a big star.

But I figured out what kind of party it was the minute he pulled down his pants and started grinding me so hard I swore the bed would break down. You ever heard of beating a pussy until you knocked it out? Well that's what Hurricane did to mine. He raised himself up on his hands and knees, slammed his hips down hard enough to crack my pubic bone, then grinded like he was on a mission to kill somebody.

"Slow down, baby," I begged, trying to catch up with his warp-speed rhythm. I wasn't a virgin, but my young ass didn't know shit about shit neither. Yeah, I'd played a little touchy-feely a couple of times, and true, I was a professional masturbator, but nothing I'd experienced had been anything like the express train that was roaring on top of me right now. I wanted to get with him, but all that pounding was drying up my juices, so I grabbed his thick arms, squeezing his muscles, then slid my hands down his back and held tight to his trim waist.

"Wait," I whispered, spreading my legs wider as I tried my best to feel him. "Is it in yet, baby? Is it in?"

He froze.

"What you say?"

Working my hips to get in his groove, I rounded under him and rubbed his ass, letting my hands work the thick muscles of his back. "Put it in *now*," I demanded, arching my back and brushing my nipples against his hard chest, eager to get my pussy stretched out and filled up until it burst. "Go 'head and slide all a' that good dick up inside me baby!"

Hurricane moved fast. He slid his palms under my hips and grabbed one ass cheek in each hand. Then he squeezed my mounds like they were two lemons, balling his hands into tight fists and digging his fingers so deep into my booty muscles he almost paralyzed me.

I screamed.

"I said, what the fuck did you say?"

Sweat broke out all over me and I arched my back and clenched my ass tight, panting against the pain.

"Candy!" he growled in my ear. "What the fuck did you just say?"

I honest-to-God didn't know what the hell I'd said. Whatever it was, I damn sure wasn't about to say it again. He rolled off of me and reached across the huge bed, searching for something under his pillow.

"I'ma put something in your ass," he said in a low voice. "Put something in there that'll shut you right the fuck up."

I almost screamed again when I saw what he had in his hand.

That crazy motherfucker was holding a gun.

And not one of those regular old Saturday night specials either. I'd seen this kind of gun before, it was Seagram's favorite piece. A .44 caliber Magnum with a hair trigger. The kind of shit you roll with when you wanna blow a niggah's brains out through the back of his head.

Hurricane cursed and slapped the barrel across my mouth, busting open my bottom lip. I swallowed blood and panicked when I saw the crazy look in his eyes. My teeth were clenched but he forced me to open them shits, shoving that barrel halfway down my throat, then taking it out and cracking it first against my collarbone and then dead on the tip of my elbow. I yelped and rolled over, balling up in a knot and cradling the black pain that ran from my shoulder all the way down to my fingertips. Suddenly he was on top of me again, and the cold metal was being pushed between my legs. All I could think was that the gun had a hair trigger and was gonna go off and blow me up from the inside out. I screamed and fought, but come on people. You know who had the wins. And then my pussy was being filled up for real. With something so hard and icy it got my whole body to shivering with pain. But as chilly and cold as that revolver was, just take my word for it and believe me when I tell you. It wasn't half as cold as Hurricane's heart.

◦ ◦ ◦

Jazzy and Danita both did the damn thang in the pit and came out sweating me with a thousand questions, screaming, 'cause Jay-Z and Kanye were both in the house, and feenin' like industry freaks to find out what Hurricane thought about their performance. I tried to tell them to play it chill, that Hurricane knew hot talent when he saw it, and if he thought the opportunity to turn a dime was right there under his roof wasn't no way in hell he was gonna let it slide.

I know I made Hurricane sound like a nine-headed monster, but actually, he wasn't much different than a lot of other entertainment hustlers out there like Suge Knight, Irv Gotti, and even P.Diddy with his crazy self. Cane kept a posse of street-hard soldiers around him ten to twenty deep, and most of them were either bangers or stone criminals who didn't have no artistic talent but were down for whatever. They would take a niggah out real quick and then show you where the bodies were buried.

From what I'd heard, Hurricane had pulled a little bid upstate for killing a drug dealer. It was up there that he made all the connections that helped him launch his record label and finance the hooked-up studio that we were chilling in right now. The real deal was that Hurricane had done something a whole lot of other hustlers wished they could do. He'd gotten in good with the right people and started sticking his fingers in all kinds of pies. Them Italians was the ones who had fronted him the seed money to build his empire, and in return he set his boy Tonk up as Harlem's number one drug distributor and used his Mob connections to make all his buys. Hurricane kept the Mob money fresh and clean by washing it through his label, cooking the books on his artists, and producing underground porno videos and selling them by the thousands as adult entertainment.

Of course I didn't hip Jazzy or Danita to none of this. The fact that I knew about it myself was bad enough, and if Knowledge hadn't been Hurricane's right-hand man and the genius behind his financial empire, a whole lot of things would have caught me blind.

"Do you work anywhere?" I asked Danita as she finger-combed the weave that was hanging down to her ass and long enough for her to sit on. "I mean, you got a job to fall back on if this don't come through, right?"

"Nah." She shook her head. "All I'm working on is my singing career. I got a baby girl and my mama works. I can't find no job that'll pay for day care, so I stay with my daughter during the day and my mama keeps her at night."

I didn't have no babies, but I knew all about working on a career because I'd worked a man's job just so I'd have enough ends to chase one.

I'd signed on as a money mule for the Gabriano family when I was just seventeen, and while the stakes were high, the payoff was lovely. Just like the two girls standing in front of me, I'd been as dumb as they come. Fresh off the corner, I didn't know a damn thing about interstate trafficking. But I was tired of fighting off horny foster fathers and getting my ass felt by a bunch of play-play brothers. Daddy had been dead for years, and Mama was living in a homeless shelter at the time so she wasn't no help. The only other family I had was my baby sister, Caramel, and she was in foster care too, somewhere out in

Queens. I was at one of those frustrated points in my life where anything could have happened. I could have swung to the left or jetted straight to the right. Nicky Gabriano had come along like a life preserver, and getting in with his crew was a stroke of pure luck. The good thing was, I had enough smarts to know it.

◇ ◇ ◇

The first time I heard the name Homicide Hitz, my girl Dominica Santiaga was screaming it in my ear.

"Did you hear what the fuck I just said, Candy?" she shrieked through the telephone, calling me at my crib in L.A. "I got a call from some chick who works at Homicide Hitz! She said they checked out our demo, and they wanna see what else we got! Girl we about to get a contract and make Destiny's Child sit their skinny asses *down*!"

Dominica was a fast-talking Hispanic girl I'd met in foster care. She'd ended up in the system 'cause she snuck out her window one night to go sing in a talent show and got back just in time to catch her house burning down and her whole family going up in the flames.

"Calm down, Dominica!" I said. "And stop talking so damn fast. Who checked out our demo, and how the hell did they get it?"

She sucked her teeth and I could tell she had her hand on her hip. "Hurricane Jackson, stupid. I ran into one of his boys at a show and slipped it to him."

"Hurricane Jackson?"

"Yeah, Hurricane. You know the fine-ass Hurricane who owns the House of Homicide in Harlem? The baddest record label in the nation? You ever heard of Big Joe or that new kid

Dolla Bill? Hennessy? Too Tall? What about Dead Moon, that hot group from Brooklyn that came out this year on his new Homicide Hitz label?"

Dominica was steady talking, but I was so shocked I couldn't answer her. Hell yeah I knew who Hurricane Jackson was. Didn't everybody? He had shit on lock all over New York and way out here in L.A. too. I just never thought we'd get close enough to make a bleep on his radar screen, let alone get him to check out our demo.

We had started singing together in foster care—me, Dominica, and our girl Vonzelle. Dominica was real pretty with big titties and a high ass, and she was also loud and ghetto. Vonzelle was just as bad, but she was sneaky and ten times prettier. She was originally from the Bronx but ended up in foster care after her mother OD'd and her and her baby brother sat locked in a room with the dead body for two days watching it rot and swell. All of us had been through some shit and none of us had had it easy, but Vonnie was the worst in our bunch. She was slick and conniving, and I swear sometimes I'd look in her eyes and see some wild shit lurking there that scared me 'bout to death.

We'd hooked up together and formed a group we called Scandalous! and when I left New York and moved out to L.A. my girls thought I was gonna flake out and leave them hanging, but I didn't. I made sure that every trip I took to the East Coast we got in some studio time, and we'd just finished recording our demo a couple of weeks earlier.

"So what now?" I cut in as Dominica flapped her tongue in about three different languages. "What does he want us to do now?"

She laughed. "He wants us to get our asses down to the House of Homicide for an audition, Candy! Next Friday at ten. The chick on the phone said he was thinking about offering us a little something in writing." Excited, Dominica screeched loud enough to bust my damn eardrum. I wanted to curse her out, but instead I laughed right along with her 'cause I was just as happy as she was. "I gotta call Vonzelle and tell her this shit," she said. "In the meantime get your chocolaty-red ass back to New York real quick so we can get in there and tear Hurricane's muthafuckin' House of Homicide *down*!"

◊ ◊ ◊

When I look back on how things went down tears come to my eyes just from thinking about my girl Dominica. She didn't deserve the terrible shit she ended up getting, and my heart twisted up when I remembered our last ride.

I followed Jazzy and Danita upstairs shaking my head. For a hot second I started to sit those two young chicks down and put them up on what was real. Hell, there wasn't no damn recording contract in their future. The most either one of them could hope for was a photo shoot for the porn calendar Hurricane put out every year or maybe a spot in one of them triple-X videos he shot and circulated underground. At best one of them might get picked as an extra ho when Hurricane produced his next video for a hot artist, but a recording contract? They had a better chance of being hit by a speeding train or getting dicked down by a vicious dog.

Something in me really wanted to tell Jazzy and Danita to jet. To warn them that the House of Homicide was really a house of horrors, with young girls like them being nothing but expendable victims. I wanted to tell both of them to head straight toward the door and put as much ground between them and Hurricane Jackson as they could. But? And? Then what? Nobody had bothered to school my ass on the way in, and even if they tried, I'd had industry fever. I was hell-bent on becoming a big-time recording star, and all the schooling in the world wouldn't have mattered.

It had taken me way too long to figure out that it ain't about how high you climb in the music business. It's what you give up in the process. It only takes a split second for things to go bad in this industry, and Hurricane played the game so well his empire was stacked strong and tall. A lot of people ask me how I got here, and others wanna know why I stay. So I'll just give it to you raw and dirty, the same way it was given to me. How 'bout I put you up on square one so you can see for yourself how it all began. Take a look at what went down before Hurricane grabbed hold of my world and spun it around like a tornado, totally out of control. Check out this snapshot of what my life was like before the passion and the pain. Before the money and the madness.

Chapter 2

Back in the Day . . .

Back in the day, I dreamed of becoming a hip-hop superstar. Salt-N-Pepa, Mary J. Blige, Faith Evans, Aaliyah—those were the singers I idolized and looked up to because for as long as I could remember, gripping a microphone in front of a million screaming fans had been my one true desire.

By the time I was seven or eight I was making mics out of toilet tissue rolls. I'd tape those cardboard tubes together and sing until my throat got sore. Back then, Mama was my biggest fan. You know how some people are all the time bragging 'bout having some Indian in them? Well my mama really did. Mama told me she was one quarter Cherokee, one quarter Navajo, and two quarters African. She had beautiful reddish-brown skin and thick jet-black hair that hung down her back in waves. And Mama had one of those all-the-way live bodies too. Her frame was graceful but curved out to the max. Mama's skin and hair mighta been mostly Indian, but her hips and ass were definitely African.

While I sang into those toilet tissues rolls and pretended to be onstage, Mama would sit on the coffee table smoking a blunt and guzzling Bacardi and watching me get down. "Damn my doll baby can sang! Work that stage, Candy Raye!" she'd scream at the top of her lungs. "Work that whole muthafuckin' stage!"

Then she'd jump up and snatch my cardboard mic and give me a drunken demonstration. "You gotta move them hips, little mama. Feel the beat deep down in the bottom of your coochie and *move* them damn hips like they on fire."

I was just a shy little kid and we were poor and raggedy, but when me and Mama sang and danced together, our living room became the main stage at Madison Square Garden and money didn't mean a damn thing. So what, we moved every other month from a roach-infested apartment to a rat-infested room to keep from getting put out on the street? So what, me, Mama, and Caramel slept huddled together on a lumpy mattress to keep warm every night? So what, I went to school dressed in grimy jeans and shirts fastened in the front with three fat safety pins? So what, we ate cornflakes mixed with cold water for breakfast and sometimes for dinner too? When me and Mama did our thing it was all about the vocals and the beat, and nothing ugly or crazy about my world could touch that.

But me and Caramel got hooked on the streets early because Mama kept us out there with her all the time. At night when other kids our age had been washed and fed and snoring for three hours, Caramel and I would still be hungry and dragging behind Mama. Going from bar to liquor store, dope house to card party. At the age of eight I saw hoes getting their asses beat, men getting shot up and stabbed, and one time we were sitting in one of the houses Mama used to work from when a woman bust up in there looking for her man and ended up with a butcher knife in her chest.

She bled out right there on the floor near the spot where me and Caramel were sitting, and I watched that lady's soul leave her eyes. Mama came out of a back room when people started screaming, then snatched me and Caramel and jetted for the door. The bottom of my plastic jellies stayed sticky with that lady's blood for three whole days.

Mama might not have been one of those model TV show parents, and sure, she had her faults, but she had a sweet way about her and was the prettiest woman I'd ever seen. Men stopped and drooled when she walked into a room, and sometimes the ones she brought home at night groaned and hollered out loud too.

Some nights Mama came in with the landlord. Or the butcher who cut meat at the shop down the street. Other times it was Freaky Calvin who ran numbers on Third Avenue. Every now and then it was Mr. Fred, who lived across the hall from us with his wife and six kids.

Mama danced in nightclubs, and she met a few high-rolling men who sometimes swung by with presents in big fancy whips and took her out riding. She always came home happy, and she always came home with cash money.

But Mama drank too much, and after a while the men friends dried up, so when she couldn't get a dancing job or the weather was too bad to take us out in the streets with her, Mama would "work" from home, and me and Caramel would snuggle together quietly on the floor. We'd press our noses together and close our eyes and cover our heads with a pillow until the moaning stopped and the man was gone.

"Ya'll can come on out," Mama would call as the door slammed shut. Then she'd laugh and light a cigarette and show me the wad of bills clutched in her hand. "Gone and get me a washcloth, doll baby, then get your sister dressed. I'm hungry! Y'all want some chicken wings tonight?"

This is how Mama kept a roof over our heads and managed to put a little bit of food in our stomachs too. Mama hustled hard, and she taught me a lot about survival. But as young as I was, I had already figured out something that Mama probably should've known a long time ago: Life got tricky for the girls in our hood. Hustlin' men were the ones who held the cards and ruled the money game. And if you were smart enough to luck up on the right one, he could set you up lovely and keep you straight for life.

◆ ◆ ◆

Everywhere I went as a kid, I sang. I sang to escape the hunger pains in my stomach, I sang to comfort Caramel when she was sad, I sang to make my mama feel good when she needed a drink. I sang just to keep on living.

The artist I admired most was Mary J. Blige. We didn't look nothing alike, but I went around walking like her, talking like her, and of course, singing like her. Mama had her favorite singers too, and she swore up and down that under the right light she could pass for Toni Braxton with a hooked-up weave.

Caramel couldn't sing at all, so we used to make her sit on the mattress and be our audience while we pretended we were hot stars in a talent show. Just me and Mama. We would strut around our room like long-legged runway models, singing our asses off, and then Mama would teach me how to wind my hips and do the back-alley booty-rock until my muscles got sore and I had all of her moves down pat.

Mama was real outgoing and liked to party a lot, and that's why she got dumped by Seagram, a drug dealer who worked out of the projects around our way. Seagram was into guns and had a whole collection of them. He'd carry ten, twenty pistols around in a gym bag, and he told us he had bodies on every last one of them. His favorite piece was a .44 caliber Magnum. He said he liked it 'cause it had a hair trigger, and when he drew on a niggah with a piece like that he was guaranteed to get a good hit. I was with him and Mama one night when two young heads from 125th Street tried to stick him up for his product. Seagram pulled out that long-barreled .44 Magnum and fired, leaving a hole in one of them kids that was so big I coulda stuck my entire head through his back. Mama tried to hide my eyes, but it was too late. I got so scared I pissed down my leg. Seagram was damn proud of himself though, and to this day I can still hear him laughing.

Seagram mighta been a killer, but he wasn't all that large in the drug game. That didn't matter to us. He was rich in our book, and he really liked Mama. When they were together he treated me and Caramel like princesses and gave Mama everything she asked for. Our lights never got cut off and we never went hungry. But Mama messed around with other men when Seagram wasn't watching her. She was only thirteen when she had me, and she told me she was trying to make up for all the fun she'd missed. When Seagram found out she was cheating he cut her loose and told her to step, but before he dropped her he grabbed Mama by the neck and mushed her face down in the floor and punched her in the mouth so hard he knocked out her front tooth. When Mama jumped up and tried to cut him with her knife, he knocked her back down again and pulled out that long .44. He told Mama that if he didn't love me and Caramel so much he woulda put a bullet in her head right then and there.

After Seagram cut out on us we were hungry again. Our one-toofed Mama could turn a dollar but she couldn't hold on to one, and I remember a lot of nights when she didn't come home at all. On those nights there wasn't even no cornflakes for me and Caramel to mix with our cold water.

When she finally did show up Mama was usually worn out and sick, and I would help her get undressed and lay down on the mattress while me and Caramel slept together on the cold, dirty floor. I didn't care that Mama smelled funny when she came in off the streets or that sometimes she slobbered down her clothes or threw up all over the place. It didn't bother me none that Mama had trouble finding her way to the bathroom when she drank too much. She'd walk right over to the kitchen chair or sometimes to our mattress and squat down and pee just like she was on the toilet. What did I do? I cleaned it up! I'd do just about anything for my mama. I had big dreams for us. For me, Caramel, and Mama. I was Mama's doll baby and she was my world. My love and devotion to Lovely Bird Montana was just that strong.

◇ ◇ ◇

Daddy died in jail the summer I turned ten. He'd been locked up since right after Caramel was born, and I didn't hardly remember much about him, except the color of his eyes. They were ocean-blue, just like mine and Caramel's.

Daddy was mixed, like Mama. His hair was red and his skin was dark olive. His mother was half white and half black and his father had come from Cuba, but other than that he didn't know much about his family. As a kid, Daddy had come to Harlem to stay with his aunt for two weeks and never left. Mama told me he was one of those pretty niggahs. Slick and fine. He was attracted to hard drugs and foxy women, Mama said, and if he couldn't get a woman, that was okay too. Just as long as he had his drugs.

Daddy used to skin-pop horse back in the day before crack came on the scene. Eventually he graduated to mainlining, and when he went on methadone and kicked the lady altogether, he jumped on the crack wagon and got lost in that drama just like everybody else.

Mama had told us that Daddy was sick in jail, and kids or not, she didn't put no sugar on it. "Rogelio got the AIDS," she told me and Caramel a few months before he died. "He say he got that shit from shooting dope, but if you ask me I think he got up there in that penitentiary and started taking it up the ass."

She took us upstate to see him before he died. We rode the Prison Gap bus from Columbus Circle up to the Elmira Correctional Facility, where they had him on an AIDS ward. The man in the bed looked old and shriveled up. He had about ten strands of dirty red hair slicked down on his scalp and didn't look nothing like the fine-ass Daddy Mama had been describing all these years.

Mama stood there for a long time, just staring at Daddy in a strange way. I kept quiet and held tight to Caramel's hand until Mama turned and spoke to me in her most serious voice.

"Get a good look at him, Candy. This is what sex and street life can get you. I been loose with my shit too, so for all I know I might be laying up here one day looking a hot mess just like him. But I'll be damned if I wanna see you or Caramel with it. I ain't been out here selling my pussy all these years just so you can lay down somewhere and give yours away. Remember, sex is good, but keep your coochie to your goddamn self. There'll be plenty of mens who wanna use it for they own pleasure, but you gone hafta be smarter than that! Concentrate on your career, Candy. You got a voice, doll baby, and you gotta use it. It's your only ticket out of the kinda life I've lived, so don't fuck it up. Use what you got, Candy Raye. Make something of yourself so that whatever me and your daddy had together doesn't end up being a total waste of a good fuck."

I wanted to heed her warnings, and I can honestly say I tried. The problem was, I had the same kind of high nature that she did and Lovely Bird wasn't the only one with a body that wouldn't stop.

I was a hottie to the max coming up in New York. At eleven I had an ass just like Mama's and a set of titties to match. Boys were forever trying to feel me up on the sly or pulling me under the staircase in our apartment building hoping they could get a few quick humps. I can't even count the number of times somebody's big brother tried to put my hand on his hard crotch or talk me up the stairs and on the roof to see the surprise he had for me in his pocket. I was scared of heights so that wasn't happening. Plus, thinking about the way Daddy died and seeing how Mama was living kept me slapping all those sweaty-ass male hands away.

But all that shit changed when I turned twelve. I was taking a bird bath in the sink and just happened to rub the washcloth over my pussy just the right way. What I felt made me break out in a sweat as I balled up that washcloth and did it over and over again. From that day forward, me and my clitoris were the best of friends. I touched it as much as possible, learning how to make my woman juices run down my thighs and to bring myself to immature orgasms by clitoris stimulation alone.

I got my first tongue fuck when I was fourteen. Living a life-style like mine had sexualized me at an early age, but as much raw shit as I'd been exposed to, not one person had prepared me for what it would be like when a man actually opened me up and touched me with his tongue.

I was spending the night next door with my girl Mercedes, and we'd stolen a few porno videos from her brother's stash and watched them. We laughed and squealed at the sight of all those big, hard dicks and what was being done with them.

"Oooh," I moaned as I watched some fine baller give it to his girl doggie-style. "That shit looks soooooo good!"

"Please," Mercedes said. "Me and Tony do it like that all the time. His shit's so long it feels like it's drilling through my whole body and coming up outta my throat!"

I bust out laughing with her, but I really couldn't relate. For as long as I could remember Mama had preached about having to sell her nookie, and somehow it had never got her nowhere. I had been guarding my pussy like it was platinum, and no-body had ever made me feel like a damn thing was coming out my throat.

People said I had odd coloring for a sistah, and my blue eyes always pulled mad attention. My skin was reddish brown like Mama's. Light chocolate, she used to say, with some pissed-off

Indian running through it. I had Mama's dimples and her big smile too. But the hair? That jungle of curly stuff hanging half-way down my back had come straight from my daddy's side of the family because Mama had said those half-ass crackers had some fire-red curls for days.

I didn't like the male stares I attracted and I used to hate the way I looked when I was a kid, but Mama set me straight every chance she got. "You got it going on, doll baby," she'd say as she brushed my hair up into a big curly ponytail. "Mens gonna love you one day. 'Specially niggers. Niggers can't get enough of a woman who got a whole lotta colors they ain't got. They gone think you some kinda exotic princess. Brown skin, red hair, blue eyes . . . doll baby, you Mama's pretty little rainbow girl."

Mama musta been right about what men liked because they were always trying to get with me. I wasn't pressed about it though, and I never let any of it go to my head 'cause being pretty had never stopped me from going hungry.

But like I said, I was stacked. I'd sprouted a pair of big, firm titties when I was eleven, and by the time I was thirteen I had the hips of a grown woman and an ass that could stop traffic. I had developed some strong urgings to go along with all that ass too, but thanks to Mama I was still handling my business by myself. I'd walk around horny all day, dying for that nighttime treat. Right before bed I'd cut on the hot water as high as it could go, then soap up my rag and drag it across my breasts, circling my hard nipples until my knees got weak.

Moaning, I'd slide that washcloth down my stomach and grab a handful of my hot pussy and rub slow rotations around my slippery spot, thrusting my mound into my own hand and fucking myself with my fingers until I exploded with heat and the water from the shower felt like tiny needles prickling my skin.

I was sleeping on the floor in Mercedes's bedroom when the door opened late at night. I looked up and saw her brother Sonny standing in the doorway, staring down at me. "Shhh . . . ," he said, coming in and closing the door behind him. He got down on his hands and knees and started feeling around on the floor.

"What you doin?" I said, pulling down my nightshirt as his hand touched my foot and ran up my leg.

"Looking for something," he whispered. "My movies . . ."

A second later Sonny grabbed my thigh and slid his hand between my legs, swiping my bare pussy. "Quit!" My legs snapped shut. "What the hell is wrong with you?"

"Shhh," he whispered again, smelling his fingers. "Let me taste that candy, girl. Just lemme get a lick . . ."

My pussy was on fire. After what I'd just seen in those movies and the way Sonny's tongue was sending chills through me as he pressed his face into my crotch and tickled my pussy hairs, I just couldn't stop him. I couldn't get AIDS like this, could I? His breath was hot on my clit as he pushed his tongue inside of me as deep as it would go.

I arched my back and damn near screamed out loud. Electricity vibed through my body, my nipples aching as I grabbed his head and gave that pussy up. Fuck Mama! Fuck Daddy! Sonny licked me from one end of my stuff to the other, pausing long enough to whip my clit back and forth with the tip of his tongue, then nibble on it as he gently sucked it between his lips.

"Oh, shit!" I was holding on to my blanket, whipping my

head back and forth and fucking his face to death. Mercedes was asleep on her bed and I didn't want to wake her up, but I couldn't hold back the scream that tore from me as he dicked me with his tongue and vibrated his whole mouth all over my clit.

I ain't gonna lie. I was still a virgin, but after all that hot tongue I was aching to feel something thick pounding inside my pussy, and as soon as I came I tried to pull Sonny on top of me, ready to give up everything I had. But he stood up and wiped the back of his hand across his mouth.

"Uh-uh. I ain't got no rubbers on me. Besides, I didn't come in here to fuck you no way. I just wanted to see what that candy tasted like."

I lay there in the darkness trying to catch my breath as my body convulsed over and over with the memory of his lips. For the first time in my life my sexual cravings were completely satisfied, and let's face it. What female you know can get her pussy licked once and not want it licked again? Sonny's tongue-down had become the high point of my life, and from then on out it would become a requirement for every guy who even thought about climbing on top of me. See, I'd finally found something that gave me just as much joy as singing, and I decided right then and there that any man who wanted to sample a piece of Candy would have to be a candy licker.

Chapter 3

The Hungry Years

Nicky Gabriano was a cool Italian guy. His family was tied to flower shops and bakeries and a whole lot of other lame businesses that were nothing but fronts to cover up how they really made their money: importing street drugs and washing dirty money.

I was hungry as hell the first time I met Nicky. Daddy had been dead for years and I was scared Mama might be sick too. She looked so bad and had lost so much weight that she couldn't even find a nightclub that would let her dance. Her skin had turned damn near gray, and clumps of her beautiful Indian hair were dusting the floor all over our apartment.

Things were getting critical 'cause Mama was having a real hard time bringing in any money at all, so in desperation she hooked up with this skinny junkie named Doc and started dragging me out on the streets with them to use as bait for unsuspecting tricks.

"Can't we take the night off just this one time?" I was whining one night as she pushed me down the street in front of her. We were walking toward a busy avenue and even though it was still pretty early the streets were already live. Mama and I were out alone this time 'cause Doc had gotten busted buying horse from an undercover officer and was locked up. Tonight I had a bad feeling in my stomach that I knew wasn't just from hunger. Doc was an old-school junkie who shot dope in his shriveled-up little dick. As much as I hated him at least he carried a gun and could protect us from the fools we tried to stick up every night.

"Shut up, Candy!" Mama yelled. "Just do what the hell I tell you to do."

"But Mama," I said, pushing my hair out of my eyes. She always made me wear my hair out at night, and my thick, wavy red curls hung halfway down my back. "We don't know nothin' about this neighborhood. What if something goes down? Maybe we should wait on Doc since he's the one with the gun."

Mama grabbed my arm and dragged me across the street to an empty corner. "Fuck Doc! I got me my own fuckin' weapon! Don't nothing but white folks live over here anyway, so it's safe. Besides. Lovely Bird Montana don't wait on *no* nigger! How the hell you think I was making money before Doc's raggedy ass showed up? Don't be so goddamn stupid, Candy! If you wait around on a man to turn a dollar, you'll forever be broke."

I wanted to ask Mama why she didn't just step out in the street and show her own damn titties, but I already knew the answer. She was too sick, and plus mine were better. They were big and firm and they sat straight up in the air. "I killed my titties breast-feeding you and Caramel," Mama said like she was reading my mind. "That's how much I sacrificed for you two. My titties use'ta look ten times better than yours, but y'all needed some milk and I was the cow! Don't be so goddamn un-grateful, Candy Raye!"

I stepped off the curb with my eyes cast down, shame caus-ing me to sweat. At least she hadn't made Caramel come out with us. That would have been too much for me to stomach. A few seconds later I heard a car coming toward us and then Mama broke.

"It's a white man! Pull up your shirt, Candy!" she hollered. "Hit him! Show this mothafucka what you working with!"

I lifted up my shirt and exposed my naked titties. I glanced up and the driver was staring at them so hard he almost ran into a fire hydrant.

"Pretty, ain't they?" Mama yelled as he pulled over and rolled down his window. "Turn to the side, Candy," she demanded. "See?" she asked, her eyes sparkling with pride as I faced toward the right. "She got plenty of junk in her trunk too, and guess what? That ain't no dye in my baby's hair neither! She's a red-head downstairs too!"

The man in the car was old and white, and he never took his eyes off my chest. "How much?" he asked, breathing hard.

Mama twisted her lips. "How much for what, mistah? I ain't offered you shit yet. Put your shirt down, Candy Raye. Yo, mis-tah. You a cop?"

The trick shook his head. "No . . . no, I'm not the police. Just tell me how much."

"Forty," Mama said. "And that's just to fuck her and suck on her titties. She too young to take it up the ass and she don't give no head."

Mama told him to park at the end of the side street as we both ran behind his car in the darkness. "You got fifteen minutes," Mama warned as he rolled down his passenger window and handed her the money. He motioned for me to get in the car, and when I opened the door I saw his hard little dick poking up out his pants.

"Get in, baby," Mama said. I got in the passenger seat and all I could smell was cheese. Old fuckin' cheese and an old fuckin' man.

Mama hopped in the backseat, and when he turned around like he wanted to make some noise she jumped bad. "This my fuckin' baby, gawdammit! I know you don't think I'ma let her get in no car with your old ass all by herself!"

He was so horny his hands were shaking. He reached over and yanked up my shirt, then dove in and slobbered all over my titties, sucking and licking like a maniac. His breath smelled like pissy dentures and old pus, and I almost threw up. I was pushing him away and wondering what the hell was taking Mama so long when she sprung into action.

"Freeze, mothafucka! Take your nasty hands offa her! Put them shits on top of your head!"

I looked back and saw that Mama had a cigarette lighter pressed to the man's neck. It was a regular old red Bic, and it looked harmless as hell. "Move, mothafucka," she said, "so I can set your old ass on fire."

Old boy was shook. "Please," he whispered. "Take what you want. Please. Just don't shoot me."

Shoot him? With what? I was so mad at Mama I wanted to jump out the car and leave her. Yeah, Doc was the one who rolled with the gun, but damn. Couldn't she at least have brought a knife?

"Give her your goddamn wallet," Mama said. "Pull it out

with one hand only. As soon as your other hand moves, your old ass burns."

He did like she said, passing me a wallet that looked swollen with money.

"How much in there, Candy?" Mama asked.

I opened the wallet. That shit was stuffed and bulging. "A lot," I said, and just as I turned to pass it back to her that motherfucker nutted up.

"Whore!" he screamed, and grabbed Mama's wrist. I swore I heard her bone snap as he twisted her arm and tried to pull her over the front seat.

"Ahhhh!" Mama shrieked, but she didn't lose control. She bit down on his fingers until he yelped and let go. Mama was all over that ass. She kicked off her shoe and started wailing him with it and flicking that Bic at his stringy hair. Little silver sparks were exploding all around his head.

The trick tried to go over the backseat and get her. Mama beat him all in the face with the heel of her shoe. "Get him, Candy!" she screamed for help. "Fuck his ass up!"

I rolled onto my knees and jumped in, but then he locked his hands around Mama's throat. She kept right on swinging home runs with her shoe.

I punched his old ass all in the back of his head and threw a few quick roundhouses at his face. I scratched the shit out of him too. Clawing my nails down his skin and raking them all over his wrinkled red-ass neck as deep as I could.

But he was trying to kill Mama.

She was gurgling now and barely swinging her shoe at all. I knew I had to do something quick, but nothing seemed to be affecting him because old boy was in another zone.

So I climbed on his back. I grabbed a handful of his face and felt for his eyeballs and proceeded to dig those shits out.

He bucked and screamed and tried to shake me off, but I dug my pointer fingers so deep into his sockets that I probably poked him in his brain. I guess it worked because the next thing I knew he let go of Mama and swung around to knock the shit out of me.

I felt my head crack against the dashboard and then he was on me. Choking me the same way he had just choked Mama.

I fought that fucker with a strength I didn't even know I had, 'cause all I could think about was my throat. My voice. My vocal cords. My future singing career.

I had landed in an awkward position with my head jammed between the dashboard and the front windshield. Dude was laying on top of me, his full weight pressing me down. We were close enough to tongue-kiss and I went for his eyeballs again.

He was smarter this time and pushed himself backward to avoid my clawing hands. He choked me with a fury, and I felt myself blacking out and got real scared. If Mama was already dead in the backseat and I didn't make it out either, who was gonna take care of Caramel?

I fought even harder. I tried to throw him off me and suck in a tiny bit of air, but my eyes felt like they was bulging and he was squeezing my breath away. There was nothing I could do and my struggling got weaker and weaker.

Then somebody snatched open the car door and there was a whole lot of noise. Cursing voices. A tall white man was punching the shit out of him, hitting him so hard the old trick let me go and fell halfway out the car.

"Thank you," I croaked as I grabbed my throat and sucked

in sweet, cool air. My savior had dragged the trick all the way out of the car, and I struggled to sit up and look over the backseat. Mama was still laid out, but at least she was moving. "Thank you, thank you, thank you," I whispered in gratitude, holding my throat with both hands. Tears ran from my eyes and my neck felt like it was crushed and on fire. But if I could talk, I could sing. *God, please let me be able to sing.*

"Thank me?" the tall man said, breathing hard as he propped the trick up against the side of the car. "Getthefuckouttahere." And that's when I heard the sirens coming down the block. "You two whores picked the wrong street to work tonight. Don't thank me because both of you bitches are going to jail."

* * *

As it turned out, my savior's name was Nicky Gabriano, and it wasn't until the cops had me and Mama up against their squad car that he realized how young I really was. He'd looked at Mama with disgust and called her a couple of dirty bitches for trying to prostitute her own daughter out in the streets, but he stared at me with pity.

I knew what it looked like. Nicky had no way of knowing it was all just a con, but there was no way I was gonna open my mouth and say some shit that might get me and Mama hit with even more charges. Still, Nicky felt sorry for me, and later on I would find out that he was really from L.A. and the only reason he had been in that neighborhood was because he was in New York on business and screwing some married woman who lived on that street.

Mama's shit was done. She'd been arrested for prostitution so many times that there was no way she was walking after a charge of endangering a minor, but Nicky did his best to talk the cops out of locking me up along with her. They wasn't having it. They hemmed my arms up behind my back and slapped a pair of flexicuffs on my wrists, and the next thing I knew I had been taken to central booking where I was fingerprinted, photographed, and on my way to jail. They hustled me out of Manhattan and over the bridge to Rikers Island.

I rode that prison bus with a bunch of other handcuffed criminals and cried inside the whole way. I'd heard all kinds of stories about Rikers. I just knew they were gonna throw me in a cell with Big Bertha, some Brooklyn dyke who liked redheads and was just itching to shove a broken mop handle up my coochie and make me wash her dirty thong.

Instead, they put me in the reception wing of an adolescent center where they housed young females, and I stayed there for two days. There were all kinds of girls in there, but mostly Puerto Ricans and Blacks. A lot of them tried to walk around looking hard, and I could tell some of them really were. I was from Harlem, and I'd seen cutthroat chicks like this all my life.

I kept my eyes wide open that first night. They had us in one big open bay and I sat up with my back against the wall, fighting my sleepiness and trying not to nod off. I'd already run into some man-looking female on the dinner line who called me Red and kept trying to tangle her fingers in my hair. You know I hurried up and put a thick braid in my shit quick fast and tucked the end under as far as I could get it. She didn't care. She ran her fingers up and down my braid and asked if she could measure how long it was. I told her to get the fuck out my face. I didn't want no trouble outta ol' girl, but I was running on so much fear I was ready to air her straight out if I had to.

The next morning I had a physical exam where the nurse's assistant told me to take out my contact lenses. "I don't have none," I told her. "These are my real eyes." She sucked her teeth like I was on crack.

An hour later I was sitting in an office with a social worker who asked me all kinds of questions about life with Mama. She told me Caramel was in the custody of Child Protective Services, and since I was only fifteen, I'd probably end up in their custody as well. She wanted to know how long I had been prostituting on the streets with my mother. I kept quiet and didn't tell that bitch shit. Mama had trained me better than that.

I couldn't keep my eyes open the second night, and I must have jumped up out of my sleep at least twenty times. They didn't keep inmates in reception forever, and I was steady waiting for Big Bertha to come get me and worrying if Mama and Caramel were okay.

As it turned out, Big Bertha would have to find somebody else to wash her prison thongs. I was waiting for my turn on the breakfast line the next morning when a CO yelled out my name. "Montana, Candy Raye. Go get your shit. CPS is ready for you, and your ass is outta here."

Years later I ran into Nicky Gabriano again by accident. Me and my girls were singing in a group and calling ourselves Scandalous! We were trying to finance our first demo, so I had taken a part-time restaurant job as a coat-check girl. Nicky was in New York on business and recognized me immediately.

He asked if Mama was dead yet. I said no, but told him how low the state had me living and he tore me off some nice cash along with my tip. The next day was my day off, and he surprised me when he showed up at my foster home and offered me a job that I figured would pay me enough to get out of foster hell and cut a recording demo too. I thought on his offer for about three hot seconds before I agreed.

"Smart decision, Candy," Nicky praised me as he looked around my fifth foster house with disgust. " 'Cause otherwise you'd be stuck in this pigpen eating dirt off the floor. You've got another good year or so until you turn eighteen and can leave here legally, but you're perfect for this job. Believe me, the state won't come looking for you, and if they do, they won't look long. Stick with me and you can live a whole lot better than the way you're living right now."

Hell, I didn't need no whole lotta convincing. I woulda followed Nicky into the pits of hell if it meant I'd have the money to finally make a demo. I didn't pack so much as a pair of drawers when I left neither. The next morning I snuck out of my foster family's house and jetted with Nicky to L.A., taking nothing but my singing voice and the clothes on my back, which was pretty much how I'd been traveling anyway.

When we got to L.A., Nicky fronted me some ends for a small apartment and some decent clothes, and a week later I was on my feet and on my new job. I was only seventeen, but I had the body of a temptress and soul of a woman. And thanks to Mama, I'd seen enough ugliness in the world to keep the innocence off my face.

Chapter 4

Runnin' Cash

Six months after I ditched the foster system and followed Nicky Gabriano out to L.A., Mama got her act together and Caramel was released from state custody. I was taking some computer classes at night, and the minute Mama's parental rights were restored and Caramel was back in her hands, I sent for both of them to come out West and stay in my small apartment.

Money mules made okay cash, but not no high yardage. I only carried drugs when I absolutely had to, so that meant I had to work extra hard to support the three of us. To keep some fun in my life, every now and then I would take a gig singing in small clubs, at weddings, or at a local talent show, and that helped.

But the more money I spent taking care of me, Mama, and Caramel, the less I was able to stash away to help my girls gear up for the Scandalous! demo. Vonnie and Dom were struggling too, so they understood. All three of us were consumed with getting a contract and cutting an album, and I asked them to be patient a little while longer and promised that when we did make it we were gonna be *large.*

It took Mama almost four months, but she finally got herself together and found a small place for her and Caramel that was only ten minutes away from my apartment. Mama had recently completed a drug rehab program that came with a job referral, and she managed to land a job at a twenty-four-hour convenience store that didn't pay a whole lot but kept a little change in her pockets. She was always complaining about being broke and whined about needing a cell phone, which she wanted me to pay for. She also bugged the shit out of me to let her make a few of my cash runs, but that was out of the question. The most I could do was give her a few extra dollars, help her out with her rent, and make sure Caramel asked me for the little bit of stuff she wanted instead of going to Mama.

Caramel was doing good too. She seemed to really come alive in L.A. She had started taking piano lessons while living with her white foster family, who claimed she was some kinda child prodigy in music. Mama swore to God they was right. After all, Mama had an excellent voice and Daddy used to be in a band, so music was in our blood. Caramel kept begging me and Mama to buy her a baby grand piano and hire a professional pianist to teach her full-time, but we didn't have it like that yet. I satisfied her by making a few extra cash runs to buy her a slamming electric keyboard, then gave her enough money for six months' worth of private lessons at a music store at the mall.

All in all, things were rolling for us in a way they never had before. I was satisfied mainly because we were together, but also because I was doing the things I loved most. Studying computers and working on getting a career. I had a computer manual in my hand by day and a mic in my hand by night. In between I jetted from city to city carrying Mob money, then came home and hung out with Mama and Caramel. Who could want more than that?

But then Dominica called and said Hurricane Jackson had offered us a chance to sing in his ear on Friday night. Not even the Gabrianos coulda kept me from going. Nicky only had me down for one cash run in the next week, a trip to D.C. on Wednesday morning. I decided it was the last transport they were gonna get out of me.

"Forget that transport. You should go back to New York right now," Mama encouraged me. "Opportunity is knockin', doll baby, and ya'll ain't been on a stage together in months. Get your ass back to New York and rehearse with your group, Candy Raye! This could be your big break."

"I can't, Mama," I said. "I gotta make that run next week." I saw where she was trying to lead me, but I wasn't about to follow.

"Gawdammit, Candy Raye! I swear your ass is stupid sometimes. Your mama is right here, girl! Care your ass on back to New York. You got any work that needs to be done here, *I'll do it.* You got some business you need to take care of, *I'll take care of it.* You got a run to make, *I'll make it.* I know it ain't always been that way, but Mama is here for you *right now,* doll baby."

I didn't even entertain that noise. Mama had a great life now, but who could forget she'd had such a fucked-up past? Plus, the least I owed the Gabrianos was to take the last run that I had promised them, so I'd show up on Wednesday, drop the cash in D.C., and then catch a Metro train up to New York, where

Dominica and Vonzelle would be waiting at Penn Station. We'd have a day and a half to knock the dust off our voices, and we'd be sitting pretty in the House of Homicide by Friday night.

Wednesday morning found me heading toward the airport, riding in the backseat of a bootleg taxi and praying like hell I didn't get knocked.

"Ain't you scared of what them greasy-ass gangstas gonna do when they find out you jetted back to Harlem?" my friend Lulu had asked before I left my apartment. Lulu went to computer classes with me and lived up the street from my house. She didn't get along with her moms at all, so when Mama and Caramel moved out I started letting Lulu stay with me, and she slept on my couch almost every night.

"Don't have them fools coming up in here tossing me up," she warned. "I've seen enough movies to know this ain't the kind of grind you can just walk away from, Candy. You they top carrier, girl. You know too much. Them Gabrianos ain't gonna let a prime mule like you just slip out the noose and escape under the fence."

"Don't worry about it," I'd told her. "Me and Nicky are cool like that. He'll cover for me. I'ma make this last drop just like we planned, then I'll call him from the East Coast and let him know I'm out for good. Nicky is down. He'll find somebody else to cover my runs in less than twenty-four hours."

I walked through the terminal at L.A. International and glanced at my watch. My flight wasn't leaving until eleven, so I had plenty of time. The security screening area was straight ahead, so I detoured right and wheeled my little laptop bag into the nearest restroom and looked in the mirror. The reflection staring back at me was perfect, but I was still nervous as shit, praying I didn't get busted just when I was getting ready to slide outta the game for good.

I'd flown out of L.A. International boo-coo times, but no matter how often I transported funds I always stayed on point and I never got sloppy. You could never tell when a rival was smelling you or when your own people might be hating on you hard enough to rob you or set you up.

Besides, moving drug money around was tricky. It had to be done just right. Crisscrossed and backtracked and flipped up and down and around to keep the feds from getting a good whiff and identifying a trail. You had to be able to dip in and glide out and deliver your package better than the U.S. Postal Service.

I ran my plan down in my mind just like I'd done no less than a hundred times over the past two years. The details were tight. I willed myself to stay calm and act natural as I walked out of the restroom pulling my computer case behind me and focusing all of my energy on looking normal while paying attention to every single thing going on around me.

There were two security screeners up ahead and I didn't recognize either one of them. That was cool 'cause it meant they probably didn't recognize me neither. I'd pulled off a whole lot of different looks while traveling, but the one I was sporting today was one of my favorites. Brown contact lenses, shoulder-length brown hair that had just the right amount of curl. Plain black pants off the rack at Target and a navy-blue shirt that covered my booty and had dark buttons down the front. As usual, I'd made sure nothing about me was eye-catching or memorable, which is what made me so good at this game. I knew how to tone myself down until I was able to blend into a crowd perfectly, which was something I could never do looking like my real self.

I'd fronted shit off in front of Lulu this morning, but in honesty, I had no idea how Nicky would react to the fact that I was leaving. He had taken me under his wing and personally trained me, so I was treated good by his people and got paid more than the average mule. But that also meant he was responsible for me and for whatever I did wrong. I'd seen the way the Gabriano family got down when shit didn't go their way.

A young Puerto Rican dude named Pappo used to transport for the Gabrianos a while back, but he lost his cool and got burnt out after just six months. Muling was some scary shit, and dude's nerves got so shook he started pissing all the time. In his bed, in his whip, on himself . . . Finally he realized he didn't have the heart for this line of work. Since his girl had just found out she was pregnant and he'd been smart with his money and stashed away a few g's, Pappo decided it was time to get outta the game and get a real job.

I guess Nicky and his boys figured on something different.

Three days after Pappo quit the Gabrianos, the police found his naked body at a landfill. He'd been beaten into the ground and tossed out with the trash. But not before the tips of his feet were hacked off and some of his toes were stuffed down his throat. I was out doing a major cash run to Texas when it went down, but the message was so loud and clear I coulda heard it halfway around the world: When you stepped off on the Gabriano family, you'd better step lively.

◆ ◆ ◆

I'd cleared the security checkpoint and was waiting at the gate to board my flight when I got the call. This was the most dangerous part of my job because if I got caught boarding a plane with dirty money it was all on me. If I got caught handing it over on the other side, somebody else went down with me. It didn't matter though. The penalty for transporting interstate was crisp on both ends, so I was always on alert at boarding time.

I flipped open my cell phone.

"Lucy there?"

The voice was scrambled, but I knew it was Nicky.

"Nah," I said quickly. "You got the wrong number."

Without another word I stepped out of line and wheeled my bag away from the gate. Nicky's call was a warning. Either the fake ID I was traveling under had come up hot or shit was on fire on the other side. Either way I needed to roll with a quickness, but I made myself walk naturally through the terminal and down toward baggage claim when I really wanted to break out and run.

I didn't get really scared until I took a taxi back to my apartment and paged Nicky. He called me back ten minutes later and there was seriousness in his voice.

"It was a bad flight, Candy," he said. "Hal fucked up when he gave you that ID. The feds were looking out for it and they had agents waiting on the back end."

If I hadn't been planning to quit the mule game before, I sure as hell was quitting now. I still needed to get to the East Coast before Friday, but Nicky had other plans for me.

"Forget this morning, Candy. I've already dealt with Hal and he's gonna need a wheelchair for the next six months. But I have something else for you. A one-day trip. Seattle. Your flight leaves Friday afternoon."

◆ ◆ ◆

I was nervous but I didn't see no way around it. I called Nicky back later that night and told him we needed to talk. He swung by my apartment in his fresh Peugeot and took me to an ice-cream parlor not far from my house, someplace he'd taken me many times before.

There was no other way to say it so I just broke it down to him straight. "I can't make the next run," I told him. "I'm already tied up for that day. I got other plans."

"Plans?" He licked his chocolate cone. "Break 'em."

I couldn't even look at him I felt so bad. "I can't, Nicky. I'm going back to New York. To sing. I've got an audition with a record label and I got a strong feeling it might lead to something."

Nicky stopped eating his ice cream and stared at me. He'd been good to me over the years, the closest thing I'd had to a father, really. I saw the disappointment in his eyes and I felt bad for putting it there, but I was on a mission and nobody was gonna stand in my way. My main purpose in life was to become a recording star, and no amount of muling in the world could make that happen.

He sighed and chucked his ice cream into the trash. "What?" he asked. "What? We're not taking good enough care of you, Candy, is that what it is? What more do you want? More money? A bigger place? What? Is it a car?"

I shook my head over and over. "I want to sing, Nicky. I want a recording contract."

He laughed. "You might get a contract all right. On your fuckin' life."

"I have to sing, Nicky. This could be my big chance."

"Forget it," he said. "Stay away from the recording business. They're all sharks, and they all work for me in some capacity anyway. Be a good girl. Make your drop."

"I can get somebody to fill in for me," I said real quick. "The job'll get done and shit will be smooth. I promise."

"Who?" Nicky laughed again, but I knew damn well he wasn't amused. "Who's gonna make your drop, Candy? That kid you go to school with? The one who's living with you and mooching off you for free? Oh, I know. Your mother, right? You're gonna let that junkie mother of yours get her hands on my money and run it for you, right?"

"My mama ain't no junkie," I mumbled under my breath. "She got herself together now."

He stood up. "I can't believe this shit! You're serious, aren't you? Your mother? You're gonna throw your whole life away on something stupid, Candy? If I'da known you were that dumb I would've left you in that coat closet back in Harlem."

He balled his napkin up and hurled it at the trash can. "I take you under my wing and put myself out for you and this is the kind of thanks I get? This is the way you repay me? I'm warning you, Candy. I care about you, but if you mess things up with the family I'll do whatever I have to do. You'll be dead to me, Candy. You hear me?"

I didn't say nothing. I had to do what I had to do too.

"Well, fine," Nicky said, standing up. His eyes were cold.

"Let your junkie mother make the drop. If she fucks it up and gets out of pocket, you'll both end up paying. Your mother is a fiend, Candy. There's no such thing as an ex-trickster. Remember that."

◈ ◈ ◈

Mama was too down.

"Don't worry, Candy," she told me. "I know what to do and I got you covered. Trust me, I can do this."

I swallowed hard. Mama needed the extra money this run would bring, but I needed Mama. She was my only backup and everything inside of me wanted to believe she could pull it off because I was between a rock and a wall. Nicky was mad at me, but Hurricane Jackson wasn't about to give us a second shot and Dominica and Vonzelle had let it be known that our entire career depended on my ass being in Harlem on Friday night.

My head was spinning. I was so stressed I couldn't think straight. Whatever decision I made, the repercussions might come back to bite me on the ass, but singing was my life. Hell, Mama was right. Opportunities like this didn't come banging on your door every day. I'd be stupid to let one this big pass me by.

Later that night I did what I usually did whenever I got too stressed. I got in the shower and turned the water on and stood under the spray until the ceiling was wet with steam. Then I turned the water pressure down and rubbed a bar of sweet soap all over my body, enjoying the lush bubbles and paying special attention to my swollen breasts and growing nipples.

I worked the soap between my hands until I was holding creamy suds. I cupped my titties and squeezed them gently, loving the thickness of them and how full and firm they felt in my hands. I held on to them, sliding my fingers forward a little at a time, teasing myself into a heat as my nipples stiffened and ached.

Finally I spread the thick suds over my nipples and massaged them in small circles, moaning out loud as my pussy started to drip. My hands had a mind of their own as they cupped and squeezed, then returned to my nipples and flicked and teased. I took the soap and slid it down my muscled belly, then worked up more lather on my mound, soaping my soft red pussy hair until it was foamy and white.

I dipped my middle finger into the suds and pressed it down hard on my clit, then climaxed as I inserted it deeply into my hot pussy. My walls clenched and collapsed around my finger as my body convulsed like crazy. Near the end of my orgasm I pushed three fingers up inside of me to feel some thickness, then squeezed my muscles tight until the very last spark of pleasure faded and my breasts stopped heaving. By the time I climbed out the shower my body and mind were both at peace. My decision had been made and I was cool with it.

The next morning I got to Mama's house bright and early, two hours before she had to leave for work. "Okay, Mama." I sighed after running the scenario down to her for almost an hour. I didn't know why I was so worried. Mama had been doing a hellified job at work, and for the first time in her life Caramel knew what it meant to have a damn near normal life. Mama had just got promoted to assistant manager, and she was seeing a guy named Greasy who worked at the station across the street from her job pumping gas and fixing cars. "Let's go over everything one more time."

I ran the rules down to Mama for the fifth time and tried to make her see just how important it was for her to present the right image when making a run. "You're too pretty, Mama," I said. "You gotta tone yourself down. Otherwise, people will remember you. Don't give those screeners no reason to even look your way. Be so plain they can forget they forgot you. No perfume, no jewelry, no makeup. Put a wig on top of all that pretty hair too. You gotta be like an actress playing a role. It should be easy too, 'cause you're traveling under the perfect cover. You're going to Seattle for World Peace Day. See yourself doing that in your head, and then make yourself believe it."

Everything I was telling Mama was what I practiced myself, especially when I was onstage. As soon as those lights hit me and the mic went live, shy little Candy Montana became a whole different person. Onstage I saw myself as irresistible, a superstar, a badass bitch. The way I moved, the things my body did, all that funky sex appeal . . . even I didn't know where I got it from. It was like I was that free little girl holding a toilet tissue roll and singing for her mama in the living room. I captivated the audience, oozing pussy. The world was mine and my performance was usually so live it brought down the house. There was no way I was gonna blow off Hurricane Jackson's offer and mess up my chance to sing in the House of Homicide.

"So when do I pick up the money?" Mama wanted to know. I stared into her eyes and for a second I thought she looked wild and hungry, but I shook it off. Nicky was getting in my head. Mama had kept herself straight since she'd been in L.A. She'd stopped drinking hard liquor and wasn't even smoking cigarettes no more. She deserved the extra ends this run would give her, and she even planned to use some of it to get a fake front tooth put in her mouth so she could feel more confident when she was talking to people.

"I'll take care of all that, Mama. You just work on remembering the rules, and leave the rest up to me."

Chapter 5

Fired and Hired

Percy Graham arrived at his office at the House of Homicide promptly at seven. He was always the first person on board each day and enjoyed the solitude of working alone for two or three hours before anyone else showed up. At a glance you might figure Percy to be a stockbroker or a corporate bigwig, but you'd certainly be mistaken. Percy was a master at keeping his appearance smooth and tight, and the three-thousand-dollar suits he wore every day and the Mercedes-Benz parked in a secure garage two blocks away were just a few of the fruits that the labor of his brilliant mind had afforded him.

Sliding his briefcase under his desk, Percy pulled a chair up to his third-floor window and watched Harlem come alive. He'd watched these same streets almost every morning during the four years he'd been working for Hurricane Jackson, and every year when spring broke he'd buy a few potted flowers and set them outside on the specially built fire escape he'd had constructed the same day he'd arrived.

An alumnus of Harvard Law School, Percy was a child

prodigy in mathematics and reasoning who had graduated at the top of his class and had twice been listed in *Who's Who in American Law.*

Percy gazed outside as commuters walked to and from the subway. Storefront shops were beginning to open, and working-class people roused winos and crackheads off their stoops before leaving for work. He loved Harlem, and loved Harlem's people even more, but it wasn't long ago that he worked a job that kept him isolated from regular people like these and focused his energies on white-collar criminals who ran empires from uptown offices with doormen and deep carpets.

At five feet eleven inches tall and weighing roughly 180 pounds with smooth chocolate skin, Percy wasn't an intimidating brother and didn't appear all that impressive unless you got caught sitting across from him in a courtroom. Only then could you see the killer glare creep into his eyes, and by that time it was always too late.

After graduating from high school at the age of sixteen and the Harvard School of Law five years later, Percy received scores of job offers from nearly every top law firm in the country, but had instead chosen to accept a low-paying position as an assistant DA with the prosecutor's office in Manhattan. Since he'd majored in corporate law with a specialty in tax codes, the DA put him to work prosecuting cases involving tax fraud schemes, drug trafficking, corruption of public officials, and loan-sharking.

Percy was tops at his job, and his handsome face and his notorious cases were plastered all over the *Daily News,* the *New York Post,* and *Newsweek.* He won countless awards and accolades for successfully prosecuting more illegal activity offenses than any other Manhattan assistant DA since Thomas Dewey. Word around the watercooler had it that Percy was in line for a huge promotion, one that was usually reserved for higher-ranking white attorneys who were well-established members of the system.

But one sunny day in December while Percy was in court ready to do battle on behalf of the citizens of Manhattan, his world came crashing down. *The State v. Jacob Freeman* was in full swing, and right in the middle of his first summation Percy was interrupted by a court clerk who informed him that the DA himself was waiting outside in the hallway and needed to speak with him urgently.

Percy glanced at the defendant who was up on the stand lying through his teeth, and then looked down at his carefully prepared notes. He was just about to drop the bombshell evidence that would introduce a paper trail that had originated with the defendant and ended with an illegal offshore account that held millions of dollars in his wife's name. Stopping now would disrupt the dramatic effect and kill the momentum he had going with the jurors.

But the court clerk was insistent, and Percy had no choice other than to turn the proceedings over to his colleague, Jim Battle, an eager white boy who had recently graduated from Yale. Exiting the courtroom quickly, Percy was surprised to be met in the crowded hallway by not only the DA, but the director of legal hiring as well.

"Percy Graham," the DA hissed, "a serious situation has been brought to my attention. A situation that can not and will not be tolerated on my watch."

The Manhattan DA was known for his honesty and above-the-board ethics, and the look on his boss's face was so grave that Percy knew this had to be something heavy.

"What's the problem, sir?"

The director of hiring stepped forward. "Kickbacks, Graham. Kickbacks and payoffs. All done under the table, and all conducted in your name."

Percy glanced at the assortment of people walking the halls, searching for a colleague who could vouch for his character, but all he saw were criminals and their attorneys conversing in small groups. He looked back at the DA, and then he actually smiled, for this had to be a joke. They could have asked anyone, Percy thought in amazement. Anyone who knew him could testify that his professional behavior was always above reproach. Yes, this had to be some sort of sick, white-boy joke. But the look in the DA's eyes and the words coming out of his mouth convinced him that it wasn't.

"You're fired, Graham!" the DA exploded. "Fired! I believed in you, and you planted corruption in my organization and tried to foul it up! It'll be months before we fully uncover the dirt you've done and years before we recover and regain the public's trust. Don't worry about getting your things from the office. I'll have them boxed up and sent to you. You're lucky I'm not inclined to have you disbarred, but if you're not out of here in five minutes flat I might just change my mind."

A hush had fallen over the busy hallway and Percy knew all eyes were on him. He also knew what time it was. He'd been set up. Framed. Railroaded out of position by the people who worked closest to him. By his colleagues who were supposed to be working on his team.

He didn't bother to ask what they had on him. Whatever it

was, Percy knew it was trumped up and bogus, but he also knew it didn't matter. He could spend considerable time and effort fighting this thing and going into court to get his job back, but for what? They'd already questioned his integrity and insulted his professionalism. He'd lost the trust, and for Percy, that was the most important part of his job.

He looked down at his right hand, the one that was missing an index finger. He remembered what his grandmother had told him as he lay in an Illinois hospital bed with a bandage covering his entire hand.

"Son," she'd said, "I know you hurtin', but some good can be found in every bad situation. So you only got four good fingers left on your hand, huh? All right, then. That means you better not never grab hold of nothing you can't let go of in a hurry."

Percy nodded at the DA, then turned around and walked back into the courtroom where Jim Battle was busy presenting Percy's findings as though he'd discovered them himself. Without a word, Percy gathered his belongings and placed them neatly inside of his briefcase. As he neared the door he locked eyes with Jim, who winked mischievously before returning to Percy's carefully constructed notes.

He was waiting for the elevator when he felt the nudge on his arm.

"Yo. Whattup?"

Percy turned around and saw a well-dressed brother who looked like he pumped iron for a living. It had been a long time, but Percy still recognized him. The last time their paths had crossed had been in a courtroom as well. Back when Percy had still been a quiet, scrawny little kid. A lot had changed in both of their lives since then. He stared at the large man with the bald head and handsome features. "What's up?"

"Hurricane Jackson," the man said as Percy held him with his eyes. "Check this. I saw what just went down. Whatever them crackers was paying you, I'll double it."

"Nah, man . . ."

"Okay, I'll triple it. My lawyer is late and I need some solid representation real quick before they put my ass in jail."

Percy's brain whirred like a computer. "All right. Then I'm Percy. Percy Graham."

Hurricane reached out for a little dap. "Cool, ak. I read the papers. I know who you be. But Percy?" Hurricane frowned and shook his head. "That's my daddy's name." He shrugged. "You can answer to that shit if you want to. But from here on out, I'ma call you Knowledge."

Chapter 6
In Da Pit

The House of Homicide was packed. There were rappers and video hoes lined up out the door and around the corner waiting for a chance to jump in the pit and impress Hurricane. Everybody wanted to cash in on the energy he had going, and all the hopefuls were bringing their best talent to the table, praying that what they had going was good enough to get an offer of a contract.

When it was our turn in the pit we got in there and performed our asses off. We had star quality and it was easy to see. I knew I was good because I worked my body into such a heat that I had a mini-orgasm right there in front of the crowd. I hate to say it but Dom and Vonnie weren't even in my zone. It was like I was down in that pit by myself in my halter top and tiny white shorts. Doing me to the fullest. The beat zapped into me at my feet, zipped up the back of my legs, then slipped between my thighs and stabbed me in the pussy. I wore that stage out, rocking it treacherously. Hurricane watched me the whole time. His eyes was crawling all over my body, checking out my ass and all my moves. Every baller and rapper in the house had lined up around the pit to see our audition. They made mad noise in the background and got crazy hot from the heat we were putting out onstage.

The response was clear. If Hurricane signed us up, Scandalous! was gonna bring something to Homicide Hitz that would knock the rest of the competition straight off the map. I wasn't even off the stage good before playas were trying to holla in my face and industry heads were comparing my looks, moves, and sounds to Beyoncé Knowles.

"But Beyoncé ain't got them fake-ass eyes," I heard one sistah say.

"Yeah," her man answered, "but this jawn's got a much phatter ass though."

I was breathing hard, trying to calm myself as we walked over to our table. I glanced around the room and somebody caught my eye. He was looking good in a high-powered designer suit. He wasn't as tall as Hurricane, but he wasn't short neither. Wasn't nothing really special about him except the way he stood apart from the crowd. Like he was in this club but not of it.

"Who's that?" I whispered to Vonnie and pointed. He wasn't dressed like a hustler, but these days you couldn't be sure.

Vonnie laughed real loud. "No fuckin' body. His name is Knowledge. He's an investment baller. Hurricane's lawyer. I tried to give him some pussy one time and his stupid ass wouldn't even take it. Don't even waste your time. He's just some analytical sherm who would rather count coochies than fuck 'em."

I wondered if that was true. When I was just a freshman in high school I had this senior liking me. He looked so much like this guy Knowledge that they could have passed for twins. Dude had been a star in our school, captain of the football team and all that. But then he got in trouble hanging with the wrong crowd and ended up getting kicked off the team for the rest of the season. Even chilling at the game as a regular spectator he was still fine and popular. He was a straight clown and made me laugh all the time. I knew how much he liked me but Mama was clocking my shit hard around boys, so that kept us apart a lot. One time I ran into him at one of our home games, and during the halftime show that crazy boy got behind me and took his dick out, then slid that shit under my skirt and between my naked pussy lips. He kept trying to push it up into me, but I wouldn't let him. I'd cock my ass back so the head of his dick slid straight across my clit, sending thick juices squirting out of me and wetting us both up. He slid his hands under my skirt and held me by the hips, then rocked me just like that. Rubbing the length of his dick against the slit between my legs. Like a hot dog sliding between a split bun. The cheerleaders were swinging, the band was bringing it hot, and his dick felt so good I screamed right along with the rest of the crowd, but my screams were for a better reason.

Vonnie touched my arm and I blinked real fast a few times. "Something's fittin' to go down," she said.

The spotlight was shining on the pit and somebody had passed Hurricane a mic. Every eye in the House was on him, but even across the room, I could tell that Hurricane's eyes were all over me.

"C'mere, you," he said, pointing and motioning me over. He walked up the steps and sat on the raised stage that overlooked the pit and the spotlight followed him. "Yeah you, Red. Bring your fine ass up here."

The noise died down as I switched my ass down into the pit and came out at the bottom of the steps on the other side. I couldn't believe that out of all of the sistahs in the house Hurricane was taking notes on little old me, but the look on his face as he watched me moving toward him said it all.

He stood up to meet me and somebody put a bottle of Cristal in his hand. The DJ gave him some beats and he broke out in a little freestyle rap:

Off the top from day one, ma, I think ya gonna be real
Step up and talk to me yo, don't let the curiosity build
It's your kinda candy my tongue is dying to touch
Your body's hot enough to make a fuckin' gangsta blush . . .

They raised the roof up off that mutha. You woulda thought Hurricane was the resurrected Tupac or somebody the way the crowd gave up the props. I thought his rap was all right. Nothing spectacular, just all right. But I ain't gonna lie. I gave it up for him too. After all, he was Big Money Cane, and he held all the cards and all the strings. Anything he did, even in a small way, was gonna be considered grand.

It was just me and him in the pit and I could feel all kinds of vibes in the air. "Damn baby," he tucked the mic behind his back and whispered in my ear. "Look like you was getting your shit off out there, shawty."

"Speak up!" somebody yelled from the crowd. "Say that shit out loud!"

The dawgs started barking. Every brother in the House wanted to be just like Hurricane, and most of the females were sipping haterade from their beer bottles and wishing they were wearing my shorts.

Hurricane started clowning under all that attention. He threw down a few more sexy lyrics directed at me, then told the DJ to stop the music as he grabbed my hand and made everybody shut up.

Every ear was perked.

"Aaight, y'all," Hurricane hollered into the mic. "I'm looking for me a wifey tonight, but she gotta be all the way real. Y'all know females are always trying to fake a brother out. Ain't that right, dawgs? You slide into a Mercedes and climb out of a Hyundai!" His boys were clapping and dapping each other out like, *Hell yeah! That shit happened to me before!*

"Or, or, or"—Hurricane hushed them—"you chilling with a Maine lobster and wake up next to some nasty tuna fish!"

Then he made a bold move by sticking his finger in my waistband. He stretched the front of my shorts toward him and took a quick peek at my naked mound.

"She's live," he hollered, jumping up and down and waving his arm. "She's all the way live! This one's for real, y'all! That ain't no weave on her head, fellas! She's a for-real, nat-ur-al, bona fide redhead!" He dropped to his knees. "C'mon, baby girl. Don't you wanna be my wifey?"

I could hear Vonnie and Dom screaming, "Hell yeah! Hell yeah!"

I looked down into his pretty eyes and couldn't believe my luck.

"Hell yeah!" I repeated after my girls. "Hell yeah!"

He was on his feet again. "Y'all heard that, right?"

More screams and whistles.

"All right, then. It's official. Candy and Cane. Just remember: Whatever gets hooked in the House of Homicide, can't nothing but death fuck it up!"

I laughed along with the crowd, feeling too damn special standing there beside him as the music kicked up again and the whole house broke live. It didn't bother me a bit that he had just claimed me without even knowing me or that he'd looked down my clothes like he had it like that. I had what every other chick in the house wanted: Hurricane Jackson's eye and his attention. And as far as I was concerned there was nothing else in the world that I needed.

◆ ◆ ◆

When the auditions were over Hurricane invited us to party upstairs in the VIP lounge with his crew, and we almost screamed we felt so lucky. Rappers like Nas, 50 Cent, and other high profilers were rolling through the house the whole night.

"Girl, he's gone sign us," Vonzelle kept saying over and over as we held our laminates and walked up to the main lounge. "That niggah is gone sign us! His fine ass is ready to put us down on paper right NOW!"

Dominica shushed her. "Calm your ass down. Don't be acting all desperate, Vonnie. You might make him think we just some regular groupies."

We were sure enough giving him groupie stares. Hurricane was so big he coulda been on steroids. Arms, chest, nothing but meat. Muscle meat. I felt myself getting warm just looking at him and I could tell Dominica and Vonzelle were turned on too.

"Damn, that niggah is so much finer in person than he is on TV," Vonnie whispered. She fanned herself with her hand, then pushed past me and Dominica to get closer to the booth he was sitting in.

"Wait, bitch." Dominica grabbed her arm. "He already stepped to Candy, remember? Sit your freaky ass down!"

Vonnie just shrugged. "Then Candy betta hook him before I jook him!"

I knew what Dom meant about acting too desperate. I deliberately turned my back when I caught Hurricane looking at me. Then I rolled my ass over to the bar and ordered a cup of orange juice with ice.

I was crunching on the ice when I felt a big hand on my waist. I turned around and got a good whiff of his cologne and dollar signs chinged in my eyes. Everything about him was fresh and expensive and the way he smelled was no exception.

"C'mon, sexy," Hurricane whispered, nuzzling my neck. "Let's go get busy."

He grabbed my hand and took me out on the dance floor. All the way out there he was using his thumb to rub small circles in my palm. Just his touch was erotic as hell, and by the time he pulled me close to him the crotch of my shorts was getting wet.

The DJ was kicking a hard rap cut, and while everybody else danced fast and furious, Hurricane had me on lock. He pressed his hard body against mine and moved like we were in the bed. I had my arms around his neck as I rubbed my big titties against his chest, scraping my nipples back and forth on him and enjoying the electric tingles that shot down to my damp pussy.

"I ain't never seen a sistah like you," he whispered, sucking on my neck and holding me by my tight waist. "Everything about you is different. Fine and different."

His tongue pushed into my mouth and spread heat. I tried to suck it down my throat. My hands were all over him. He massaged my ass like he loved its thickness. People were dancing all around us but we carried on like we were alone. I spread my legs until his thigh was between them then moved up and down, crushing my clit against him so deliciously that I came. Hurricane held me up as my orgasm rushed through me, kissing my neck and lips and winding his fingers in my hair.

A moment later he surprised me by slipping his hand down the front of my shorts and sliding his fingers through my tangled pussy hairs. He touched my clit, and I arched my back and moaned, then thrust my hips toward him as he slid one thick finger into my tight, wet pussy and moved it slowly back and forth as I bent my knees and bounced gently up and down.

I came again as he brushed his thumb lightly across my clit, and he massaged my pussy with the handful of juices he'd collected, then pulled his hand out my shorts and licked his fingers.

"Damn." He grinned, kissing my cheek. "You look good. You feel good. You taste good. Who's your man? Wait. Don't tell me. I might have to kill that niggah!"

I laughed and leaned against his chest as the music thumped. Hurricane let go of me and started fast dancing, so I did the same, shaking my ass all over the floor. My moves were wild and hot, and people were starting to notice. I enjoyed the stares as me and Hurricane worked it out to "P.I.M.P." by 50 Cent.

I was amazed at what had just went down between us, but I didn't feel bad about it though. Things were falling in place for me and it was turning out to be the best night of my life. My group had performed for the baddest label out there, and its owner had just let me know with his fingers how much he liked me. I had turned around to give him a couple of views of me from the back when someone caught my eye. It was the same guy I'd checked out earlier. Knowledge. Everybody else was moving and he was holding still. He busted me eyeing him and turned and walked away.

Chapter 7

Mob Money

Hurricane got distracted by one of his boys and disappeared somewhere, leaving me standing by myself on the dance floor. I worked my way back over to my table with people stopping me every few feet to tell me how hot our audition had been.

I was chilling in a booth with my girls and sipping another glass of icy orange juice when my cell phone vibrated. I slipped it off my waist and looked at the caller ID. Mama. The last thing I'd told her was to call me after she made the drop in Seattle, but I hadn't heard shit from her in over eight hours and I'd been waiting on anxious for her call the whole night.

I grabbed my purse. "Let me out, y'all," I yelled, practically pushing Vonnie and Dominica out of the booth. "I gotta go to the bathroom."

Mama had been calling from her house, and I ran into the ladies' room to call her back. Females were all up in that mug doing everything except peeing. One chick had her curling iron plugged in over the sink and was frying her weave, two others were bent over a fifty-dollar bill, sharing a couple of lines of hit, and three older sisters were checking their shit out in the floor-length mirrors, sucking in their stomachs and stuffing tissue in the bottom of their bras to make their titties sit up higher.

One of the stalls had an OUT OF ORDER sign taped to it, so I stepped past the crowd and went into the other one and locked the door. I pressed Mama's number on speed dial and breathed a sigh of relief when Caramel answered on the first ring.

"Put Mama on the goddamn phone!" I said. I'd been so scared she'd gotten knocked that now that she was back all I wanted to do was curse her out real good.

Caramel sniffed. "She ain't here."

"What you mean she ain't there, Caramel? She just called my cell phone a minute ago!"

"That was me, Candy," my sister said, and that's when I heard the tears in her voice. "I called you 'cause Mama still ain't made it back yet."

My heart sank. This was not good news, and I didn't even want to think about the possibilities that were trying to creep into my mind.

I spoke calmly 'cause I could tell my sister was already scared. "Okay, Caramel. Did Mama call to say she made the drop? Did Nicky come by the house? What about that niggah Greasy she be with? Do you know if he heard from her yet?"

Caramel sucked her teeth into the phone. "Candy, you don't even know. You think Mama been on the real with you, but she hasn't. You know how she usually calls both of us every day as soon as she gets to work?"

"Yeah?" Mama had a ritual. As soon as she made it to work each day she called her house and let Caramel know first, and then she called me. I think she was happy to have an actual job and thrilled to be able to call her kids and say she was there.

Caramel went on. "Well, lately Mama been calling you from right here in this house. She's not working anymore, Candy. Her and Greasy been staying out all night and they don't even go out looking for jobs during the day."

The only thing that saved me from falling was the fact that I was already sitting down. Mama must didn't understand who she was fuckin' with. Those Gabrianos wouldn't hesitate to deal with me and her both. All I could think about was Mama and the money. The money and my mama. Either she'd gotten knocked or she'd fucked it up. Either way, we were both in trouble.

"Hurry up, I gotta piss!" some drunk heffah banged on the bathroom door.

I took a deep breath and tried to think. "Okay, Caramel," I said, trying to stay calm, "you gotta listen to me and do exactly what I say. Cool?"

She sniffed through her tears and it killed me that me and Mama had made her jump into this dangerous trick bag with us. "Okay."

"Keep the door locked and stay by the phone. Don't let nobody in the house, not even Greasy. The minute Mama calls, I want you to call me. If anybody else calls, just act like they dialed the wrong number and hang up, okay? I don't wanna scare you, Mellie, but if for some reason shit gets hot, then you gotta call the cops, okay? You gotta dial 911."

Caramel started crying harder and that bitch on the other side of the bathroom door started banging harder.

"What the fuck is your problem!" I screamed, kicking at the door. And then to my baby sister, "No, Caramel, not you. Just some crackhead trying to get in this bathroom. Please, I'm not trying to scare you. Don't be scared. I just want you to know how to handle shit if something comes up. Just remember what I said and everything'll be straight. Mama's on her way, okay? I love you, Caramel. Call me every thirty minutes until she gets there."

I dashed out the bathroom and went looking for Dom. She was on the dance floor shaking her ass. I searched for Vonnie too, but she was nowhere to be found. All of a sudden the music was too loud for me and my heart was beating too fast. I walked back to our booth and made myself sit down and take a bunch of deep breaths. The party was still live and the mood was high, but I was so nervous and stressed out all I could do was sit there shaking and praying that Mama would call and say the drop had been a success.

"Whattup, wifey?" Hurricane joked all sexy-like the next time he rolled past our table surrounded by his crew. I was sitting there biting my fake nails and gripping my cell phone in my hand. Hurricane looked so good standing there, so big and strong and powerful that I wanted to jump back into his arms and hide from the storm I felt coming.

Instead, I gave him a cute look and made myself smile. "I'm cool, baby. I'm just watching the drinks until my girls get back. The music is live, though."

He nodded, searching my eyes, then turned away as a rapper named Thug-a-licious, who was also a recent number one NBA draft pick, interrupted us and pulled him away to introduce him to a wannabe rapper trying to get signed.

I was glad when they walked away. I was so worried about Mama till I didn't know what to do. I had no way to get in touch with her and I cursed myself out for not getting her that cell phone she wanted. If I didn't think she was ready for something small like a cell phone, then what in the world had made me think she could be trusted with the Gabriano money? The House of Homicide, I realized. I sat there breathing hard and gripping my phone, praying it would all be worth it.

Fifteen minutes later Vonnie and Dom weren't back. I was still sitting in the booth praying my phone would vibrate and it would be Caramel telling me that Mama had made it home. Instead, some thugged-out-looking ruffneck stepped up to the table, then looked down at me and stared.

"Hurricane want'chu."

I gave him a look. "Who you?"

"Omar."

I'd seen psycho dudes like him all over Harlem. He looked high as hell. Buggy too.

"Where is he?"

"You asking too many damn questions. The man said he want'chu. Step wit me."

I tried to spot Dominica on the dance floor but she was in too deep. I walked behind him feeling creeped out. Omar was tall and slim, but nowhere near bony. He looked just like every other young head walking around the streets of Harlem until you looked in his eyes. There was nothing good in them.

I followed him up a flight of stairs I hadn't even noticed before. He walked me down an archway that stretched like a bridge high above the pit. Directly over the center of the pit was a small vestibule area where a big king's chair with a footstool covered in red crushed velvet sat between two smaller, less-royal-looking chairs. We continued down the archway, and he led me down a narrow hall that had a bunch of closed doors.

"Go 'head in. It's the door on the right. He's waitin' for ya."

I stepped into a big room where wall-to-wall playas were gambling, playing pool, and shooting cee-low. Drinks was being served by big-hipped sistahs wearing thongs and high heels, and more than one head was bent over a table inhaling thin, neat lines of cocaine. I was standing there trying to take it all in when some huge, high-yellow brother with three necks and girlie hips walked up to me.

"You got the wrong room," he said, trying to sound hard. But then somebody hollered, "She good, Butter," and I heard my name called. Hurricane was sitting at a card table with two other men and a sistah wearing a pair of dark shades who looked a little older than him. He waved me over. They were talking shit and playing Spades, and when he patted his leg for me to sit down, I settled my ass down on his muscle-hard thigh.

"All right, y'all," he said, rubbing my hip and thigh so that everybody could see him. "I got my good-luck charm with me now! Ain't gonna be no rise and fly on this side of the table so get ready to lose all your damn money!"

His partner groaned.

Hurricane laughed. "While you moaning, niggah, get your ass up!"

He patted me on the ass two times real quick. "Get up, Candy. Go take that fool's seat."

They were playing sandbags and passing three and under. Each hand was worth a bill, and Hurricane put me in. The rules were easy. If you got set, you lost your money and the other team won the pot. If both teams made their bid, the pot stayed on the table. Blinds started at seven, and if you or your partner got caught reneging y'all gave up the pot and paid an extra two bills to the other team.

I sat across from Hurricane and jammed my cell phone between my legs. He introduced me to the chick on my left.

"This my sister, Jadeah," he said, shuffling like a Vegas shark. "Jadeah, this Candy. She's gonna be my wife."

Jadeah picked up her cards one by one. She turned to me. "Your wife, huh? Go 'head with it. I saw her in the pit. Making herself known." Then she cracked a little smile. "Nice to meet you, Candy. You must be pretty hot 'cause my brother don't be taking too many wives."

I recognized Jadeah's partner as a West Coast rapper named Mo' Troubles. He'd been on the underground for a while and had just got his first legitimate single released.

"How many you got?" Hurricane asked, studying his hand.

I counted. "Three and a possible."

"Can you pass?"

I shook my head. "Nah."

"Damn!" he cursed. "We shoulda took a blind. Okay," he told Jadeah, "give us a eight."

I kept squeezing my cell phone between my thighs, waiting for Caramel to call, and when the phone finally did vibrate it scared me so bad I dropped half of my cards trying to get to it. Mama's number was on the caller ID, but before I could click it on, Hurricane lunged across the table and bitch-smacked the phone clear out my hand.

"No fuckin' phones up here!"

I froze, then looked down at my cell laying on the floor. The entire faceplate had come off and it wasn't ringing no more.

"Well damn," Jadeah said, still studying her cards. "The girl didn't know. Omar should've told her. C'mon, Junius. It's your play."

Hurricane played the ace of diamonds and Mo' Troubles leaned over and scooped the cell phone up off the floor. He clicked the faceplate over it and passed it back to me.

"Turn it off," Hurricane demanded.

I did. I was so shook and distracted that I played out of turn once, slept a book twice, and almost reneged too. All that sweet shit Hurricane had been dropping on me went out the window. He got mad like we was playing for millions and started slamming his cards on the table all crazy. His sister gave him a chill-the-fuck-out look and he calmed down a little bit, but he didn't want me to be his partner no more.

"Yo, baby," he told me, shaking his head. "You got to go." He looked around the room then hollered, "Yo, Knowledge! C'mere!" Then to me: "Get up, shawty, and let my man sit down. This here is money we working with. You gone need a little more practice before you get back at my table."

I knew how to play Spades better than I had shown him, but I got up gladly. My mind just wasn't on no damn card game. It was way over on the West Coast in a city called L.A., worrying about my mother and waiting for my little sister to call.

The guy Knowledge came up and dapped Hurricane's fist, then sat in my seat. He had smooth chocolate skin and clear brown eyes. His gear was expensive and pressed, but nowhere near flashy.

"What's up?" He nodded at Mo' Troubles. Then he leaned over and kissed Jadeah on the cheek and looked from her to me and asked, "How my sisters doing?"

Jadeah patted his back like he was her little brother. "Good, baby."

"I'm good," I said quietly.

Jadeah started shuffling the cards.

"Knowledge," he said, holding out his hand to me. One of his fingers was missing.

I glanced at Hurricane then shook it for just a second. "Candy."

"Cool," he said, picking up his cards and setting up his hand. "Cool."

Chapter 8

The Scene of the Crime

We left the House of Homicide at 6:00 A.M. and decided to go to Vonnie's place for the night since her sugar daddy was locked up and she had the most room. I'd seen all kinds of stuff transpiring at the House, and my head was swimming from the size of Hurricane's operation. I'd found out from nosey Vonnie that he washed West Coast money through legitimate businesses, but here on the East Coast he was a straight baller. He controlled his gambling and drug operations from the upstairs rooms, and there was porno filming, dick sucking, and all-night fucking going on downstairs.

My girls were amped about me and Hurricane hooking up. I told them all about the finger fuck he gave me on the dance floor. Dominica gave me a sick look and called me a cheap ho, but Vonnie gave me big props and said I should have slurped his dick down while I was at it so we all coulda got paid out the ass.

"Now, Candy," Dominica said, talking to me like I was a little kid, "we do not let men treat us like chickenheads on the first date, remember? They are *not* entitled to the poon-poon just because they have mad dollars. If we expect the hustlers and Hurricanes of the world to respect us and treat us like talented, independent sistahs, we can't be grinding our pussies all over their fingers in public."

Vonnie laughed. "And why the hell not? Candy ain't no real baller catcher. Ain't no way I woulda let no playa get up in my na-na and make me lose it like that on the dance floor. I woulda had his dick so far down my throat he'da been calling for the fire department to come get it out. And then he woulda been paying me cash money to do it all over again!"

I loved my girls, but even their craziness didn't help me relax. Mama wasn't back yet and that didn't make sense to me. Caramel had called me four times in the past two hours. My phone had lit up and vibrated every thirty minutes just like I'd told her, the last time just as we got in the taxi to come to Vonnie's place. But now the calls had stopped. If I thought I was worried before, I was close to cracking up now.

Dom said she was hungry, and Vonnie went in the back to take off her skirt. I was sitting cross-legged on her living room floor hitting speed dial every fifteen seconds and trying not to flip the fuck out when Dominica came out the kitchen eating an apple.

She raised her eyebrow when she saw the look on my face. "What's wrong?" She frowned. "Don't tell me Hurricane's sticky fingers got you calling his ass for some more."

I had taken off my shoes and shirt, but now I got up off the floor and started putting my shit back on.

"Something ain't right, Dom. I can't reach Caramel, and she's supposed to be waiting by the phone." I went in the kitchen and got the number for the White Diamond Cab Company off the refrigerator and dialed it. The dispatcher popped her gum all in my ear, then finally told me to be outside in ten minutes.

"But where's your mother?" Dominica asked, setting her apple down on the table and coming toward me with worry in her eyes. "She did you that solid, right? Everything went cool with the drop, didn't it?"

I was so shook I couldn't even talk about Mama. By now it was becoming probable that she'd dipped with the Gabriano cash, and somebody was gonna have to pay.

I slipped into my heels and made sure I had everything I needed in my purse. I'd get my ticket changed at the airport. Fuck my suitcase that was still at Dom's place, fuck last night's little hot hoochie ho shorts I still had on too. I needed to get back to L.A. and find out where Mama and Caramel were before Nicky got suspicious about the drop and put us all in the ground.

"I'm out, Dom," I said, pushing past her on my way toward the door. "I'm going back to L.A. I'll call you when I get a minute."

I was almost out the door when Vonzelle came out the bathroom wearing just her bra and a skimpy thong. "Where the hell you going, Candy?" she hollered.

I didn't even turn around.

She ran out in the hallway half naked and leaned over the banister as my shoes click-clicked down the steps. "Bitch, don't you walk outta here! Hurricane wants all three of us to be in that pit at two o'clock tomorrow afternoon!"

I just threw up my hand like, *Whatever.*

"Your stupid ass! You gonna ruin this deal for all of us!"

I was almost out the building when I heard Dominica snap, "Leave her the fuck alone, Vonzelle. There's more to life than sucking industry dick."

◆ ◆ ◆

I caught a 9:00 A.M. flight back to L.A. and arrived a little bit after six, West Coast time. By now I had called Mama's house so many times my finger was sore from pressing REDIAL, but still no Mama. No Caramel either.

I waved down a taxi outside of the baggage claim area, and when it pulled up in front of Mama's house I felt my first bit of relief in over twelve hours. Mama's car was in the driveway. That heffah had finally showed her ass up, and I wanted to hear the damn lie she was gonna tell me about where she'd been.

My mind was racing and rationalizing as I paid the driver and walked up the path to the door. Maybe her flight had got canceled or rescheduled or some shit. Or maybe she'd missed her return flight and couldn't get on another one until real late last night or early this morning. Or maybe, I told myself, knowing my mama she probably took that niggah Greasy along with her to make the drop, then decided to hang out in Seattle until she felt like coming the hell back.

But reality hit me the moment I pushed on the door.

I was stepping into a crime scene. The place had been totally tossed, but somebody had put up one hell of a fight. Shit was everywhere. Furniture was turned over and curtains had been snatched down. A heavy smell was in the air and a trail of blood ran from the front door all the way to the back of the house.

For a second I just stood there clenching my teeth and gripped in fear. Sweat beaded between my titties and under my arms. My feet wouldn't move. But then Caramel flashed in my mind and I crept cautiously. Silently. Deeper into the house. The further back I went, the more blood there was. But there was something else on the floor back here too, and when I crouched down to see what it was, vomit gushed toward the back of my throat and I heaved up spit and air. My skin crawled and my whole body spazzed as I stared at the sticks of flesh, some of them recently manicured, that were pointing the way toward Mama's bedroom.

The tiny part of my mind that was still almost rational understood that there were too damn many fingers there to have come off just one person, and when I rounded the corner to Mama's bedroom terror fell down on me and the reality of what I was seeing became as clear as day. The Gabrianos had gotten hold of Mama and her boyfriend, Greasy.

They'd gotten Caramel too.

Chapter 9
Domestic Violence

Aunt Jessie was driving too fast. She whipped down the street running traffic lights and honking her horn like crazy whenever somebody got in her way. Jessie's husband rode nervously beside her in the passenger seat, and every few seconds he glanced over his shoulder out the back window and shook his head in disbelief.

"Dial 911, Jerlynne!" Jessie yelled at her sister, who was huddled in the backseat with the kids. "Get the goddamn po-lice on the phone!"

"He's right up on us!" Jerlynne wailed, looking over her shoulder, the car phone almost slipping from her trembling hand. She sat in the backseat with her sister's sleeping twin infants and her own thirteen-year-old son. The twins were in car seats, but her son sat right next to her. Jerlynne's voice was full of fear, and it seeped from her and touched her child. She wrapped her arm around the boy and held him close to her. He was small for his age, but she knew he was strong.

"Hello?" she shrieked into the phone. "Yes! Yes! This is an emergency!"

The car lurched as Jessie tried to pass a garbage truck. She slammed on her brakes and her husband hollered and thrust both hands against the dashboard as they came close to rear-ending a school bus.

"Lawd," Jessie cried out. "Look what that fool almost made me do! That crazy motherfucker gone kill all of us!"

The boy in the backseat remained quiet as they fled. He had no use for the man behind them. He hadn't spoken more than two words to him since the night of the fire. The boy bore thick scars on his back and vivid memories in his mind of the night he'd been forced to jump from the burning window of a blaze that his father had set. Only once or twice did he turn around to look as his father chased them down, waving his arm for them to stop and cursing and threatening what he was going to do the moment they did.

"Yes!" Jerlynne cried into the phone. "My name's Jerlynne Jackson. I have out an order of protection against my husband! He molested my niece and he's not supposed to come anywhere near me. My sister picked me up from work this morning, and now he's chasing behind us and waving a gun out the window!"

"Tell 'em we coming down Spring Street!" Jessie yelled. "We headed their way and we ain't stopping for no motherfuckin' lights!"

Her husband spoke beside her. He was a big man, but when it came to Pug there was no courage in him. "Yeah. That's what we should do. Drive straight to the police station and drop Lynne and Percy off. Them boys kin handle Pug from there."

Percy's mother spoke into the phone, then leaned against him shaking and crying. She was still wearing her nurse's scrubs and she looked scared and exhausted. He reached out and touched her small brown hand, patting it and stroking it as her tears fell on his face, warming his skin.

"Keep your head down, Percy," she sobbed softly, trying to scooch herself down lower in the seat as well. *"Baby keep your head down."*

"All right!" Aunt Jessie hollered from the front seat. *"We going in!"*

She turned the car left, directly into the police parking lot, and the maniac behind them followed. The station sat in the center of a U-shaped paved area, and there were lined parking areas on all three sides. The front door was propped open, but there were no officers in sight. *"Shit!"* Jessie cussed, searching for help. *"Ain't no-where to park. Them motherfuckers knew we was coming. Why ain't nobody out here waitin' on us?"*

Jerlynne let go of Percy's hand and dialed 911 again as her sister drove around to the back of the station and pulled into the only spot that was available. It had a sign that read SHERIFF'S DEPUTY ONLY.

Jessie hadn't even put the car in park before her sister started screaming into the phone again. *"We're right out back! Outside your station! Help us! He's out of his car and he's got a gun!"*

Percy looked to his right and things got slow. He saw his father moving toward the car as if in slow motion. Veins stood out on his bald head, and his handsome face was contorted in rage. His work vest was unbuttoned and his paint-splotched jeans rode low on his waist. The powerful muscles on his chest, arms, and stomach bulged, and he held a Saturday night special gripped in his right hand.

"Pug, noooooooo!" Jerlynne screamed, and grabbed at her son. She flung the boy down to the floor of the car and threw her body over him.

Percy felt his shoulder slam against the edge of the babies' car seat, and then he was on his back. He struggled against his mother, *trying to flip her over and switch their positions. But his father was right outside the window. Their eyes met and Percy stared into the face of a sadistic wife-beater who had a thing for teenage girls. His father blinked, his pug nose flaring, the black hole of his revolver aimed and deadly.*

Percy hugged his mother to him with his left arm and instinctively threw his right hand out, palm forward. "Noooooo!"

The window exploded, and Percy felt his index finger snap backward and fly off.

Bak! Bak! Bak! Bak! Four more shots rang out as Jessie screamed in the front seat and the babies woke up crying, covered in blood and shards of glass. Her husband flung open his door and jumped from the car, crawling beneath the cruiser parked next to it and leaving his wife and twin daughters to their own fate.

Percy felt his mother's body twitch and convulse. The car phone fell from her fingers as a long breath escaped her and she went still.

And then the car was surrounded. Officers with drawn guns closed in on his father, ordering him to drop his weapon or die.

Percy gazed through the tiny pieces of glass that were covering his face and looked into the face of his mother's killer. Pug's left eye swung downward, but the right eye glinted with pure evil. Pug stared at his son for a moment, then spit through the shattered window and into the car, striking Jerlynne on the side of her bloody face.

"Bitch," he spit before the wall of policemen rained down on him. "Trifling bitch."

◊ ◊ ◊

Knowledge Graham swung open the metal safe in his office and removed a stack of ledgers. He had taken several basic accounting courses in college and two or three corporate accounting classes in law school too, just for fun. His understanding of numbers and financial equations came naturally to him, which made keeping two sets of books a minor issue.

Like his boss, Knowledge was fearless. Hurricane might have been the muscle behind the House of Homicide, but Knowledge was the brain. He had an air of loyalty that was unquestionable, and Hurricane trusted him explicitly. Knowledge showed his boss the highest respect, and had never forgotten how Hurricane had hired him on sight and paid him triple what he was making at a time when no other law firm in the country would have touched him.

Working the other side of the fence was just a matter of shifting perspective to Knowledge. For years he'd played by all the rules and followed the correct protocol at the Manhattan district attorney's office. Those white boys had seriously underestimated what dicking him would cost, and it wasn't long before they realized it had been much better for them when he was playing on their team. Sitting across the table from his old colleagues made Knowledge twice as deadly because he'd mastered the game from both ends of the field.

In the four years he'd been with Hurricane, Knowledge had tripled his boss's net worth. True, the feds had come after them a time or two, but as soon as the name of Hurricane's attorney was disclosed, they knew they were outclassed and would end up with an L in their column.

Knowledge Graham was an expert at finding tax loopholes, but he was a real genius at hiding and diverting corporate funds. He dealt in offshore accounts, secret stocks and securities, tax-exempt entities in Bermuda, holdings in Latin America, and untraceable Swiss bonds.

Knowledge washed his boss's money like he was an old lady with a box of Tide and a gallon of bleach. Not a penny could be linked back to Hurricane, and he kept his boss rich and happy and left the feds and their task-force agents scratching their heads in amazement on a regular basis. And what he did for his boss financially he also did for himself. What kind of investment strategist would he be if he didn't follow his own advice?

The Italians who did business with Hurricane were happy too. They began funneling larger and larger amounts through Hurricane's main drug czar, and even offered bigger pots of seed money to start other front businesses like funeral parlors and restaurants. The only hustle they wouldn't share was their arms operation. They didn't mind supplying the guns that gang-bangers used to take each other out, they just didn't want to share any of those mega-profits.

Still, all and all, Knowledge was satisfied. There had never been a moment when he felt a single pang of guilt for taking from white people what they'd already taken from poor blacks. They had created the game and etched out the rules, but he had put a twist on it and was playing it like he owned it.

The one thing that bothered him was his boss's insistence on where he should rest. Hurricane was heavy on control and was adamant that his most loyal soldiers live with him in his Long

Island mansion. While Knowledge was a loner by nature, he agreed. The mansion was big enough for everybody to have their own space, and since Hurricane's entourage spent most of their time either at the House of Homicide or on the road, he was usually there only to shower and catch a few quick hours of sleep.

For tax purposes and to maintain his sense of individuality, Knowledge also kept a nice loft apartment downtown on Seventy-ninth and Broadway. Thanks to his healthy investments, his paycheck was fat enough to afford him that private escape and the midnight-black Benz that he pushed to work most days. And it still left him a whole lot left over.

The only thing missing from Knowledge's well-ordered life was a good woman. Sure, there were wall-to-wall females at the House day and night, but he had never been attracted to loud, flashy women. His mother had been sweet and naïve but too swayed by criminal-minded men for her own good.

As a kid, Knowledge had never had adequate clothing. He'd worn the same pair of shoes from the sixth grade through the eighth, which is why as an adult he favored expensive leather shoes and a wide variety of designer suits.

Occasionally he broke down and got with a woman. Usually an old acquaintance from law school or some other professional, educated woman he'd met outside of the music industry. He never made any promises, but he always treated them right. He did all the expected things like taking them out to dinner and buying them gifts. He paid attention to their desires and actually listened to their conversations. Knowledge looked good and treated them generously. He was a gentleman and a hot, unselfish lover. He just wasn't ready to commit himself to any woman. Or maybe he just hadn't found the right one yet.

Whatever it was, Knowledge was on a mission, but he'd been content with his life since coming to the House of Homicide. Not happy, but content. Until that sexy little honey-skinned redhead had come to audition for Hurricane and damn near blasted the walls down with her sensual, powerful voice. Knowledge had seen a lot of hopeful singers over the last few years, but hands down, this one was the best.

Something about her had stayed with him, and since he wasn't the kind of brother who preferred women of other races, it wasn't her red hair or her blue eyes. It wasn't those sexy-ass white shorts that had fit her like a bikini bottom either. He'd seen right past all that, and yet something about her still intrigued him.

Knowledge looked down at himself and grinned at what was rising in his lap. Shifting his dick in his pants, he opened the ledgers and began his examination. There were plenty of computer programs that would do this ten times faster than his pencil and his brain, but he was much too smart for that. Relying on machinery was the lazy man's way of making money—and the fastest way to get caught stashing it.

He touched his dick again, then put that hot little redhead out of his mind and got down to business.

Chapter 10

Paying Dues

I don't even remember dialing 911. Just that the cops were suddenly there, and then the ambulance was too, covering my mother's face with a white sheet and taking my sister away on a stretcher. I was hysterical, but not blind enough where I couldn't see that Nicky was a man of his word. His hand had been all over this and I was scared out of my mind.

The LAPD was sorry as hell. They kept on restating what was totally fucking obvious. The murders looked like a professional hit. Of course they wanted to know who did it, and they put me in a little room and tried like hell to drag some names out of me, but I stuck hard to my lie. I just kept crying and telling them over and over again that all I did was come back from a studio audition in New York and walked into my mother's house to find three bloody bodies.

Was your mother hustling drugs? they demanded. Was she a thief? Is that why her fingers were cut off? Who were her enemies? Who were her close friends? Does your sister associate with any known gang members? What do you know about the man, Darren Kendall, who was also found murdered?

I answered their questions the same way each time they asked. I didn't know who shot my sister and killed my mother. I came from good people and I had no idea who would have wanted them dead. No, Mama didn't steal and Caramel wasn't banging, but maybe it was that dude Greasy or Darren Kendall or whoever he was that the killers were really after and my mother and sister just happened to be in the way.

Caramel was in intensive care with an armed guard posted at her bed. The doctors said she was lucky. She'd gotten shot in the head but it was only a skim. The bullet went in above her ear at a downward angle and came out behind her ear on the same side. They couldn't tell if there would be any long-term effects on her faculties yet, but it was standard procedure to put all gunshot victims in intensive care.

It took me almost a week, but somehow I managed to plan a funeral for Mama without collapsing in a heap of grief. I was getting shit done through a thick fog, and it took everything I had in me to have her body moved from the morgue to the funeral home and prepared for cremation, but I did it.

All I could see in my mind was those hacked-off fingers and all that blood. Throats cut, bodies mutilated, Caramel with a hole in her head. I didn't have time to think about my situation or to dwell on the fact that me and Caramel were two broke-ass females all alone in the world. I sure wasn't gonna let myself acknowledge that the people who had brutally shot my sister and killed my mother were probably looking to do me too and that it was probably just a matter of time.

Vonnie and Dominica arrived by my side while I was at the

funeral home. Caramel had gotten out of ICU by then and was now in a regular room, but she still had a twenty-four-hour guard at her side. I was busy making arrangements for Mama to be cremated when my girls showed up. I was so grateful that they'd come, and so glad I wouldn't have to stand there and put my mama away all by myself, that I broke down so bad they ended up taking me outside the funeral home and splashing water all over my face.

I had barely eaten two spoonfuls of anything in almost a week because every time I even thought about touching some food the smell from Mama's place crept up in my nose and throat and made me sick. Dom and Vonnie were hungry though, so they took me to get a burger, which I picked over for about an hour before throwing it in the trash. I knew they had a lot of questions they wanted to ask, but after the grilling I'd gotten from the cops I was in no condition to go through all that again. Instead, we went to visit Caramel, who was sleeping when we got there. I talked to her nurse and she told me my sister was doing damn good for somebody who had got shot in the head. She was opening her eyes and talking and going through a bunch of tests to find out if she had lost any memory or normal functioning.

Later that night I got real tired so the three of us went back to my place and climbed in my bed together and cried. Dominica had seemed kinda uneasy all throughout the day, but as usual, Vonnie was the one to keep it real.

"Candy," she sniffed, wiping away her tears. Even at a time like this Vonzelle was pressed out and her hair was hooked. "Girl, I know I called you a dumb bitch when you left the other day and shit, and I'm sorry. You know I didn't mean it. I just wanted us to get with Hurricane so bad." Then she sat up in the bed and unsnapped the back of her lacy push-up bra and threw it on the floor. Her titties were full and perfectly round, and her brown nipples pointed straight toward the ceiling when she laid back down. "But for real though"—she wiped her eyes again—"we need to get our asses back to New York with a quickness. If them motherfuckers could bust up in your mama's place without a problem, what's to stop them from coming up in here right now and rolling us out too?"

I'd been thinking those same kinda thoughts but I owed it to Mama to see that she got put away right, and I owed it to Caramel to make sure she was going to be okay. I refused to let myself dwell on my fear. I'd been scared in some kinda way or form for most of my life, and I wasn't stupid enough to think that fear could get me away from a family like the Gabrianos. If they wanted my black ass, they would come for it. Whether I stayed in L.A., jetted to New York, or caught the next shuttle to the moon. There was no place I could hide, and I told my girls that.

The next morning we held the service in a small parlor of the funeral home. The casket was kept closed and the cremation was scheduled to take place immediately afterward. As fly and pretty and outgoing as Mama had been, I felt bad that there were less than ten people there to see her off, but I couldn't afford to fly her body back to Harlem where all her running partners still lived. The manager at Mama's old job had showed up, and so had my girl Lulu from computer school along with her mother. Lulu had gotten her shit out of my apartment and ran straight home after the murders. She saw what Greasy had gotten for hanging with Mama, and she was scared the same thing might happen to her if she stayed too close to me.

A few of Caramel's friends from high school came out too. They had been visiting Caramel in the hospital pretty often, and now they sat sniffling in the back row by themselves. Caramel's music teacher had really liked Mama. She thought Mama had the most amazing voice, and looking at Mama's casket she cried so hard she got hysterical. "What a damn shame," she kept moaning over and over again. "Such an amazing waste of talent. That lady had promise! She could have been somebody! She could have been somebody. . . ."

The funeral director held her in his arms and led her out the room, but aside from Vonnie and Dom, there was no one in the world to hold me, and my tears just wouldn't stop falling as I realized that the last physical reminder of my mother was laying there in that cheap wooden box.

I was crying even harder on the inside than on the outside because I felt guilty and I shoulda known better. Instead of chasing some damn recording contract I should have been out there on my business. Nicky had been right. I'd put Mama in a situation that she couldn't handle, knowing full well how weak she was when it came to drugs and quick money. Mama's past behavior should have been a clue that she couldn't resist that much cash, especially when she had a niggah talking in her ear. And Caramel. My baby sister. She'd been right there to see it all, and there was no doubt that she would keep seeing it in her mind for the rest of her life. I'd done a bad job on my own family, and the fact that I'd thrown everybody's life away for a chance to sing in front of Hurricane Jackson messed me up most of all.

Dominica and Vonnie helped me get through the funeral

and were down for me 100 percent. They were flying back to New York later in the afternoon, but they had begged me to go back with them.

"Candy," Dominica said when we were back at my apartment and she was packing her bag. "Girl, I got a funny feeling in my nose. Why'ont you grab your gear and hop on this bird with us. C'mon. Caramel got a guard, but you ain't got shit. I ain't trying to leave you sitting like a duck in no death trap all by yourself."

I shook my head.

"Well what in the fuck is keeping you here?" Vonnie wanted to know.

I shook my head again. Vonnie couldn't help it. She just didn't understand what it was like to love somebody more than you loved yourself. She didn't know shit about how I loved my sister. She hadn't seen or heard from her little brother since her mother OD'd and they got sent to foster care, but Mama hadn't raised me and Caramel like that. I'd die before I left Caramel stranded in some hospital way out in L.A. by herself. That shit just wasn't happening. "My sister is keeping me here, Vonnie," I said. "My baby sister."

"Well," Vonnie said, styling her hair in the mirror. She turned around and peered at her plump ass to make sure it still looked good. "Before we left New York I got with Hurricane and put him down on what happened to you. He's got mad connections out here in L.A. and said if you needed anything to just call."

Yeah. Okay. Picture that shit.

That night after Dom and Vonnie had gone, I laid on the floor by my bed staring at a small snapshot of me, Mama, and

Caramel and wondering how the fuck my life had ended up so empty and what I could do to get it back on track. I could see Mama smoking a blunt and yelling, "Damn my doll baby can sang! Work that stage, Candy Raye! Work that whole mutha-fuckin' stage!"

Fuck singing, I thought. I didn't care if I never sang again.

And then I thought about the message Hurricane had sent by Vonzelle. *If you need anything, just call.* That niggah would be the last person I called. But I did need something, I admitted as I rolled onto my side just as another wave of tears hit me.

I needed my mama.

◊ ◊ ◊

Hours later I opened my eyes in the darkness and my whole heart started pounding up in my throat. The last thing I remembered was crying myself to sleep on the floor, and now I was wide awake, listening. I'd heard footsteps. Somebody was in my kitchen and moving toward my bedroom.

I didn't even think about it. I scooted my ass under the bed like a crab, bumping into shoe boxes and stacks of computer repair manuals and magazines and praying like a motherfucker.

There were two of them. I could see their shoes coming down the short hall, and I held my breath hoping they wouldn't hear me. They were white men, I could tell by the sneakers. Some off-brand tennis shoes they probably only wore when they were out on jobs like this.

My room wasn't bigger than a minute, and it didn't take them long to find me. One of them flipped the whole damn bed over while the other one dragged me by my feet across the floor. They started giving me man-blows. I got punched in the

face and I felt my nose explode. Blood went everywhere, choking me as it gurgled in my throat.

I tried to scream but only managed to cough. They were
kicking me like a football, back and forth between them, banging my ribs and stomping their feet up in my lower back. One
of them grabbed me by the neck and flung me into the dresser
so hard I cracked my face on the wood and howled, holding
my jaw. *Yeah,* I thought, fighting to stay alive through the
punches and the pain. *These are Nicky's boys all right.* I could
tell by the way they beat me and the shit they talked. This ass-
kicking wasn't business. It was strictly personal, and all I could
do was close my eyes, roll up in the fetal position, and pray I'd
die fast.

They beat my ass unconscious, and when I opened my eyes
again I was surrounded by darkness and my arms were throbbing with pain. My hands were tied behind me and I was under
a blanket or something. I was moving too. In a small tight
space, the trunk of a car. I tried to scream but realized there was
tape across my mouth. Kicking a taillight out wasn't gonna
happen. I couldn't see shit, and plus my feet felt like they were
tied together at the ankles.

I couldn't even think I was so scared and in so much pain. I
started praying, talking to God, Mama, and Caramel all at the
same time. Minutes later the car lurched hard to the right like
it was skidding off the road. I slid with the momentum and
cracked my head up against something hard. The car slowed
down and I braced myself as we rolled to a quick stop.

Doors opened and then slammed shut, and a moment later
I heard loud voices. Men talking. Arguing. And then the trunk
popped opened and cool air rushed in. Somebody pulled the

blanket off me, and if my mouth wasn't taped shut it would have fell the hell open.

"This you?" I stared at the Italian guy standing over me. His fat behind was the one who had kicked me all up my ass, and if my feet wasn't tied together I'da punted him straight in his dick.

The man he was talking to nodded. "That's right, Victor. This is *me*. You heard what the fuck Nicky said on the phone just now. I'm pulling in a favor from an old friend."

"Okay." Victor shrugged. "You can have the bitch. But remember, if you ever take your hands off her, she's ours again."

Seconds later the tape was ripped off my mouth, and my arms and legs were freed. I was helped out of the trunk, and I hobbled into the sports car that looked like it had forced the Italians off the road. My aching ass felt like it was being cradled in warm cotton as I sank back into the plush leather seats.

"Thanks," I whispered as tears filled my swollen eyes.

Hurricane Jackson just looked over at me and nodded.

Chapter 11

Back on the Block

Hurricane took me to his place and let me heal for about a week. He had a condo in La Brea, and I chilled and laid low there while he handled his West Coast business with them same Italians who had almost killed me. Every morning he brought me doughnuts or scrambled me some eggs, then had one of his boys drop me off at the hospital where I stayed next to Caramel's bed until late at night. He didn't try to sex me once. In fact, he didn't even stay in the same room with me. He said I needed time to heal and he didn't want to mess with that.

I looked ten times worse than my sister did and couldn't sit down without a pillow, and when the cop who was guarding her saw all my bruises he called his sergeant and blabbed his damn mouth. The cops were back in my face in less than an hour. They wanted to know who kicked my ass, where I was living, and if I would come down to the station and look at some mug shots.

You know what I told them. I was in the wrong place at the

wrong time and got jumped by a gang of bitches who were banging. They stole me from behind, so I never saw their faces. Mug shots? Like I said, I never saw who hit me so there wasn't no need in wasting their time.

Caramel's doctors said her condition was stable. She'd gotten away with just a deep graze, and they said the only thing she might suffer was some short-term memory loss. She'd told them she didn't even remember getting shot, and she was mad at me 'cause the whole thing had gone down in the first place. She was gonna be discharged from the hospital in a few days, but I didn't have anywhere to take her when she was released. Going back to my place was totally out, and Mama's place was still a crime scene.

Hurricane was pressed to get back to Harlem to meet with some producers for an upcoming video shoot, and he said I had to roll out with him. "You heard what the man said, Candy. I gotta keep you close, girl. If they find out you walking with no protection, they'll kill you."

The only way he could get me to agree to leave my sister was to hire a nurse to fly back to New York with Caramel as soon as she was discharged and cleared by the doctor.

"Don't stress nothing," he told me. "Your sister can stay with us. We got plenty of room where I rest."

I hated to leave Caramel alone, even for a few days, but she seemed to understand what was up and I really didn't have no other choice. It was either do things the way Hurricane said or die a hardhead's death.

I did what I had to do.

● ● ●

The next morning we caught a flight back to New York. Hurricane had a white Jaguar waiting at the airport that was driven by some guy Vonnie was fucking named Quadir. The whip was phat as hell, and any other time I would have been memorizing every detail so I could brag on it to Dom, but so much had happened over the last two weeks that I couldn't relax enough to enjoy it at all. The only thing that mattered to me was that in a few days my baby sister would be coming back to Harlem to live large with Hurricane and me.

Even though my short-term problems—like Caramel, a crib, and some pocket change—had been solved, all kinds of other issues were running through my head as we drove through Queens and out to Long Island. It was a relief to be safe from the Gabrianos, and I wanted to prove to Hurricane that his decision to snatch me and Caramel out of L.A. was the right one. We'd talked on the airplane and he told me how Vonnie had run my whole situation down to him.

"It's fucked up what happened to your people," he said. I was looking out the window and thinking that out of all the trips I'd taken as a mule, this was my first time traveling in first class. Hurricane was drinking his ass off and had them ditzy little flight attendants running back and forth and getting him ice, crackers, you name it.

"But that's how it goes in this hustle," he was saying. "You was a little girl playing stupid games with a lot of big boys, Candy. That was a lot of money your mother tried to hustle off. You lucky Nicky's my nuccah and I got to him in time. You was almost out."

"Well, thanks for looking out for me and Caramel," I said,

not knowing what else to say. "I just don't know what I can do to pay you back on that kind of solid."

"Oh, you gone pay me back," he laughed, shrugging his big shoulders and snapping his fingers so they could bring him another drink. "Believe that." Then he looked at me and laughed again. "Them Italians add mad interest to their debts, little girl. There ain't no ceiling on what they can ask for, and they asked a whole lot for you. But it's all good. You mine now, and me and you gone do a lot of shit for each other, ya know? You, sexy Candy, are gonna ring me up a whole lotta money. And I"—he took a big swallow of cognac—"am gonna take care of you and make you a hot new star."

I didn't have no complaints about being a star or about being his. Big Money Cane was talking just the kind of noise that I wanted to hear, and any way he wanted things to roll was good with me. Mama had taught me to think on the move, and I was impressed by getting claimed by a baller like him. Hurricane Jackson could have had any female he wanted. Three and four of them at a time if he wanted them that way. Knowing that he'd hopped on a plane because he wanted to help me and my sister out and then hearing him make a promise to launch and back my singing career let me know my future was set.

We got to Long Island and slid up in front of a house that was bigger than some of the office buildings I'd seen in the city. The crib was a mansion for real, all on one level and with three different wings and an intercom system that ran throughout the whole thing. The bushes and shrubs were trimmed so tight I thought somebody had gotten out there with a nail scissor. There was an inground swimming pool off to one side and a basketball court and two tennis courts on the other. Mad expensive cars were lined up near the garage, and a huge onyx sculpture of a dragon stood guarding the doorway.

Hurricane took me inside to introduce me to his posse, the crew that was closest to him and had his utmost trust. Five of his most loyal soldiers lived with him in the house, and four of them had girlfriends who were known in the industry as "housewives."

The mansion had fireplaces and smoked marble floors and every imaginable comfort you could want. There were mad corridors, and it felt like we walked at least a mile before Hurricane opened a door on one of the family rooms and introduced me to a pretty, light-skinned sister with long curly hair who was bent over a sewing machine. I couldn't tell what she was making, but she was wearing designer everything. Crazy jewels dripped from her neck and her fingers were rocked out.

"Candy, Fatima. Fatima, Candy." Then he turned to me. "I got some business to see about. Teema'll take you around to meet everybody and help get you set up straight."

I saw surprise in her eyes as she looked me over real quick. I wondered if I passed her little test because she still looked shocked as she turned to Hurricane and said, "Where you want me to put her, Cane? In that empty room on the right?"

Hurricane laughed, then reached out and touched my hair. "Nah, baby. This me. Her sister's shit can go on the right when it gets here, but put her fine red ass dead in the middle."

◔ ◔ ◔

Teema waited until Hurricane walked out then got up in my face and said, "So what did you do?"

"What?"

She waved her hand like, *Bitch, please. You know what I'm talking about.*

"What you say your name was again?"

"Candy,"

"Oh, okay, Candy. So how'd you hook Cane?"

I just looked at her, wondering what her game was and why she was here. She had a big ass and a tight waist, but she seemed too together-looking to be a video ho. "I didn't know he was hooked. Thanks for the 411."

She bust out laughing. "Girl you good. I'm just tripping. It's been a long time since we put somebody in the middle. Wait till I tell Sissy. I hope you last longer than the other one did, though, 'cause that stuck-up bitch couldn't hang for more than a month."

She took me through the front of the house into a huge kitchen that had two stoves and one of those industrial-looking refrigerators. "This right here"—she opened it up and all I saw was Colt 45s, frozen pizza, buffalo wings, and Bulls—"is ours. That one over there"—she pointed toward a smaller fridge, and when she opened it there was fresh fruit, vegetables, bottled water, yogurt, and milk—"belongs to Cane. I was gonna say don't touch his shit, but since he said to put you in the middle maybe you got it like that."

I found out later that there were two maids who cleaned the mansion and shopped for food and a Mexican guy who took care of the big-ass lawn and maintained the pool. I also found out that the middle of the house was the part of the mansion that Hurricane had all to himself. There was his big-ass bedroom, two guest rooms, three bathrooms, a weight room, and a small kitchenette. The left side of the house was where Teema and I had just come from. Over there I had seen three big suites that were laid out like separate apartments. Teema stayed in one of the larger suites with her man, Joog, and Butter, the brother in charge of Hurricane's gambling operation, lived on that end with his woman too. Butter's woman had recently had a baby and he'd sent her to Detroit to stay with her mama 'cause he said she wasn't acting right. Some guy named Vince stayed in the last suite with his housewife, Sissy, who Teema said was busy watching a movie.

The right side of the house was where that dude Knowledge stayed, and there were a total of three suites on that end too. Knowledge had one of his own, and Long Jon, Hurricane's chief of security, and his girl, Peaches, lived in one, and the other one was empty.

Teema switched her gangsta booty down the hall ahead of me. "I'ma introduce you to Peaches, but don't fuck with her 'cause she ain't right upstairs, and if you ever see that crazy bitch anywhere near the kitchen watch her like a hawk. She so scatter-brained she'll be tryin to make toast and fuck around and burn the whole house down."

We walked what seemed like another mile to the right side of the house. There were three doors and we stopped outside the one in the middle.

"Peaches! Peaches!" Teema hollered, then knocked real quick, opened the door, and clicked on the light. I saw her from the side. Sistah had been sitting there in the dark checking out the wall. Teema had to call her twice before she even turned our way, and then she looked around like, *What? Where am I? Who are you?*

I glanced around the huge room. Wide-screen TV, nice stereo. The furniture was da bomb, but the covers were tossed off her bed, clothes and junk were all over the floor, and the suite had a funky odor like she needed to open up the windows.

"Peaches, we got a new girl in the house."

She focused her eyes on me and I was shocked to see how beautiful she was. "Good," she said, " 'cause all them other bitches livin' up in here are past tired."

"Who's tired?"

Peaches cut her eyes. "That bitch Laniqua for one."

"No, girl." Fatima shook her head. "Remember, Laniqua drowned, Peaches. She *been* gone."

Peaches shrugged. "Whatever. The bitch was tired."

"Hey," I said. "I'm Candy."

She stared at me for a second then said, "Hey your damn self. Who you? You cute, but them contact lenses are played. You got that red weave working but them blue eyes gotta go."

"I'm Candy," I repeated.

Peaches yawned and stretched, ice glinting from her ears, neck, and wrists. Her soft brown hair hung down her back in loose curls. "Teema, what I told you about busting up in my room? I'm hungry. Tell Long Jon to bring me something to eat." Then she stared at me again. "Who you? Girl don't be so damn fake. Them blue eyes gotta go. . . ."

Teema grabbed my arm and pulled me out the doorway. "That's Peaches. Like I said, don't fuck with her. She cool, but she been beat down too much. The bitch has brain damage."

I followed Teema down a hall and into a room with a drop-down movie screen and a bunch of soft velvet love seats. A hot new flick called *G-Spot* was playing on the screen, and stretched out on a sofa near the front of the room was one of the flyest chicks I'd ever seen.

"Sissy," Teema said, grabbing my arm and parading me in front of sistah who had rich ebony skin and wide eyes. "This is Candy. She's a new singer getting ready to sign a contract. Hurricane dropped her off and she's staying in the middle."

Sissy swung her feet to the floor and stared at me. Her bone-straight hair seemed to say *whissssh* before settling around her shoulders. "What? Girl, stop lying and get out my face. I know that crazy motherfucker ain't bring no bitch up in here to put in the middle!" Then she stood up and grinned. "Oops!" She covered her mouth. "Damn. I didn't mean you a bitch. Girl, how you doing. I'm Sicily, but you can call me Sissy."

I nodded and said hey, even though I didn't see why these hef-fahs were so damn shocked to see me. Hurricane was a grown-ass man. He was probably what? Thirty-five pushing thirty-six? I couldn't have been the first piece of pussy he had brought home.

"Yeah," I said, giving them both slight attitude. I'd just lost my mama, almost lost my sister, and had flown across the country from one coast to another. I was tired, and it was time to let my position be known because I knew how minor and jealous chicks could be. "I'm Candy," I said real straight-up-like. "And that's right. I'm Hurricane's new woman. I'm a hot-ass singer and a badass bitch, and I'll be chilling in the middle."

I had put my mark down with boldness and confidence, but that's because I was dumb and didn't understand that Fatima and Sicily had been through all this shit before. They knew some details about the mighty Hurricane that I didn't know yet. They knew that before the night was over my new man would come home and give me a long kiss and a hot bath, then stick his .44 between my legs and threaten to splatter my pussy all over the mattress.

Chapter 12

The Rules of the Game

We walked back down to the kitchen where Teema and Sissy put me up on the house rules. Rule number one? Hurricane was king and his word was the law.

"He snaps on the regular, and he don't take no shit from nobody," Sissy said, "but he got these niggahs up in here so vexed they don't give him none neither."

I stared at her with her pretty black self. "Vexed? For what?"

She laughed. "You must ain't seen your contract yet."

"Rule number two," Teema said. "Don't touch shit in this crib that don't belong to you. If Hurricane didn't personally give it to you, that means you stole it."

Sissy jumped in next. "And rule number three . . . the attic is a badland. Don't go your ass up there. Never. Not for anything."

"What's up there?" I asked.

Teema gave me the stupid face. "If Cane wanted us to know what was up there, he wouldn'ta put the shit off-limits! You better learn real quick not to ask no whole lotta questions around here. Don't nothing but men's business go on in this house, so keep your mouth closed and roll with the program."

"So what do the females do?"

They thought that shit was funny.

Sissy hollered. "Suck dick!"

"Fuck their men!" Teema laughed.

I found out that Teema liked to sew and made most of her clothes. Cooking was Sissy's thing, although she was so bony I doubted if she ate much. "Cane owns a rib shack but he don't allow no hog in this camp," Teema told me. "But Sissy be sneaking that shit in here anyway. She seasons the hell out of our food with it, then feeds the evidence to his dog, Predator."

As tired as I was I sat talking with them for over an hour, but it had only taken me a minute to see what was really going on. Sissy, Peaches, and Teema had flawless skin, banging bodies, silky hair, and empty lives. They were made up, dressed up, iced out, and bored as hell living way out in the boonies on Long Island.

I was glad that I had talent, and if I stuck with Hurricane, I knew I would have a booming career. I liked looking good and having fun, and I loved sex more than most men. But sitting around all day while the fellas was out there getting recognized wasn't my thing. I needed much more than that.

◊ ◊ ◊

Hurricane had been sexy, sweet, and generous while we were in L.A., but less than two weeks later things had changed between us in a hurry. For one thing, he had been perpetrating that night he finger-fucked me on the dance floor at the House. Wasn't nothing hot or sexy about his ass. All that licking pussy juice from his fingers and thangs had been a big act designed to get me where he wanted me, and from then on my orgasms were my own damn responsibility. And all that mutual dream building and conversating about my singing future went out the window too. He let me know real quick that there was no questioning him about his business or about my career. He immediately signed Scandalous! to a two-album deal that named Knowledge as our lawyer and Joog as our manager, and as soon as my bruises healed we got busy in the studio, working day and night to lay down our tracks and produce our hit album.

My shit was still live and you know I held it down on the mic, but I was grieving bad for Mama, and being in the studio was hard. It took me a minute to get past the guilt I was feeling because in spite of everything that had went down, I still wanted to sing. I still needed to sing. Hurricane simplified shit for me real fast though. He said I *had* to sing.

So I did, and I can honestly say it still made me feel good. Mama always said my voice was a gift from God, and since she had always got so much joy out of listening to me, maybe in some sort of way she could still hear me.

When Caramel arrived she moved into the empty room on the right side of the house, but I was in the studio so much that I didn't have a lot of time to spend with her. In a couple of weeks I would have to take a day off and get her enrolled in school, but in the meantime I ended up leaving her at the mansion, as long as Sissy or Teema was home. I didn't trust Peaches to look after her. That would be too much like the blind leading the damn deaf.

But then I found out that Teema and Sissy weren't much better. Those two chicks were devious and conniving, and as soon as the door closed behind me in the mornings they started putting my sister up to all kinds of stupid shit. And Caramel was down for whatever too. I don't care what those doctors said. That bullet had done something to my sister. Caramel before she got shot was not the same Caramel after she took that bullet. She was still beautiful and the way she wore her hair covered her bullet wound almost completely, but something wasn't connecting upstairs and it seemed like her whole personality had changed.

Where before the shooting she was a gifted pianist, these days she acted like she'd never even read a musical note before. And all of a sudden she wanted to be a rapper. Lil' Kim, if possible. Hell, even if she could rap, Caramel had too much ass to be walking around dressed like Lil' Kim. She had major attitude with me all the time too, and that was new. The doctors said all these changes were because of the violence involved in her trauma, and I believed them. Who knows what afflictions I mighta walked away with after having a gun stuck to my head and hearing the trigger pulled.

But more than Caramel's personality had changed. A few weeks after she got home she told me she wanted to come down to the House of Homicide and party. This is from a quiet little mouse-girl who never even had a boyfriend. Caramel was seventeen years old and Mama had recently bragged to me that she'd never even been kissed. Let alone felt or fucked. And now she was flossing around in shorts that showed her crack and wagging her round ass under the greedy eyes of grown men.

We had never gone back into Mama's house after the murders, so Caramel had lost all her clothes and everything else that she owned. Her little stuff hadn't been worth all that much, but

Hurricane had given her several grand so she could buy some gear and get herself right again. I'd asked Teema to take her into Midtown to shop at Macy's and Nordstrom, but as soon as I saw the plastic bags they came dragging home I knew for sure they had been on Pitkin Avenue in Brooklyn, or Fordham Road in the Bronx, or maybe even Jamaica Avenue in Queens.

Everything Caramel had bought was too short, too tight, and too loud. My baby sister was walking around looking like one of those desperate chickenheads who posed outside the House of Homicide hoping to hook a baller every night. All her shit might as well have been neon and silver-studded and screaming, Fuck me, fuck me, and fuck me *hard.*

Another thing that bothered me about Caramel was that she acted like she wasn't bothered about Mama. She never wanted to talk about her, and whenever I mentioned something about Mama she brushed me off and acted like she didn't wanna hear it. I couldn't figure out what she had against Mama all of a sudden. I understood why she dissed me, because she had every right to be mad at me. I was the one who put them in that situation in the first place.

"You and Mama was the ones tight, Candy," Caramel had the nerve to say to me. "Y'all was the ones always talking and singing and doing shit together. Y'all left me by myself most of the time, and neither one of y'all came to see me when they had my ass locked up in foster care."

"Uh-uh, Caramel," I protested. "It was always all three of us. You don't remember? We slept on one mattress together, and me and Mama always put you right in the middle! We did everything together, Caramel. Mama didn't play favorites with us. She loved us both the same."

She looked at me with my same blue eyes, then turned her lip up and walked away. I really didn't know what to do about her. I had to go to the studio, so I couldn't stay home and baby-sit her all day. Vonnie said to leave her crazy ass back at the mansion 'cause it wasn't like she could walk way out to Harlem from the boondocks anyway, but I got the feeling Vonnie just didn't want Caramel around. Baby sister had a banging body, and she mighta been looking just a little bit too fly and too hooched out for Vonnie's tastes. Vonzelle Desiree Greenley did not like competition. Standing onstage next to me every night was bad enough without having my younger image blocking on the scene too.

But Dominica told me to just deal with the changes in my sister and to bring her on down to the studio with me. "At least there you'll be able to watch out for her, Candy. It don't matter how grand Hurricane's mansion is if it's way out in south hell. Caramel probably feels like a prisoner up in that camp. Coming down to the studio will be like getting out of lockdown."

I thought about it for a minute and then I agreed. Later, when I looked back at how it all went down, I would say that was the only piece of bad advice that Dominica had ever given me.

◊   ◊   ◊

Caramel was off the chain. The day after I talked to Dom and Vonnie about her I broke down and let her come with me out to the House. I should have known she was scheming from minute one, because as soon as we walked through the doors she took off on me talking about she needed to "investigate" the layout so she could know her way around.

"Can't you wait?" I said. "We just walked in the door two seconds ago. Ain't nothing up in here for you anyway, but gimme a few minutes and I'll show you where the bathroom is and take you down the street to meet Shyreeka. She'll hook you up with some ribs for lunch."

She kept right on moving, heading down the walkway that led to the pit. "You ain't my mother, Candy. And I don't need no tour guide. I can find my way around."

I wasn't feeling her snooping everywhere. The House of Homicide was supposed to be for an over-21 crowd, and there were some places in this joint where her little ass didn't need to be. Like that mini dope distribution center Tonk had going upstairs. Or the triple-X video room downstairs where Hurricane filmed them poor young girls doing the nastiest shit you could think of with some of the most high-rolling rap artists on BET and MTV. But Caramel was right. I wasn't Mama. Hell, I was only nineteen and Caramel was already seventeen. Mama had trained me to take care of her since I was little, though, and since she was the only family I had it was hard for me to stop thinking she was a little girl and treating her that way.

"Well come right back then," I hollered after her. "Meet me downstairs in Studio B."

I didn't see that girl no more for the next two hours, and when she did show up she knew the House of Homicide like the back of her hand.

"Long Jon's security office is hooked the hell up. Cameras and equipment out the ass. But why they got all them bars all over the windows? And why are all the exits locked and chained up?"

"Damn," I said. She was telling me some things I didn't even know. "You been looking that deep?"

"Hell yeah," she said all happy. "This place is it for me, Candy. I got a feeling I'ma be spending a whole lot of time around here."

I didn't even like how that shit sounded coming out her mouth. The House of Homicide was home to some hard, thugged-out criminals and playas, and Caramel was so new she had just come out the house. I watched the way she looked around, running her hands all over shit, grinding her hips, then bending the mic down to her lips and acting like she was singing. Mama had once said that even a blind rat could find himself a hole, and something told me that my little sister had just found hers.

◆ ◆ ◆

Make no mistake about it. I was grateful to be where I was and doing what I was doing. I was on the verge of a hot singing career and just about to bust out and show the world what kind of talent I had and what I was made of, but I was also starting to have some for-real for-real doubts about my new life and my new man. Hurricane had about ten different personalities, and there was some new niggah living up in his head every other night.

I'd come up on the streets with Mama, so I knew all about the cold-blooded, nasty hustlers who were walking around looking for victims. But Hurricane was past nasty. He was nasty, cold-blooded, ruthless, and cruel at the same time. No bullshit, he was sick in the head. He had two faces: One he showed to get who or what he wanted, and the other one he showed once he had people where he wanted them. He was so heartless and vicious he gave a fuck who he hurt if it made him feel good.

And lately a whole lotta things about him were working me. First of all, Hurricane liked to play around with animals.

That nut had birds, fish, and turtles, and even a little rat-looking hamster that he let out the cage and allowed to run around our room while we was sleep. I was too scared to even get up in the middle of the night and go to the bathroom. Some mornings I woke up having to pee so bad my stomach was cramped.

But that wasn't the worst part. Hurricane was into snakes and dogs too, two animals that flat-out terrified me. The snake's name was Savage and he kept her in a cage in one of the guest rooms. She was a baby ball python and only about five feet long, which Hurricane said was small but looked pretty damn big to me.

"This my real bitch. Ain't she fine?" he would say, holding her all up in my face as I tried not to freak out. Miss Savage scared the shit out of me, and Hurricane knew it and he liked it. "She bites," he told me one day, which just scared me even more. "But she ain't got no poison, so she won't kill you." He made me go in there with him whenever he had to clean her cage, and he even made me thaw out the frozen mice he kept in a little freezer for her to eat.

If the damn snake wasn't bad enough, the dog was even worse. Hurricane had a big, nasty-ass Doberman named Predator that he took with him almost everywhere he went. Hurricane had him trained to obey his every command, but I'd seen him play around and sic that beast on plenty of flunkies out at the House.

I didn't do animals in the first place, but I could have sworn that dog wanted to fuck me. He would run up to me and try to stick his whole head between my legs, then snap his jaws and act all crazy when I wouldn't let him get a little sniff.

Predator had claimed his territory in the backseat of Hurricane's Yukon XL Denali with the size 24 shoes. Wherever we went he was right there riding between us with his scratchy paws up on the middle console and his big wet mouth drooling stank spit.

"Damn, Cane," I'd said one morning on the way to the studio when I got fed up with all that damn panting in my ear and slobber being slung on my shoulder. "Why can't we leave his nasty ass home sometimes?"

That crazy dog slapped his paws on my arm and started growling and snapping. I was scared to turn and look dead at him, but I could sure see all them long, pointy-ass teeth out the corner of my eye. "Get your dog, Hurricane," I said, pressing myself against the window. "What the hell is wrong with him?"

He wouldn't even call the dog off. He just circled his ride around and headed in the opposite direction saying, "Nah, what the fuck is wrong with you?" The next thing I knew we were back at the house and my ass was being kicked out the whip. I had no choice but to take my tail back in the house with the rats and the snakes and chill until he felt like coming back for me.

But that wasn't the worst of it.

Hurricane had some strange shit about him in bed. When I tell you he was dickless, I'm not playing. Brother was short. He needed a dick weave. Some Krazy Glue and a couple of dick tracks. I didn't understand how the rest of his body could be so banging and he be so jacked below the belt, but he was. The bad thing about it was when he got hard his shit was nice and pretty for the whole two inches there was of it. Then it just fell off to nothing. It had a man-sized thickness and a baby-sized length, and the sight of it kinda freaked me out.

One time I got careless enough to make him think I was laughing at it. He punched me in the back of the head so hard I saw bright flashes for two days. I was laying on the throw pillows thinking about the last time I'd had my pussy eaten real good. It had been a long time, back when I was still in foster care. I'd just gotten a job working in an upscale restaurant as a coat-check girl. People would pass me their expensive furs and leathers to hang up and keep safe until they had finished their meal. The door to the coatroom had a top half and a bottom half. The top half swung wide open, of course, but the bottom half usually stayed closed. I kept a big tip jar halfway filled with coins and dollar bills up front on the ledge of the bottom half, you know, to encourage the customers to pay me for my service.

Well this fine Puerto Rican kid named Javier, who bussed tables, had his eye on me and wouldn't let up. He had dark skin and a long ponytail that was real black and curly. His dimples were devastating, and his lips were so pretty I could have sucked them all night. Javier went out of his way to walk past me several times a night, and when he did he made sure I saw the fat bulge in his pants. He said it was just for me and that I could have it anytime I wanted it. Well I wanted that shit. It looked so huge and stuck out from his body like a little flagpole and he had to carry his plastic dish bucket in front of him to hide it.

It was a Wednesday night, and little did I know it but in

three days I would run into someone from my past and leave that job for good. The restaurant was pretty empty. I'd been working for two hours, and I'd only hung up about twelve coats. Javier walked past me a few times, and each time he'd grab his big dick and shake it at me. I rolled my eyes at him and all, but my pussy was wet on the real tip, and I wouldn't have minded checking him out and seeing what he was all about.

About an hour before closing he came up to me bringing a line.

"Why don't you let me get in there with you," he said.

I gave him a look like *Be for real.* "Why don't you go back out there and do your damn job?" I said with a whole lot of attitude for somebody whose nipples were almost poking him in the face.

He just smiled, running his pretty pink tongue over his lips. "For real," he said, turning the doorknob and damn near knocking over my tip jar. "I'm only gonna stay for a minute."

I didn't know what the hell he thought he was gonna do to me in that coatroom, because waiters and waitresses and an occasional customer were still walking past every now and then, but I wasn't about to let it happen.

He came in quickly and closed the bottom half of the door. Then to my surprise he got down on his knees and touched my hip. "Turn around," he urged.

I stared down at him. "For what?"

"Shhh . . ." He pushed on my hip and grabbed the hem of my black skirt. "Face front before somebody asks you who's in here!"

I turned around and tried to look normal. He tapped my

foot, urging my legs wider. He yanked the back of my skirt up, rolling it past my hips, and my whole ass was exposed. I couldn't believe it when I felt him on me back there. He tried pulling my thong all the way to one side, and when that didn't work for him he ripped it, letting the center string hang free. He kissed my ass murmuring softly, his soft lips smacking every inch of my cheeks. Then he spread me open wider, forcing me to lean my elbows on the counter and bend my knees. That boy stuck his whole face up in me. His hot tongue licked my slit as he pressed my swollen clit between his lips.

All I could do was moan deep in my throat as I spread my legs wider and leaned on that little ledge trying my best to keep a straight face. Javier was eating the hell out of my squirting pussy. Lapping up my juices before they could fall from me. His tongue was like a little snake. Darting between my lips, flicking my clit, probing my asshole.

I came about four times before I couldn't take it anymore. I was sagging at the knees, and sweat was running from my hair and down my back.

"Stop," I panted, slapping behind me at his face. "Stop!" I tried to bump him off with my ass, but he held on tight, keeping up the rhythm with his tongue and making me come again. I was biting my lip and working my hips. I fucked backward, humping his face and rubbing my own nipples. Javier's tongue was doing some shit to me that had to be illegal. He lifted and massaged my ass cheeks with both hands, tooting it up so he had a clear path to the na-na.

I almost freaked when I realized two customers were coming my way. I'd taken their coats earlier and they'd left a nice tip. I was standing too wide-legged, and at the sight of them I tried to straighten up real quick as another orgasm ripped through my pussy and wobbled my knees.

"People coming!" I hissed, and slapped at his head again. That motherfucker had become one with me. My pussy was now a permanent part of his tongue.

And now the white couple was standing in front of me and I didn't know what the fuck to do.

"Hi," the wife said brightly. "We had the brown trench coat and the black wrap."

Javier sucked my clit between his lips so good I almost started humming. Instead, I coughed and tried to smile. "Okay. Um . . . excuse me. Uh, do you have your ticket?"

The husband started patting himself down, searching for the little blue stub. "I must have left it on the table," he said, and walked back toward the dining room. I was praying his wife would follow him, but instead, she was staring at me like she was trying to figure me out.

"You don't look so good," she said, peering closely into my face. "You're perspiring and your skin looks flushed. Are you coming down with something?"

"Yesssss," I sighed, my eyes rolling upward as I tried not to throw my head back. Javier's tongue was teasing my asshole, and he'd inserted his thumb in my pussy. He pumped it slowly in and out, and he used his other four fingers to massage my wet mound. "Um . . ." I wanted to moan, but instead I let out a weak, fake-ass *ha-choo*. "Something's going around. Don't come too close. It must be c-c-catching."

She got out my face real quick then. "I'll just go help my husband," she said, backing away. "You know, look for the ticket."

The minute she turned her back on me I reached back and pinched Javier's ear until that shit bled. He yelped and took his suction-cup lips off me and pulled his hands out of my pussy.

"What you do that for?" he said, cupping his ear. "You was getting off girl. You liked it!"

He was right. I liked it all right, but I wasn't trying to get caught with him in no coatroom! I was so tongue whipped I could barely stand. By the time the couple came back for their coats I had them off the hanger and ready for them.

"Sorry," the husband said, shaking his head and holding out his hands. "I guess I must have lost it. I can show you ID if you want, but those are our coats."

I gave him a big smile as the wife stood back, eyeing me suspiciously.

"That won't be necessary," I reassured him. "I know these are yours. I remember you from when you came in."

I gave them their coats and then asked one of the waitresses to watch the room while I went to the bathroom. I got in there and wet my face with some cold water, then soaked a paper towel and went into a stall and dabbed at my damp pussy. Javier had eaten me out until I was sore. If I could have snapped his head off his body and taken it home with me, I would have slept with his face between my legs all night long.

My pussy had got to percolating as I thought about Javier's tongue, and I was just about to slip my fingers into my pants and get me a quick nut when Hurricane walked into our bedroom. He had just finished working out in his gym, and he stood in the middle of the room and stripped out of his sweaty clothes.

I must have been in a serious need-some-pussy-licking zone, because I damn near committed suicide.

"Whassup?" he said standing in front of me butt naked and scratching his balls.

I glanced up, saw his baby dick, and chuckled. "Not a damn thing."

The next thing I knew I was flat on my face with monster punches raining down on the back of my head. I screamed and tried to run up the steps and jump on the bed, but he followed me right on up, kicking me in my back and fucking me up. I scrambled around on the bed trying to get away from him, and that niggah snatched me by my shirt and tossed me into the air. I landed on the floor by the dresser, banging my shoulder and yelling for Joog or Butter or anybody to come help my ass.

Hurricane leaped off that bed like a goddamn frog, and it was only God who helped me roll over fast enough to keep him from landing on my head.

"Bitch!" he screamed, and dragged me into the bathroom.

"Please, Cane!" I begged. I was trying to get away, but I wasn't crazy enough to swing no blows like I was bad enough to fight him back. "What I do, boo?" I screamed. "Huh? What did I do?"

He yanked me over to the toilet bowl and lifted the seat. Rage was in him as he stared down at me and he looked like the devil. "You gone make me kill your simple ass."

I screamed for real when I saw what he was planning. That niggah was fittin' to give me a swirlie, and when he tried to dunk my head in the bowl I fought him like he was that old white trick who had almost killed me and Mama.

For a minute I took him by surprise.

Then he regrouped. "Oh, so you a bad bitch, huh? You wanna fight back?"

My whole head was in that bowl before I could draw a quick breath, and I sucked in a mouthful of toilet water that should have been air.

I came up sputtering and choking, freaked the hell out. But Hurricane wasn't finished with me yet.

"All you trifling bitches are just alike!" he screamed. He grabbed the back of my head and dunked me in again, then reached up and flushed the damn toilet. Still cursing, he squeezed my neck between his fingers as cold water ran up my nose burning and choking me, and all I could do was hold my breath and pray the toilet would hurry up and flush and the water would empty out.

When he finally let me go I sat on that bathroom floor and cried loud as hell. I knew Long Jon and them other niggahs had probably heard me hollering. But I was Hurricane's housewife, his property, and playas like them believed whatever a man felt like doing to what was his was his God-given right.

Hurricane just stood there and stared at me like, There. Talk some more shit about my dick if you want to, then he turned around and walked out the bathroom.

I was trying to stand up when I heard his voice.

"Stay your black ass down there."

"W-w-what?" I sniffed back tears as toilet bowl water ran from my hair.

He spoke in the voice of a maniac. "You heard me, Candy. Crawl your ass in here. On your hands and on your mother-fuckin' knees."

I was so scared, what could I do?

I crawled.

Out of the bathroom, across the plush carpet, and over to where he stood, water dripping from my hair and tears falling from my eyes.

"Wash me."

I looked up at him, confused as hell. He never even wanted to take a shower with me, let alone asked me to wash his body.

"Gimme a bath, Candy."

I was about to stand up and head back in the bathroom when he brought his foot up and mushed me dead in the mouth with his big nasty toes. "With your tongue, bitch. Gimme a bath with your *tongue*."

That's right. I had to lick that rusty niggah from his ankles to his ears. It was all about humiliation, and I knew it. First his and now mine.

He had salt coming all off of him. Salt and funk, and he stood there grilling me as I licked him like he was my favorite flavor Tootsie Roll Pop. He had the nerve to cock open his legs when I got to his heavy, sweaty balls, and he wanted those licked top and bottom, under and above. My mouth was dry and I was gagging inside the whole time, but I made damn sure he didn't see it.

"No," he said as I lifted his mini-dick and held it with two fingers. He slapped my hand away and covered up his cheesy little wee-wee, then turned around.

"Now lick my ass."

I got to licking.

I was finishing up the right cheek and starting on the left one when somebody banged on the door.

"Cane!" called a deep voice. "It's Knowledge, man. We got

some hot business to handle, boss. Let's take a quick ride. There's money to be made."

They say money talks and bullshit walks. Well, Knowledge represented money, and little old me? Hey, I was just some old bullshit that Hurricane had rescued out of a mobster's trunk.

I walked.

Chapter 13

Fuckless and Frustrated

The day after he gave me that nasty toilet swirlie, Hurricane surprised me with a gorgeous gift.

"This for you, ma," he said. We'd just come home from the House after a big all-night recording session. Butter was sitting right in the front lounge getting his dick sucked by some groupie he had brought home, and everybody else was chilling in the kitchen where Sissy was cooking breakfast for us. Hurricane made sure the whole household was watching before he gave me the gift. I took the box and just stared at it.

"Go 'head." He waved his hand. "Open that shit up. I ain't got all day."

I opened the box and stared into it before taking out my gift and holding it up so everybody could admire it. It was a 24-karat bracelet that had a trio of nice-sized diamonds on the band and three classy little charms.

And that was just the first peace offering. I noticed real quick that every time Hurricane dogged me out he bought me something def. By the end of the month I had three new pairs of diamond earrings, a platinum and pearl choker, and two dainty white-gold rings rimmed in rubies. That might sound phat, but believe it. For every piece of jewelry Hurricane gave me, he put a scar on my body to match it.

And I wasn't the only one taking blows. Now I knew why the chicks in his mansion stayed iced out. Fatima was a straight redbone, and she had more black-and-blue bruises, busted lips, and black eyes than I could count. But her man Joog kept her gear tight. Jewels, hair, nails, shoes—she had it on lock in all those areas. That's when she wasn't too dented up to leave the goddamn house.

And Peaches. We won't even go there. Fatima had been right. That chick was brain damaged to the bone. Long Jon was a master bitch-beater. I'd seen him mush her in the face with his size 13 boot. While that shit was still on his foot. Later on I found out that this was the usual for some high-profile thug rappers and even a few of the more hard-core ballers. They got so hyped on their money and their gangsta image they started believing they were entitled to kick a bitch's ass whenever she got out of pocket. Just look at them chicks who hung heavy with some of our big-name rappers. Bruised up and hiding behind designer glasses 'cause they tripped over their pussies and banged their eyeballs on the floor. Remember Big Pun's housewife, Liza? And all that shit that was said by Charli Baltimore? I ain't saying all rappers and ballers were wife-beaters, but a hella whole lot of them coulda hung that label around their necks right next to them phat-ass platinum crosses.

So where did that leave sistahs like me who had uncontrollable niggahs who liked to throw blows? As much as I had dreamed of having my name in the media and my songs on the charts, I was beginning to wonder if it would actually feel as sweet as I thought it would. My life was too damn controlled for me to be so young. If I wasn't in the studio rehearsing I was at the crib ducking blows. When I wasn't doing that, I was sneaking on the spare computer and hanging out in sexy chat rooms or participating in hot cybersex. Basically, I was abused and defiant and bored out of my mind. I was tired of masturbating and fantasizing. I wanted to be handled. I wanted my shit done right. I wanted my titties sucked. I wanted to feel some tongue on my clit and a nice thick pipe in my pussy. Instead, I had to satisfy myself with future visions of stardom and get off on that.

I'm not gonna lie. In the back of my mind I'd known shit wasn't all the way right with Hurricane almost from the beginning, especially in the sheets, but I'd ignored it because he was a true warrior when it came down to making music, and he knew exactly how to cut top sellers. He got hold of Scandalous! and made changes in our style and in our pitch that fucked all our heads up they were so good. It didn't matter how much he beat my ass or how bored or horny I was laying next to him in bed. Hurricane was putting it down heavy for me in the studio, and careerwise, that's where it counted.

Plus, Vonnie and Dom were hyped. We were excited as hell about this new direction our lives were taking, although it seemed like I was the one who had to pay all the dues. Anytime Hurricane got his ass on his shoulders, something of ours went out the window and it was my job to get it back. They didn't understand that I was just another possession to Hurricane. They thought since I was in his bed that meant I had his heart in my hand and my mouth to his ear, so my girls were pimping the mess out of me for stuff we hadn't even earned yet like limo service, jewelry, clothes, restaurants, you name it. He even sent us on shopping sprees when he was feeling nice. Saks, Nordstrom, Macy's, Bloomingdale's. We tore them stores up. But let Hurricane get mad because somebody was a half a second late for rehearsals or one of us wasted studio time by forgetting lyrics or singing off-key. That fool nutted up like he was Ike Turner. Fuck sending the limo down to Brooklyn. Y'all bitches betta walk or take the train. Oh, so y'all hungry and ain't had lunch? No more freebies up in my rib shack. Dig some damn Tootsie Rolls or a bag of Doritos outta that goddamn purse.

Hurricane was a slavemaster, but like I said, he also knew how to get top results. He'd learned a lot from music vets like Dr. Dre and Jermaine Dupri, and everything he touched shined like diamonds. He was grooming us to be big stars, and since that was our ultimate dream, none of us could fault him for that.

But belonging to Hurricane meant I had to watch my every move. He was mad jealous and his temper was ridiculous. One time I saw him pistol whip one of his new artists just because the guy messed around and used Hurricane's private bathroom. Hurricane liked to sit down and pee, and I'm sure you can understand why. But not only did this new kid use his toilet without asking, the stupid boy left the seat up when he was done, which pissed Hurricane off so bad he bust up in the bathroom and dragged him out, then went upside his head with that same hair-trigger pistol he had shoved up my stuff.

"Who da fuck"—*wham!*—"told you"—*wham!*—"to piss in my"—*wham!*—"fuckin' bathroom!?" *Wham!*

The guy was so stunned he didn't even have a chance to put

his dick back in his drawers. He rolled over on the floor with his sausage hanging out, and after getting a real good look at it I turned my head right quick and looked the other way. The only niggah pissing on his nuts up in here was Hurricane, I laughed to myself, because that skinny little dude he was beating on was straight hung.

It didn't take us long to complete the first eight tracks on our album 'cause Hurricane kept us on it night and day until we had it right. We argued with him over the title but he wasn't hearing it. The three us of had come up with *Urban Soul,* but he said hell no, the album was gonna be called *Scandalous!* because that's exactly what we three bitches were. He fronted all the money for our pre-release hype, and between him and his sister, Jadeah, our names were hot before the album was even done.

Now I done told y'all about his animals, but the second problem I had living with Hurricane, which was really the biggest problem of all, was my steaming-hot pussy and his little-ass dick. C'mon, like I told you, anytime I was outside of the recording room I was bored. Get real. My hair wasn't red for no reason. I was a hot-ass sistah with a bouncin' booty and a tight waist. I had between-the-legs needs that I couldn't keep handling on my own. But Hurricane didn't fuck. His dick wasn't really long enough to call it that since he couldn't achieve any kind of decent penetration. He liked to use his fingers on me, but hell, I had ten of those myself. When he really needed to get off he would climb on top of me and smash my pussy hairs up until he came, but to tell the truth, he liked sticking other things up in me and pretending they were his dick.

Flashlights, hairbrushes, anything. Hurricane was cruel and sadistic, and when he got to feeling like less than a man below the belt or just felt like hurting me sexually, he didn't hesitate to go into insertion mode. All the Big Berthas of Rikers Island put together didn't have shit on Hurricane, because he got down with a mop handle. He actually shot his thang off by hearing my screams.

"Hold that pussy open, Candy. That's right. Let Papa know he doin' it right. Scream when you getting yours. I wanna see that pussy get nice and wet. I mean straight dripping nookie juice, and, bitch—you *better* come."

Believe it or not, oral sex with him was even worse. He never wanted me to do it to him, and I wasn't sure I could put his little pee-pee in my mouth without laughing anyway. It would have felt like I was sucking on a pacifier. A binky. A nee-nee.

But the first time Hurricane went down on me it was like nothing I had ever known. He got real drunk and then called himself holding me down and eating some pussy. I hollered and screamed and scratched his neck up so bad he let me the hell go. That freak was down there biting and chewing and gnawing on my clit like it was a piece of teriyaki beef jerky. I wasn't bleeding when he finished, but I was so raw I kept checking to see if I was. Two days later it was still burning like a mug when I peed, and if I hadn't been so embarrassed I would have gone to the doctor to get myself some kind of treatment.

Regardless to that fool's sexual issues, I needed a few healthy orgasms to help me chill out. I was masturbating and fantasizing a whole lot, but none of that self-stimulation really satisfied me. Sissy and Teema were all the time bragging about how much good meat they were getting and how sore their pussies were all the time. I wanted to get my nookie sore too, and not from some crazy niggah's teeth or a bunch of unnecessary pelvis banging or frantic friction with no penetration. Hurricane kept plenty of porno flicks around, but watching other people get down didn't do nothing for me. It just encouraged more masturbation, and I was already doing enough of that.

I thought about ordering myself a strap-on dick from the Internet, but then who was I gonna strap that shit on to? Hurricane's manhood would be threatened by anything that resembled a normal-sized dick, so I knew that was out. I considered ordering an extra-large dildo and fucking my own brains out, but then where would I hide it when I was done? Hell, where could I even have one delivered to? Hurricane checked the mail at the mansion, and Jadeah got the mail at the House. That wasn't gonna work either. I felt trapped and frustrated in a situation that gave me little room to move and almost no options.

My frustration burned me inside because while Hurricane was large in the industry and on the street scene, deep inside he was one of those small, insecure niggahs who needed to keep a hottie like me smashed tight in his fist. There was no way he'd leave me enough breathing room to sneak in some real dick on the side. He wanted me to stay stuck up in his bedroom when we was at the mansion. If we was at the House, then I had to stick close to his side or park my ass in his private booth until he gave me permission to move. He didn't even allow me to hang out with Dominica or Vonzelle unless we were rehearsing or laying tracks. To keep me even deeper in check he stuck me in the front office to sit up under Jadeah on a lot of days, and gave me permission to work on some of the House's broken electronic equipment on the side.

Jadeah was cute and had an uptown ass, but when she took off them shades she had a lazy eye that looked down at the floor. As much cash as her baby brother rolled with I didn't see why she didn't just go get her eyestring fixed and be done with it, but since Hurricane had told her to watch me in between studio sessions and keep my ass in check, she put that one good eye to work.

Jadeah was responsible for the front office and for appearances around the House in general. That meant she had the miserable job of grooming Homicide Hitz artists so they looked good on television, spoke right in interviews, and didn't pull out their dicks and piss down the side of the stage during concerts. It was all about presentation. Jadeah mighta had a loose eyeball, but she knew how things was supposed to look. She understood that beef, controversy, and shit-talking between artists equaled to-the-ceiling sales, so she made sure Hurricane's artists kept enough drama and hoodlum rivalry going with competing artists that their names were constantly on somebody's lips and their cuts were constantly on somebody's radio.

Unlike her brother, Jadeah was laid-back and had an easy personality. Crackheads and dope fiends would come to the door selling hot shit they had stolen from major stores in the city, and Jadeah would always buy a little something of what they were offering and give them a few dollars more than they asked for. She was good at handling the artists too, and even good at running Hurricane's office, but she wasn't up on computers like I was, and I used that shit to my advantage. She had asked me to set up a database file in Excel so we could track studio hours for the label, and every other day I would sneak and disable something minor on her system, then claim I had to go in the smaller office and use the spare computer up in there.

Most of the time I did it just to get out of the same room with her, but sometimes I did it 'cause my body was on fire and I needed something to play with. I put a protected password on the second computer and signed up for a free Internet account, then started an online blog called LickMyFlicker.blogspot.com that spelled out all the freaky things I fantasized about doing with a brother who was interested in licking my candy all night long.

I got all kinds of responses too, from HotSauce out of Texas, who said he wanted to slide a jalapeño up my coochie then use his tongue to put out the flames, to Lickerish from Richmond, who said he'd never met a pussy he didn't want to lick and offered to fly me out to Virginia and pay me cash money to grind on his face all night long.

One of the hottest posts I got was from a guy who called himself TongueTwister. Every response he sent was steaming. I'd sit back in the chair with my hand in my panties as he described all the delicious ways he could lick my flicker. His game was so good I could actually feel his tongue parting my pussy lips and sliding up inside of me. The more I read, the wetter I got, and by the end of his message my fingers would be soaked with juice as I bounced my ass around on that chair until I came so hard I needed a nap.

It got to the point where I was so horny that I set up a webcam and had "web" sex with a total stranger. His dick was long and black, but it had a crook in it near the head. He held it up to his camera and stroked it, and I nearly fainted as that shit grew bigger, and bigger, and bigger. It was like somebody had one of them bicycle pumps hooked up to his nuts. That dick was blowing up like a tube balloon.

I was careful not to let my face get near the camera, but I did press my titties up there. I would have loved to have felt that gigantic dick sliding between my breasts, tickling my nipples and slapping against my face. I figured out how he got that crook in his dick, though. Boy was working that thang. He was a professional stroker. His right arm was probably twice as big as his left one. I damn near licked my computer screen when he came, shooting quarts of cum all over his camera lens and rubbing it over his entire dick.

The sight of all that brought me to a quick climax, but then I had to face the biggest part of my problem. What next? What kind of chick slept in a bed with a man every night but depended on fantasies and the Internet to get her sex thang off?

Nah, I needed a real man. I wanted a kiss to go along with a real fuck. I wanted to feel a man doing me and digging me at the same time. I needed somebody to put his back in it and fill me up with more than the two blunt inches Mr. Jackson had to his name. Bottom line, I needed a man who could satisfy me without causing me pain. Mentally, physically, and emotionally, and just because Hurricane Jackson couldn't handle his business like a real man should didn't mean there wasn't a bigger and better playa out there who wouldn't.

◊ ◊ ◊

Whenever I got a few minutes alone in the front office I dipped in every file or folder I could find. In the three months

I'd been working for Jadeah I had already learned a lot about Hurricane and how things went down at the House of Homicide by snooping through all the computer files, but there was still a whole lot of stuff that wasn't on the computer system that interested me too. I didn't know exactly what I was searching for, but if I ever ran across something hot I'd surely figure out what to do with it.

I found out that Hurricane had all kinds of dirty cops on his payroll. He'd paid to have a fake liquor license issued for the House, and he even had a local councilman or two in his pocket. Their old asses swung by the House of Homicide every so often to splash in some young, hopeful pussy. These so-called ethical, respectable, married men waded all in that pool of eager hoes Hurricane kept dangling from a long string. Just being seen with Hurricane or at the House of Homicide was enough for some of these young girls. For others, he yeasted their heads up promising them all kinds of flash and fame just as long as they did what he wanted.

My eyes and fingers was all up in Jadeah's desk. I knew her inventory better than she did. One day I slipped though, and she almost busted me.

She was searching through her bottom file cabinet so hard she had to take off her glasses. "I think I'm gonna need you to copy some more permission forms, Candy."

"You got a whole stack of them," I answered without thinking. "Midway toward the back of the drawer behind that yellow tab."

I knew I'd messed up even before she gave me that so-you-been-in-my-shit look.

"How you know?"

"Because," I said, still crunching on the pretzels I was eating, "Hurricane asked me to get him one the other day when you wasn't here."

She didn't press it, but my nosey butt would have to be more careful in the future.

The next time I was in the office all by myself the printer was acting up. Instead of calling the repairman Jadeah had asked me to take a look at it while she went downstairs to talk to Hurricane in Studio C, where he did most of his writing. The printer was one of those laser joints. The kind that prints real fast and the pages slide out one right on top of the other. I had just unplugged it and removed the toner cartridge when the phone rang. Jadeah was still downstairs so I snatched it up.

"Homicide Hitz, how can I help you?"

"Hey, this is Knowledge. Is Jadeah there?"

Knowledge. That quiet niggah. The one with the nice eyes and fine smile.

"No," I said. "Jadeah's out of the office right now, but this is Candy. Can I help you with something?"

He paused for just a second. "Actually, I was calling for you."

"For what?"

"Well, I heard you're good with computers and I think mine might have crashed. I wanted to know if you could fix it for me."

"Umm," I said slowly. "I'm kinda working on something right now, but I can come up and take a look at it later on when I'm done."

"That'll work. I'll be here all day. Thanks."

I clicked off the phone and just stood there for a minute. That Knowledge was something real. Fine motherfucker. He had some kinda shit about him that made him stand apart from every other brother in Hurricane's circle. He was a baller, no doubt. But he didn't dress like a regular playa, he didn't talk like one, he damn sure didn't look like one. And if he had turned down Vonnie's rotten poon-poon that meant he didn't fiend like a regular playa neither.

Suddenly my ass was on fire and I didn't even try to fix that damn printer. Hell, Hurricane was paid. Let Jadeah call the repairman or tell her brother to buy her another one. I skipped to the bathroom real quick and checked myself out in the mirror. My nipples was so hard they could have cut holes in my shirt. I washed my hands and dabbed two drops of body oil on my wrists and jetted my horny ass upstairs, ready to fix whatever Knowledge had that was broken.

◊ ◊ ◊

Even his office was different from the rest of the House. It was up a narrow staircase at the end of a hall and had big windows and a corner view. I liked the whole openness of it. The panoramic feel I got the moment I stepped inside. The blinds were pulled way up high, and there were no curtains on the windows at all. Colorful flowers sat on a ledge right outside. The immediate sense I got was one of a clear view, live from Harlem. The sights of urban people hurrying up and down the streets just doing their thing.

"Whassup, Candy," Knowledge said, nodding for me to come all the way in. "That was quick, though."

I shrugged, closing the door behind me. "I can leave and come back later if you want me to."

"Nah, nah. Now is good for me. I accept assistance whenever I can get it."

He got up from his desk and motioned for me to sit down. Just standing in the same room with him was giving me a charge. He wasn't as tall as Hurricane, but his shoulders and arms looked strong as hell and I found myself wondering if he could pick a sistah up and put her in the face-mask position so I could ride his tongue and scream all night long.

My coochie was thumping, but my eyes were supersonic. They crawled all over his desk looking for pictures, cards, anything that would give me a clue to the kind of man he was. "What was the last thing you did before it shut down?" I asked softly.

"Nothing out the usual," he said, putting his hands in his pockets. I'd done a lot of shopping with Hurricane for awards dinners and other events, and the suit Mr. Knowledge was styling hadn't come off nobody's rack. It was custom-made from high-quality material, which fit right in with his image. "I did install some additional memory a few days ago, though, and come to think of it, it's been acting crazy ever since."

I felt him looking dead at me as he spoke, but I was too hot to meet his eyes. Instead, I followed his power cord to the wall outlet and unplugged it.

I blurted, "You don't use a surge protector?"

I glanced up and caught his smile, and I swear one of his dimples stabbed me right in the coochie.

"What's that for?"

"It's to regulate the surge of electricity through the system. You know, so your computer doesn't get overloaded and short out or blow your modem out."

"Nah, I don't know much about computer systems, that's why I called you."

"Don't worry," I said, heading toward the front of his desk and making sure he saw what I was packing in my tight jeans. "I'ma hook you up."

I looked at him and saw something flash in his eyes. "You promise?" he said, standing there with his hands in his pockets and digging me with a sexy smile.

I laughed. "Yeah. I promise."

Chapter 14

Breachin' Security

Peaches's fifteen-year-old daughter showed up at the mansion a few months after me and Caramel moved in. Her name was Asia, and she came from down South. I didn't even know Peaches had a child. She was a real cute little church girl too. Long straight hair, wide eyes, nice skin. A younger, even prettier picture of her crazy mother.

But Long Jon wasn't Asia's father.

When Peaches was thirteen she had kicked it with Tonk, the hard-hearted drug czar who distributed heroin and crack out of the projects for Hurricane. Asia told me that Tonk's grandmother had been raising her down in Mississippi and that the old lady had had a stroke and got put into a nursing home. Tonk's people had broken their necks to put Asia on a Greyhound to New York City. They gave her ten dollars and three chicken wings and told her not to get off the bus until she saw her mother.

I liked Asia. She was real country and real sweet. She was musically talented and had a decent singing voice too. She'd been playing the church organ practically all her life, and she was shy and naïve, kinda like Caramel used to be before she took that bullet. I figured having her around would be good for Caramel. She needed to be around somebody who was closer to her age and who wasn't so damn hot in the ass, 'cause I was about to check Sissy and Fatima over the yang they'd been putting in my sister's head. Those bitches could see Caramel wasn't totally correct, but they kept her around as their private entertainment because she was so easy to influence.

Hurricane had said to put Asia in the same room with Caramel, which was cool with me, but not with my sister.

"I don't know that down-south trick!" Caramel stomped around her jacked-up room like a spoiled little kid. She had on a pair of tight yellow shorts that was so dirty they probably stank. Caramel had some big firm titties, just like me, and the tube top she was wearing was so flimsy and narrow it looked like a dingy little headband that covered just her nipples. "Why she can't stay in the room with her mother?"

"Because her mother stays in there with her man, that's why!"

Caramel shrugged and kicked a paper plate under the bed. "That ain't my fuckin' problem. Let her sleep on the floor in there with them, then. I just don't want her in here."

"Cool," I said. "Tell Hurricane that."

She smirked at me and grinned like she knew a secret that I didn't know. "No problem. I can tell Hurricane *anything*."

I didn't pay Caramel no mind. But I worried about that girl because she was acting like a real nut. I had gotten her back in school, but at least twice a week her teachers were blowing up my cell phone. She cursed the math teacher out, stole a sandwich from the cafeteria, and when they sent her to the principal's office she jumped up on that mug's table and started dancing like she was on a stage with a pole.

To top it all off, I had a feeling she was out there boosting too.

Before Sissy got with Vince she used to be a professional thief. She had boosted high-priced merchandise from top department stores in every borough of New York City. But even though she was kept now and didn't need to steal no more, thievery was still in her blood, and I wondered if she'd been giving my sister private lessons.

Caramel didn't make no money, but every time I looked up she was laced up in something fresh. Most of her gear was cheap, but some of it sported labels from top designers, and there was no way my sister could afford to buy those kinds of rags. Hurricane was a tight-ass baller unless he was trying to impress somebody, and whatever little bit of money he tore me off I usually split with Caramel, so I knew how much change she was working with. Almost none. It damn sure wasn't enough where she could afford to shop the way she did. For all I knew Sissy was busy teaching my sister how to boost with the best of them, which straight pissed me off.

Regardless to all that complaining she had done, two weeks after Asia moved in her and Caramel were tied together like shoestrings. I hate to say it, but my sister was a real bad influence, because it wasn't long before you couldn't tell them apart. Asia was still cute and country, but everything else about her was changing. The way she walked, the clothes she wore. Her whole attitude was getting some snap on it. Caramel had found herself a protégé, and Asia was now a certified hooch-in-training. Peaches woke up on that and tried to put a halt to her groove right quick.

"Don't be so fast, Asia," Peaches warned, cutting her eyes at Caramel when her daughter walked in the kitchen wearing a pair of shorts that were cut so high her fat little butt cheeks were falling out the bottoms. I knew Peaches didn't want Asia picking up no bad habits from Caramel, and I couldn't front and say I blamed her. She turned Asia's ass around at the door and told her to go find the other half of her shorts. "You got too much going for you to walk around looking so stank, Queen Asia. There's plenty of time to be grown."

Peaches was crazier than a pregnant roach, but I could tell she really loved her daughter. Let Fatima tell it, Peaches had been truly handling that motherhood thing until she hooked up with Long Jon and he started flying her head left and right. Asia's father, Tonk, had been busy selling dope in the projects, but he didn't want his baby being raised by no battered woman so he scooped Asia up and sent her down South to live with his people.

I tried to talk to Caramel a little bit. You know, Asia was only fifteen. I wanted Caramel to watch out for her like she was a little sister, not turn her out on all the ills Harlem had to offer.

"Candy, please," Caramel tried to diss me when I told her how I felt. "For one thing, she ain't my little sister. For two, me and her ain't connected at the brain or at the ass. If she wanna get out there and get hers, I sure won't be the buster who tells her not to." She rolled her eyes up in her head. "Humph. I ain't trying to regulate a damn thing."

I stared at my sister. Where this little ghettofied, booty-licious heffah had come from was anybody's guess. I'd gotten so used to dealing with Mama and all her forty-nine cases of drama that I had never really noticed how much like her Caramel really was.

A couple of weeks later I had to reassess my tune.

Even though I didn't want Caramel hanging around at the House of Homicide and Peaches damn sure didn't want Asia there neither, both of them were drawn to it like kids to a playground. To make things worse, Long Jon and Hurricane acted like it was okay for their young asses to be there. They went as far as to send cars to the mansion to pick them up whenever they called, and one night I busted Caramel slow grinding with some rapper clown and drinking gin. That probably wasn't all she'd been doing either.

It was true that Caramel had been through the streets a lot growing up with Mama, but she had always been sweet and in check. I got to really wondering why these two youngsters were all of a sudden so hot in the ass, and when I looked at things closely, for some reason my eyes kept swinging over to Long Jon.

Every time I looked up Caramel was in his grill. Asia was too. And not like no father-daughter thang neither. Matter fact, the three of them was in the movie room real late one night watching porno flicks together. I heard Peaches hollering and thought she was wildin' out because her teenage daughter was in there drooling over a bunch of hard black dicks, but when I got down there I saw that wasn't the case.

"Get your ass up off his *muthafuckin'* lap, Queen Asia!"

Damn if he didn't have that girl sitting between his long-ass legs. In a flash I wondered if he was fucking her. He laughed and pushed Asia to the side as Peaches screamed, "Long Jon ain't your goddamn daddy!"

I was mad too, because Caramel had been snuggling up under him like he was her man. They had a big old blanket covering the three of them up, and there wasn't no telling what had really been going on. When Caramel saw me standing there she stood up and posed, I guess to show me that all her clothes were on so nothing had been happening. I just looked at her. Then I looked at Long Jon with his slimy ass. He was *supposed* to be running security for the House and the mansion, but instead, he was up in here trying to mug the young poon-poon he got paid to look out for.

I started wondering if Long Jon and his boys were passing Caramel and Asia around. Snake, Grip, Das—I didn't trust none of those niggahs, and at one time or another I'd seen every last one of them acting a little bit too friendly with Asia and my sister.

I glanced at Long Jon and turned my lip down. That fool knew just what I was thinking. He mighta been the big bad man who ran the cameras and carried the Glocks, but I was the big bad sister who would be watching his ass.

Chapter 15

Music and Madness

Five months after we signed with Hurricane our self-titled album was released and all three of our lives took a sharp turn. Our first single was a sexually aggressive ballad called "Rett Ta Go" that debuted at number 15 on the Billboard 200 album chart and made a lot of impact on the streets. I sang the lead on the sexy little rhythm-and-blues/hip-hop cut that Hurricane had laced with catchy hooks and sassy funk, and suddenly things were happening for Scandalous! and we were in hot demand. All the radio stations in major cities like Detroit, L.A., New York, Chicago, and Atlanta were spinning our cut and trying to get us in their studios for interviews.

Six weeks later "Luver Boy" was released and we didn't know what hit us. The slinky cut was a straight club banger and an instant hit. We recorded our first music video, and MTV snatched it like a hot potato. We were invited to the Essence Music Festival in Nawlins, and we performed at the Soul Train Music Awards too. We were living large and loving it. There were makeup sessions out the ass, hairstylists were all in our faces, tailors were throwing more clothes at us than we'd ever seen in our lives, and to top it all off, Hurricane chartered private jets to shuttle us back and forth between cities and events like they were yellow taxicabs.

The response we were getting was so crucial that all three of us got the big head and it took a black-hearted playa like Hurricane to put our asses back in check.

"Don't start acting major just 'cause they rotating your shit on the radio," he warned Dominica when she challenged him over something minor like a stage costume she thought looked too hoochie on her. Hurricane and Jadeah controlled everything from what we said in an interview to what kind of outfits we wore on the stage, to how our hair was styled. "Bitch, I own your ass, and if you fuck with me you'll roll outta here wearing the same rags you rolled in with." Then Hurricane said something that made all of our hearts pump apple juice. "But not until y'all jawns earn out all the funds I been fronting for ya. Don't act stupid. Y'all bitches is broke."

We went on to perform at the Apollo Theater that night to a sold-out house, and while we gave 100 percent onstage, later as we rode in a limo back to the studio everybody was kinda quiet and I knew what my girls were thinking. If we were racking up the kind of quick sales everybody said we were, then when in the hell was we gonna get our hands on some of that money?

It was after 4:00 A.M., but the House of Homicide was just coming alive as we pulled up to the curb and climbed out the car. We were walking through the door when I went ahead and said what we all were thinking.

"I'll be glad when we finally see some ends."

Vonnie broke. "Aw, stop fronting, Candy. You probably don't give a fuck whether we get paid or not," she accused me. "That big old niggah feeds you lovely and puts mad clothes on your back and crazy jewels around your neck. Me and Dom still living in Brooklyn trying to get enough hot water rolling through the pipes to wash our asses every night. I don't care how many *things* Hurricane sets us up with. We still need to feel some *money* in our hands."

I nodded real quick. "I'm there with you, Vonnie. I might live with Hurricane and all, but I still need my own money. Remember, I got a sister to take care of and ain't nothing promised to me neither. I wanna get paid in cash dollars too."

I was talking loud, but I knew that wasn't happening. Hurricane had made it clear that I had to work off my Mob debt before I saw a dime of my royalties, and if I didn't like it he offered to call Nicky and tell him I was ready to take over my own payment plan.

Dominica just looked scared. "I had a funny feeling in my nose that something like this would happen. I dreamt we worked our asses off and Hurricane jerked us around on our contract. We ended up owing him everything and walking away with nothing."

"That's not happening," I said real fast. "There's no way that could happen."

Vonnie cut her eyes at me. "How the fuck do you know, Candy? Just 'cause you suckin' that niggah off don't mean you know how he rolls with his artists. Don't be defending his ass."

I wasn't trying to defend Hurricane, I just didn't like seeing my girls so shook. We went upstairs to a lounge room we chilled in after shows and started taking off our clothes and makeup.

"Nah, y'all." I tried to soothe the aggravation that was still rising. "That's not gonna happen. There are other artists on the label who are making money, right? If nobody else is complaining then they must be getting paid, right?"

Vonnie smirked. "Girl, all they asses is broke."

"And it's because of their contracts," Dom agreed, stripping out of the hoochie dress that had started the whole thing. "A two-thousand-dollar advance and 6 measly percent of the first 500,000 copies sold—8 percent if we go platinum and sell over a million. He should've started us out at least at 10 percent since we have to split everything three ways. See, Hurricane knows how to catch talent when it's young and desperate. That's how he gets his artists to sign shit that doesn't promise them anything. By the time you pay the producer and the label, then add on fees for the studio, video shoots, clothes, travel, promotion, and every damn body else who got their hand held out, you're left with five dollars to your name and a bunch of ho clothes you'll never wear again."

Vonnie took a blunt out of her purse and lit it. "We oughtta do like TLC and 'em did. File for bankruptcy and be done with that niggah. I was talking to Butter and he said plenty artists get out of their contracts that way. And they get to keep their houses and their cars. All the stuff that we don't even have yet. Butter said going that route ain't nothing but a thing. All it takes is filling out a simple form."

I got real quiet then. If Vonnie had been stupid enough to go running her mouth and complaining to Butter, wasn't no

telling how much Hurricane had already heard about our dis-
satisfaction.

"Well," I said, fanning the sharp smoke away from my face.
Weed didn't do nothing but stink up my hair and I wasn't trying to get no contact neither. "I think we should just wait and
see how things fall before we start getting all hyped. We still
have other singles to be released. If they hit anywhere near as
hard as the first two did, we *gots* to make some money."

Dom nodded. She had changed into a pair of red pants that
showed off her basketball booty and her slim waist. "True.
We're just at the beginning of all this. Let's wait until the rest of
our singles drop and see what kind of digits Hurricane is talking then."

◈ ◈ ◈

The following Friday night was live at the House. Right after
the pit auditions were over, Hurricane called for a freestyle battle of the mic. All the rappers were pumped and couldn't wait
to get in the pit and get theirs. I half listened to the lyrics because my mind was on other things. Like money and sex and
where the hell I was gonna get me some of both.

I'd been hollering right along with Vonnie and Dom about
our royalties, but I knew I didn't have none coming to me.
Hurricane was forever reminding me that I was just like an in-
dentured servant, working off Mama's debt, and he wouldn't
even tell me how much interest he'd paid the Gabrianos for me.
How could I work on paying my bill if I didn't know how
much I made or how much I owed?

I was feeling stuck like hell when Dom nudged me as the
crowd went crazy.

"Oh! She straight dissed her ass!"

I looked down and saw this young girl rapping in the pit. She was holding her own against a crew of other rappers and apparently the crowd respected her for that.

> Save all that shit you tryna spit to me
> You can't be a weak rapper tryna get with me
> I write my own rhymes and I make my own cheddar
> There ain't a MC male or female who can spit no better

Dom hollered. "That's my kinda girl! Sistah breaking off some dicks on that mic!"

"Who is she?" I asked.

"A rapper named Nasty Nisaa," Dom said. "She been goin' at it real hard with some girls she used to rock it tight with in Brooklyn. You didn't hear about it? They been talking shit about her all over the Internet. Blowing her up in chat rooms and rap groups just because they think she wrote a hot song without telling them. They all got their own contracts and do their own thing too, so she didn't see what all the noise was about, but they been trying to put shade on her anyway. Nisaa said they just jealous 'cause she did something they all wished they could do, so she challenged her haters to get off the Internet and battle it out with her on the mic. Now everywhere she goes she lays it on their hatin' asses verbally and to a vicious beat."

I *had* heard about this girl. I heard she was real good too. She had a lot of talent and was doing thangs, but sometimes even your so-called friends could have a problem with that. I thought

about how Vonnie had been acting lately and then listened to
what Miss Nasty Nisaa down in the pit had to say.

You's a undercover hater
A sheisty alligator
You jealous of my rhymes
And your mouth is like a crater

You front like you my girl
Throw your salt around the world
Then you smile up in my face
Bitch you make me wanna hurl

Since when!
I gotta get permission from you
To do my thang
Just like I do?
I didn't steal these words
I wrote 'em myself
You just jealous 'cause you flat
And my rhymes are top-shelf

You spreadin' ya hate
Thru that nasty e-mail
I got a ass
Bitch you got a tail

Hiding behind
That phony screen name

Your ass is skraight skurred
'Cause my flow is game

You just a desperate housewife
Who needs to steal a life
dissing on the sneak tip
'Cause u losin' ya grip
just running ya mouth
all day and nite
Try stayin' ya black ass
up off my website!

You just do you, and let me do me
'Cause that's the way
The game's supposed to be
But I'm telling ya now
1st skank'ta step to me
Is gonna get stomped out
By a sistah OG!

Nasty Nisaa almost brought down the house. Insecure rappers who were scared of competition mighta been mad at her, but music lovers didn't give a damn who wrote what. They were straight feeling what she was saying 'cause they went crazy over her power rhymes.

At the bottom of the battle only two rappers were left standing. Some cute brother from Brooklyn who was rocking some sweet cornrows, and a rapper from Harlem who had just signed a contract with Hurricane.

"Check this out." Dom nudged me like I couldn't hear for

myself. "They said the guy in the blue is from downtown. Brooklyn. They call him Reem Raw. You know who that other rapper is. Dolla Bill."

"Aaight," Hurricane hollered over the mic. "We fittin' to get us a *costly* competition up in the House right now! Dolla Bill recently got him a contract, so let's see can he keep it. Yo, Dolla, if this niggah cracks you on this stage, he's walkin' out holding your papers tonight."

Now that's the way to stir shit up between rappers and keep them beefing and lunging at each other's throats. Hurricane was a trip, but he knew what the fuck he was doing. Pit one against the other with a recording contract as the prize, and watch them niggahs tear each other to pieces trying to get a hold of that paper.

Reem Raw climbed up on that stage and started doin' the damn thang.

> Look, ak, I ain't even gotta put the shooters on you
> I was hustlin' back when niggahs was flickin' boogers on you
> Come on now,
> it's time to turn it out.
> I'm still on fire
> while you burning out
> Reem Raw is something you should be concerned about.

Dolla Bill went up next.

> Whut up dawg, yeah, you really sweet
> But your rhymes is soft and not raw in the least
> You can't battle me, my flow is too real

Plus you broke
And I got all the dolla bills.

And then Reem Raw fucked him up for real.

Dolla you was never 'bout it to bang
'Cause when shit jumped off your whole personality changed.
You come at my click wrong, it's costing you your throat
Then I'ma bury your pops for fatherin' a joke
You better get to know me
Before I flip out
and blow three
Leave you crippled,
Fuck if you a triple OG.

Dolla Bill tried to bust him back.

How you coming at me
When I got the same
Pump that flipped
Tony over the balcony
You don't wanna battle, Reem
You ain't nothing but talk
I'm the motherfuckin' rapper who runs New York.

Dolla Bill had handled his, but not hard enough. And at the
end of the night Hurricane had made a loyal friend. Reem Raw
walked up outta that pit on top. And he walked out the door
with Dolla's contract too.

Chapter 16

How Low Can You Go?

The next Saturday night Hurricane hosted a "Drop It Like It's Hotttt" contest.

You shoulda seen them hopeful chicks cracking their backs down in that pit. Vonnie, Asia, and Caramel were right in the middle of it all, trying their best to shine.

Vince was on the mic, and five girls got eliminated during each round.

The first girls to go were those with flat asses. Why they were up there in the first place I didn't understand. How you gonna come to a rump shaker and don't bring no rump? The next group of girls to get tossed were those with little asses or no hips. I didn't understand them either. Like Vince told them, the same rules applied.

"Okay, yawl," Vince screamed from the stage. "Now we gone check out some legs. All yawl jawns standing up on two chicken bones, squawk your asses up outta this goddamn pit!"

Now I didn't think that shit was fair. This was about backing that thang up, not holding it up. Some of them sistahs had gangsta booties and knocked knees. Did that mean they couldn't drop it down low?

Vince shooed three other females out the pit on looks alone. "I don't care how phat that ass is!" he clowned. "If your teef is crooked and your nose been broken at least twice, get your ugly asses up outta my goddamn pit!"

When it was all said and done, Caramel and Vonzelle were the last sistahs left standing.

"Oh, boy," Dom said, crossing her legs and turning her head. "It's down to those two? I don't even wanna see this shit."

I'd been thinking the same thing because Caramel and Vonnie couldn't stand each other. Quadir was the main reason, although he wasn't the only one. I'd already stepped to him and told him to stop playin' with my sister trying to make Vonnie jealous, and he'd just looked at me and laughed. "Tell your little sister to keep that sweet pussy out my face, and Vonnie won't have no reason to get mad."

They cranked up the music as 50 Cent started hollering, "Shake, shake, shake your ass, girl," and Caramel and Vonnie went at it strong. Both of them had ferocious bodies, but Caramel was the more crucial bitch 'cause her back had an S curve in it that drove niggahs wild.

Vonnie was doing some wicked winding, but Caramel was out there busting some of Mama's old moves. She thrust her round ass out and went down, down, down, dipping her chips. Niggahs screamed and whistled, urging her on.

Vonzelle looked over at all the commotion and picked up her pace. She dropped her apple bottom to the floor and started cherry picking, her toned stomach clenched and sexy as her booty damn near mopped the pit.

But then Caramel stepped it up. Baby sister was out there popping it, and popping it *right*.

"I think I hear a bowl of Rice Krispies in them shorts!" Vince screamed, pointing at Caramel as she bucked her back, va-wumping that thang. " 'Cause this one here got the snap, the crackle, *and* the pop!"

Caramel went buck wild. She started rotating her hips like she was doing the hula hoop while her ass was steady vibrating and humping the air. *Ka-thunk-a-thunk-thunk! Ka-thunk-a-thunk-thunk!* Then she got it to quivering and jiggling, and niggahs went crazy and started jumping over the railing, rushing the pit. Vince barely had time to pull her up on the stage before they could swarm her, and right then and there he held Caramel's hand up in the air and declared her the winner.

I didn't even wanna see the look on Vonnie's face 'cause I knew it would be twisted. It was hard enough for her being second to me onstage. Taking second place in an ass-shaking contest, an area she specialized in, just wasn't supposed to happen. Yeah, I thought, following Dom's example and turning my head away. Vonzelle could be real minor sometimes. She needed to be the queen bitch at all times, and having Caramel come in and knock her off her throne wasn't something she was just gonna take and roll over.

◊ ◊ ◊

Hurricane was one of those rare brothers who was into watching baseball. The next weekend he rented a five-thousand-dollar Hall of Fame suite at Yankee Stadium and invited his regular crew to the opening game of the season. All of his top niggahs went and left their housewives at home. Long Jon and Butter were out there flashing their bling and frontin' like important artists as they tried to cop white pussy all day long.

The suite was phat, but I wasn't interested in no damn baseball. I was busy trying to keep my eye on my hot-ass sister, who I had tried to make stay home.

"What?" she'd said, looking at me like I was stupid when I told her she needed to stay out at the mansion. "This ain't your party. Hurricane already said I could go, so that's where I plan on being."

I couldn't believe Caramel. It was like she was brainwashed or something. Where before she'd been shot she had looked up to me, these days my little sister acted like everything about me was ill. There were times when I wanted to put my foot in her ass or knock the shit out of her, but I kept reminding myself of all she'd gone through.

I barely said a word the whole day. Wasn't nobody to talk to anyway, except Caramel, and the way I was feeling I mighta smacked her teeth out if she got smart with me again. I was glad when the game was over and it was time to roll. I'd been sitting down for so long I had a cramp in my ass, and Hurricane had only let me get up to use the bathroom once. We were leaving the suite through the VIP entrance when one of the younger rappers on Hurricane's label stepped to him all serious.

"Yo, Cane," the kid said, "I need to holla at you for a minute, ak. It's about my contract, ya know?"

Right away I knew his ass was in trouble. He wasn't all that smart, but I respected him for having the heart to approach a killer like Hurricane like that, especially with all his niggahs around.

Hurricane had been saying something to Butter. On the

word "contract" he stopped and swung his head toward the young boy, and something cold and dark jetted from his eyes. "Lil muthafucka, you talking to me?"

That kid was either psycho or more man than any I'd ever met. Hurricane used fear to control his people, but I didn't see a drop of it in that kid when he nodded and said, "Hell yeah, man. You the one write the contracts and sign the checks, right?"

Hurricane snatched his little ass up by the neck and pressed a big black gat to his head. "Little niggah, do you know how many bodies I got on this piece? You questioning me about my muthafuckin' *contract*?"

And then out of nowhere, that niggah let him go and snatched *me*!

"See this bitch right here? This my moneymakin' artist and my number one bitch. If *she* opens her fuckin' mouth with some beef about the way I write my contracts, I'll put a hot one in her too." He let me go and I stumbled, falling against Butter's soft ass. "Now get the fuck outta here before you make me mad. If I catch your black ass back down at my studio again you gonna become another Harlem statistic."

I was so mad I could have fried his ass. Here I'd sat around like a statue all day not doing nothing, not saying nothing, and this maniac sticks a gun up to my head like it's nothing. Like *I'm* nothing. Hurricane was out of control. There was no other way to explain him.

We started walking toward the limo and I reached out to touch Caramel's arm. Tears were running down my face I was just that mad.

"Whaaat?" She shrugged me off like she was aggravated at

the sight of me. "Damn, Candy!" she said, and rolled her eyes. "You ain't got *no* fuckin' heart."

I didn't say a word as Caramel ran up a few steps and grabbed Hurricane's arm. They walked toward the whip together and never looked back.

◐ ◐ ◐

It was Sunday afternoon and we were having ourselves a braid-a-thon. Hurricane was still out with his baseball posse from the night before, and I didn't give a fuck if he never came back. Fatima had popped two bottles of Hypnotiq, and Peaches had broken out with some chronic she had gotten from Tonk. I left all of that get-high shit alone and concentrated on the chicken wings Sissy had fried and the deviled eggs with sweet relish and paprika she'd fixed to go with them.

We were taking turns doing each other's hair, and it shocked me to learn that everybody's hair was real and that none of these chicks had a weave. Sissy had already hooked me up with some medium-sized box-braids that looked really fly. She had greased my scalp with some Bergamot Lite and brushed a little gel into the soft "baby hair" along my edges, then lined it down with the tip of the comb like Mama used to do when I was little.

I was returning the solid by throwing some tight, skinny cornrows in her hair, while Peaches was straight jacking Fatima's hair up with some fat cornrows and crooked parts going every which way she pleased.

"So what went down at the game last night?" Teema wanted to know.

I shrugged, playing it off. "Hold your head still," I said to

Sissy, trying to make sure I parted her hair straight. She ignored me and swung her whole damn head around.

"Nah, hooker. Don't be holdin' out on us. If something went down just give it up. We in the same boat you in, girl. Hell, what you know might save one of our asses."

"Let Teema tell it," I said, pulling Sissy's head back around where I needed it. "She brought it up."

"Well from what I heard," Fatima said, her head to the side as Peaches caught the fine hairs around her edges and pulled them tightly into the cornrow, "somebody pulled out his gun and stuck that shit to your head."

Sissy hollered, "What! That niggah pressed his shit to you?"

"Whut?" Peaches said real nasty-like, turning her lip down at Sissy. "Whut? Like a motherfucker ain't never put the barrel on you? Remember, bitch, I was here when Vince dragged your skinny tail through the door way back when. You probably got barrel burns on both sides of your ass!"

I was waiting for Sissy to go off and show her ass on Peaches, but instead she surprised me.

"Yeah. You right. Vince used to do stupid stuff like that to me all the time. But I was young then. I didn't know no better."

Teema sighed. It was so deep it sounded like she pulled it up out her toes. "Yeah, all of us was young when we hooked up with these fools and came out here. All of us had stupid dreams of living the high life too. That's what the bling do to you. It lures you in."

"And spits your ass right back out," Sissy agreed.

Peaches shook her head and gave Teema another jacked-up part. "That's if you let it. Tell the truth and shame your big daddy. Every one of us wanted this life. Ain't nothing turned us out but our own greed. We got high on status. We let the dollars and the dick turn us out. We let the whips and the jewels turn us out. Some of us even wanted it so bad we got turned out on the ass-whippings and head bangings. Y'all might say I'm fucked up in the skull and crazy like a mug, but you gotta agree with that."

Heads got to nodding like they were in church. Mine was nodding right along with them too.

"I used to wanna be a chef," Sissy laughed. "Ain't that some stupidness? I even went to school for it when I lived over in Philly, but Vince made me quit before I could graduate. He said he was too tight in the game to have his wife knocking somebody else's pots. So he brought me out here to the mansion and had them put in two damn ovens. He told me to have at it. Said I could burn the whole damn kitchen up if I wanted to. As long as he was getting his joint sucked right, he was cool."

Peaches had Fatima bent over at the neck, but I heard her anyway. "That's how Joog did me. He said fuck a Fashion Institute and brought me a sewing machine and told me to set that bad boy up and stitch together my own rags."

"Whatever," Peaches said, her fingers swirling as she took a braid all the way to the end. "I forgot all my little dreams a long time ago."

My fingers stopped braiding in the middle of a row. "But what about your daughter, though? What's gonna happen to Asia and her dreams?"

Peaches turned to me, and for the first time since I'd met her she looked all the way fuckin' sane. "I want Queen Asia the fuck out of here," she said coldly. "I don't give a damn what Hurricane says. Asia ain't no singer and he ain't no dream maker, Candy. That motherfucker is a straight-up dream slayer. He's supposed to be settin' her up with a contract, but in my heart I think his evil ass is just settin' her up, period."

Sissy nodded as I picked up my braid again. "I don't doubt it," she said. "She won't be the first one he set up either."

When Sissy said that I stopped braiding for real. I had been dying to know, so now I asked. "Why was y'all acting so surprised when I first got here? Where are all the other females Hurricane used to roll with before me?"

"All what females?" Teema asked. "For a minute Cane had me wondering if he even liked pussy. Cherry was the only female I ever seen him bring home. And he wore her tight ass out so quick it wasn't funny."

Peaches laughed. "You still a baby in this camp, Fatima. I been here almost five years. That girl Cherry wasn't shit. She didn't last a good month. Last time I saw her she had a drop-lip and her nose was crooked. Aside from her and Candy, only one other female has ever lived in the middle. Her name was Laniqua."

"So what happened to her? When did she leave?"

Peaches shrugged. "Who, Laniqua? Didn't Teema just tell you Cane wears his bitches out? Laniqua was live too. She used to be a model. She got messed up, though. One night she was here swimming in the pool with Hurricane, and the next morning he was dragging her shit up to the attic saying she drowned. She had a tight funeral, though. Every rapper in the universe turned out to show off they shine."

"What's up there?" I stared at Peaches, damn near whispering.

Sissy broke free of my fingers and swung her head around. Teema turned in her seat until she could see me too. "Damn, Candy," Sissy said. "You's one of them hardheaded heffahs, ain't you? We already told you don't be worrying about that attic. That niggah of yours is into keeping freaky-ass animals, so he probably got him a killer crocodile up there or some shit."

I gave her a look.

"Don't be rolling your eyes, girl 'cause you better than me living in the middle like it's a damn zoo. Don't you watch the news? Crazy shit happens all the time and plenty of nuts like Hurricane keep wild animals in they house. Like that stupid-ass brother in Manhattan who got caught keeping a tiger and a alligator up in his little-ass apartment last year. Fucked his neighbors up when they saw him up there on CNN talking about how he wanted to make his own Garden of Eden."

"Forget them animals," Teema said. "I heard it was bodies up there. Probably some big-ass freezer where Hurricane keeps all his bodies."

Sissy got back in the game. "That's stupid. Cane is too smart for that. Keeping bodies at the crib? That's just keeping evidence of your crimes. He ain't stupid like that."

"Oh that niggah got bodies," Teema smirked. "Plenty bodies. His ass went on trial with Irv and his brother, didn't he? I knew the drug dealer the cops said they beat to death. A guy named Cooter. Stutterin' motherfucker. Used to work the bar over at the G-Spot. And remember when that little boy got kidnapped over on 135th Street in a beef behind some contract money? Them cold motherfuckers cut that baby's finger off and sent it to his father. That was Hurricane's shit too."

Sissy shook her head. "How you know all that shit is true,

Teema? If you listen to what the streets say, Cane's responsible for every fool who gets popped on a corner. I'm not saying he ain't got a filthy rep, but he ain't the only one out there filling up the morgues."

"Well it ain't drugs," Teema came back. "That distribution room he has at the House is just the tip of what he sells. Tonk runs the main operation through the projects, and that stash comes straight out of a warehouse downtown."

"Y'all all wrong," Peaches finally said. "It's guns. Glocks, AK-47s, .45s, Machs—they even got lasers now. Long Jon found a sweet connect who steals them out of some underground shipments to the Mob. Hurricane runs them in trucks across the country and then resells 'em. He's one of the biggest suppliers for the street gangs and the rest of them fools out in L.A."

Teema's eyes got big as hell. "Peaches is lying her ass off! And if you ain't, don't be telling us all that shit. I ain't trying to know nothing I ain't supposed to know!"

"It doesn't make sense, though," I said, ignoring Teema's scary ass. "Hurricane is Mob-favored. This I know for a fact. Why would he risk selling any hot shit that falls off the back of their trucks?"

"And how the hell do your crazy behind know anyway?" Teema hollered.

Peaches looked at us like we were the crazy ones. "Just because I act whack don't mean I am. I got that niggah Long Jon on foolish! He think he can bust my ass, bust a nut, and then handle his business all up in my face 'cause my brain supposed to be busted too, right?" She nodded and winked like she had one on him. "WHUT!"

We were all hollering laughing now, but I was only halfway

with 'em. As far as I could see Peaches mighta been slick, but she was still riding that little yellow school bus.

"Still," I insisted while they were still laughing, "even Hurricane ain't stupid enough to fool around with Mob money like that. If he wanted to run guns for them he wouldn't have to do it behind they backs."

Peaches got real quiet for a second, and when she opened her mouth she made me feel like I was about five. "Now, Candy. Don't you know shit about shit yet? Shit about your own niggah? Hurricane is one greedy bastard. Just like them gangsta-ass Italians got it figured out, he got it figured out too. Next to drugs, guns are the biggest moneymakers on the market. Hurricane's connect is sweet, and them Italians don't know every damn thing. If he can get a tiny piece of what they got going and get away with it, don't think he won't try."

We got quiet then, 'cause she was right. The comb slipped out of Sissy's hair, and we all jumped when it hit the floor.

"Well," Fatima said, moving out of range of Peaches's hands. Her hair was totally jacked up. Her parts were crooked and her cornrows were twisted and lopsided, thick and thin. "I'm with Sicily. Cane is smart. So don't tell me nothing else, because like I said, I really don't want to know."

Peaches shrugged, and I watched that dumb, half-retarded look creep back into her eyes. "Don't wanna know what? Don't be listening to me. Y'all know I'm crazy." She stared at Fatima. "Who braided your hair like that? Girl, they straight fucked you up! Y'all go find Long Jon for me. I'm hungry. Tell him to bring me something to eat."

Chapter 17

Shockin' Us to Death

The shit hit the table about four months later at the BMI Urban Awards. Scandalous! had five number 1 singles and had just been certified 4X platinum by the RIAA after winning three nominations for the Soul Train Lady of Soul Awards in the Best R&B/Soul Group category.

We'd just recorded a cut on the soundtrack for a new movie starring Halle Berry and Mos Def, and we'd been invited to do a cameo for another promising black film starring the hot NBA rapper, Thug-a-licious. It was about that time that Vonzelle started going off on her own little private missions. She was still messed up over Quadir and had started hanging out with crackheads and jetting for days at a time, and then coming back acting all nonchalant like she'd never left. Don't let us ask her where she was. She'd black out and wanna kick somebody's ass just for asking.

One time she skyed up for over a week and missed Dom's birthday party and a major press conference, and we were left looking stupid on camera and stammering over questions about where she was.

I thought she was either smoking crack or totally dick whipped, but Dominica took it more personal. She said Vonnie was a selfish little heffah who put herself and her own ambitions over the group.

Right before we left to attend the BMI Awards, Hurricane called us into his office and said our sales were high and our records were climbing the charts like spiders. In fact, he'd already recouped a lot of what he'd spent on us. He said he wanted to pay us a little bonus and promised we'd each have a nice check in a couple of weeks.

It was the moment that we had all lived and prayed for, and finally our dreams were coming true. I was happiest because he had actually included me when he said *we* were getting checks.

"We fucking them up!" Vonnie screamed later that evening as the MC pronounced us the winners in our category. We had on dresses made from similar slinky fabric, but each one was cut in a unique pattern. Mine had a huge diamond shape cut out of the front that showed off my tight stomach, and Dominica's was styled low down her back nearly to her ass. Vonnie's was the cutest, though. It had thin straps and a V cleavage that dipped all the way below her navel. Her big, firm titties were bouncing all over the place and I laughed like hell as I followed her and Dom up to the stage. "We did it, y'all!" Vonnie kept yelling as the cameras flashed and the crowd screamed while we sashayed down the aisle. "My sistahs, we fuckin' made it!"

I glanced at Dominica and saw she was crying. She didn't even front like she wanted to wipe those happy tears away. We were onstage waiting for the applause to die down when she reached out and hugged me and Vonnie close, kissing both of us on our cheeks. "We came a long way," Dom whispered. "From foster care to the Fountainebleau Hilton. Ladies, we some badass bitches!"

I can't remember everything that was said up there on that stage. I stepped back and let Vonnie and Dom go up first, and I'm sure they babbled all the usual yang, thanking their homies and giving shout-outs to our friends. But when it was my turn I took a minute to say a few words to Mama and Caramel, and just being able to stand there on that stage and speak their names in front of the world almost made me cry.

"I'd like to dedicate my little portion of this award to the memory of my mother, Lovely Bird Montana, and to my baby sister, Caramel Rose Montana." I paused and took a second to touch the locket around my neck that held a tiny picture of the three of us. "Mama, you had the talent, but you never had a chance to use it. Stay in my heart and I'll take you all the places you never got to go. Rest in peace and sweet dreams. I miss you, your doll baby."

The crowd went wild and Dom and Vonnie were both crying and hugging me as the three of us waved and blew kisses into the air, but just as we were stepping off the stage, Hurricane was there with his arms around us. He was laughing and grinning and pushing us back to center stage.

"Ladies and gentlemen," his voice boomed as he stood up there looking like a superfine black Hercules in a tailored suit that had to have set him back at least seven grand. The audience roared and gave him much respect. Sisters were moist in the panties just looking at him, and every man out there wanted to take a walk in Hurricane's three-thousand-dollar French leather shoes. "Let's give it up one more time for the hottest sisters to hit the stage this year, Scandalous!"

They gave it up too. For us and for Hurricane, 'cause that niggah had swole pockets and a magnetic smile. "But tonight," Hurricane continued, "we have some extra-good news to hit y'all with. Even though Scandalous! is off the chain and dropping big nukes all over the charts, we got our eyes steady aimed on forward. We're looking at progress, ya know? Homicide Hitz is all about creating new opportunities for our artists that'll help them progress and express the range of their creativity. So tonight I got something great to lay on y'all. Tonight you're looking at the next phenomenon. Not Ciara, not Ashanti, not Kellis, not Beyoncé . . . but the lead singer of the group formerly known as Scandalous! and now our newest, hottest, and sexiest soon-to-be solo artist . . . Candy!"

I felt the air go cold around me and the next thing I knew Hurricane had shoved the mic in my hand and the crowd of people were on their feet clapping and screaming like crazy. I didn't know what to say, and even though Hurricane was showing all his pretty white teeth, the naked truth was right there in his eyes. That niggah had set me up.

"Thank you," I forced myself to whisper before the crowd lit up with noise again. Cameras were really snapping now, and all those flashes looked like demented strobe lights. "Thank you."

Hurricane snatched the mic from me and I heard him tell the world to look for my first solo album to hit the stores in ninety days. I walked off that stage numb as hell and filled with guilt up to my neck. I reached out to hug Dom and Vonnie, and both of them gave me looks so full of hot hate they burned right through my heart.

They didn't even wait until we got outside. "You stupid fuckin' sellout!" Vonnie yelled, stepping up in my face like she was gonna do a little something. "Dominica, this dirty bitch sold us out! Fuck you, Candy. You no-good traitor-ass bitch!"

"Can't you see what he's doing to you?" Dominica pleaded. "This ain't about no new challenges. He's pulling you away from us for a reason, Candy. That fool wants to keep you in a box. A box where only he has the key!"

I turned to her with my mouth open. "Dom, you know I didn't know . . . I would never do nothing like that to y'all—"

"Stop fuckin' lying!" Vonnie swung on me, and with the cameras flashing we got to scuffling right there in the aisle. "You was always trying to sing in the middle! Always hogging the goddamn mic!"

I fought back, but I wasn't trying to hurt Vonzelle. I knew how hurt she already was, and I was just as hurt too. I was even more confused. I let her talk her shit and throw a few blows. She wasn't doing nothing though, and I basically just slapped her hands out the way and pushed her off of me a few times, but the way she was screaming and showing her ass you would've thought we were fighting for real.

"I'ma hit your heart where it hurts, Candy!" She screamed and kicked as three of Hurricane's boys pulled her toward the door. "You think you cute, but you ain't shit, bitch. And you can't fuckin' sing neither! Just wait. I'ma get your ass back!" She was going wild as the dudes hauled her toward the exit, backward by her arms. One of the straps had popped off her slinky dress, and the press was snapping mad photos of her big juicy titty that made Janet Jackson's little titty look sad and saggy.

I turned to Dom, pleading. "I didn't have nothing to do

with this, Dominica. I swear on my mother. I didn't do it, and I don't want it either."

"Yeah," Dom said sadly with her hands on her hips and her bottom lip trembling. "But you had a chance to deny it right then and there when he said it." Her eyes flashed. "And you didn't."

Chapter 18

Who's a Fuckin' Snake?

I cried for three days straight after Hurricane split Scandalous! up. I wouldn't talk to him, I wouldn't get up out the bed, and I wouldn't go in the studio to record. I even missed a live radio interview about my new solo career with HOT 97, but I didn't give a damn.

Hurricane wanted me to get behind this whole solo shit, but I wasn't with it. He tried to talk me up first. "C'mon, Candy. You the real talent of the group anyway. Them other two jawns can be replaced with anybody. Whose name you hear them screaming when y'all onstage? Yours! All those moves you got, that sexy red hair and that ass . . . Ain't nobody hollering Vonzelle or Dominica! They yelling for *you*, ma. You the star!"

On the morning of the fourth day that niggah lost his patience and made his move.

It was about six in the morning, and I had to go to the bathroom. Or rather, I was having one of them dreams where you know you gotta pee, but you don't want to wake up and go. I felt pressure in my lower body, and in my dream I was doing like Mama used to do, walking around the house blind drunk and searching for the toilet bowl.

The pressure was getting worse on one side of me, and I forced myself to wake up. I opened my eyes and felt even more pressure. On my right leg. I glanced down, and my blood went cold.

Savage had me. The bottom half of her was wrapped around my leg from my knee to my thigh. She squeezed real hard, then flicked her cold tongue out at me.

I shrieked and tried to scoot back.

"Don't move," Hurricane warned. I let out a moan but kept my eyes on the snake. "Or she'll think you a mouse. Just do what I tell you to do. Savage ain't gone hurt you. But she *will* get your ass up outta that bed."

By now I knew that begging only excited Hurricane and made him meaner and more powerful. But I didn't give a fuck. I begged. Begged my ass off as that cold bitch with the beady eyes wrapped her body around my leg and lifted her top half in the air.

Then she slithered her head straight up my stomach, over my navel and between my naked titties. She was inching toward my face and licking her tongue out at my chin when I freaked straight out.

"Hurricane, NO!" I screamed, then peed. I was out of control. Hot piss gushed from me, soaking the sheets as I grabbed that fat cold snake around the back of her head and tried to fling her ass away from me. Her head smacked the bed between my legs then bounced back up and she was right in my face again. I pushed out with two hands and she dipped her head low, striking my leg. I felt a sharp pain and lost all my senses.

"HELP! HELP! HELP! MAMA! CARAMEL LORD JESUS SOMEBODY HELP ME!!" I was hysterical, my heart jumping outta my chest, and then Hurricane was there. Handling Savage like she was his woman. He started unraveling her gently, laughing the whole time.

"All right, Candy. You all right, girl. Stop making all that noise. Savage can't hurt you." He wiped at the tiny row of bloody spots burning on my thigh, then held the snake by the head and forced her mouth open. "See? Just some real little teeth in there. They sharp, but they ain't poisonous. She ain't even got no venom in her. And she just ate so she ain't hungry enough to squeeze you too hard."

I was straight wailing. Holding my thigh as more blood eased out and down my leg. "It was just a joke, Candy," he insisted, wiping at my leg some more. "Goddamn, girl. It was a joke. See, watch this."

He lifted Savage in the air and held her mouth open again, then pressed her mouth down onto his forearm. She sank in so fast I almost didn't see her move.

"Okay?" he said, holding his arm up to show me. "You feel better now that she bit me too? I told you the snake can't hurt you, so now you know it's true." That fool draped Savage over one shoulder and snatched the blanket off of me. "Now get up and go wash your ass. Brush your teeth too. You got another radio slot at HOT 97 today, and this time you better not fuckin' miss it."

I rolled outta that bed in a hurry. I limped into the bathroom and poured some peroxide on those little bloody dots, crying my ass off. Later that afternoon on the way to the radio station Hurricane told me I better not say nothing about it to nobody. "And don't be walking around here like you got shot in the leg neither. I got bit too, and you don't see me whining."

I showed Caramel my snakebite that night and she didn't even seem impressed.

"Oh, it don't look that bad. It's just a kiss. You such a drama queen, Candy. The way you was talking I thought you had a big hole in your leg or something. Just put a Band-Aid on it. It'll be all right in a few days."

She was lucky she was my sister. Caramel and Hurricane could both go somewhere far. That kiss from Savage was both a mark and a memory that I was gonna carry with me for the rest of my life. All the way to my grave.

Chapter 19

IRT to Brooklyn

If I didn't know any better I would have sworn Hurricane's big bad ass was shook. It was almost ten in the morning and we were still in the studio. He'd made me stay up almost the whole damn night, rehearsing and re-rehearsing a cut he felt was coming out less than perfect. At five in the morning he'd told me to go downstairs and catch a catnap in one of the video rooms, but I don't think he'd slept at all. He was still hard at work. His shirt was off and his eyes were red and tired.

His cell phone rang, lighting up in all colors. "Yeah!" he snatched it up and barked. He had certain ring tones for certain people, and I knew this tone meant a 911 was in the works. Some hot shit was going down.

"Yeah, whassup Mr. D?" He listened for a moment, then sat straight up. "Whoa, whoa, whoa! Hold the fuck up! That shit is already paid for! I swear to God, I took care of that. They 'posed to have two fuckin' crates set aside for you. You sure about that?" I peeked over at him. He was so hyped his titty muscles had started twitching. "Aaight. Tell 'em to chill the fuck out till I get there. Lemme round up my niggahs and we be up that way in a minute."

Two seconds later he was on his feet. "Damn! Get your ass up outta here, Candy 'cause I got some business to handle. And oh yeah, I forgot to tell you. You gotta be down in Brooklyn today at two for a photo shoot with XXL."

"Cool," I said, and just stood there. He'd been cooped up in this office for too damn long and I could tell he was stressing. Mess was all over the place. Half-empty juice bottles, orange peels, cracked-open nuts. "What time we leaving so I can call Dom and Vonnie and let them know when to be here?"

He glared at me with those red devil eyes. "Did I say anything about them hoes? I said *you* got a shoot to do today, Candy. You. Your ass is a solo act now, remember? Goddamn! How many fuckin' times do somebody have to tell your stupid ass something? You act like you can't live without them bitches. Which one of them you fuckin', Candy, huh? That stank-ass ho Vonzelle? Or that undercover pussy licker Dominica? You need them jawns more than you need me? Either one of them doing more for you than I'm doing? I got shit lined up for you that them two hoes can't even understand. You gone be up there with all the top stars and you wanna drag them two project bitches around behind you, right? Just what the fuck is your problem, Candy, huh?"

I knew better than to answer. I just stood there looking down at the floor while he went on and on, letting him rage and talk shit until he got tired. Hurricane was under a lot of pressure 'cause he did a lot of jobs. I didn't get mad behind the noise he was making because I understood it. Scandalous! had busted out on the scene undeniably large, and he just wanted to take advantage of that by keeping my face in the media so the fans would be begging for my solo release.

He was slaving in the studio for me day and night because he was trying to get me out there in a big way, and that's what it was all about. Hurricane had visions of taking my career to the next level. He'd gotten me mad radio spots, cable TV shows, BET and MTV interviews, and a couple of hot photo shoots too. All of this was important because he wanted me to be able to rub shoulders with artists like Beyoncé and Missy Elliot and Eve as often as possible.

"How am I getting all the way to Brooklyn?" I asked as he damn near knocked me down going out the door. "I don't know where their studio is."

He spoke over his shoulder. "Call Knowledge. He'll take you."

◈ ◈ ◈

Knowledge was already at the House but his car was being serviced at the dealer, and since Cane and his boys were taking the limo and the Yukon, we were gonna have to take the train to Brooklyn. Hurricane had given me some money and told me to go around the corner to the Puerto Rican hair salon and get my hair and makeup done. When I came out of there two hours later my hair was live, my skin was fresh, my jewels were large. I was looking delicious and I knew it. But I was nervous too. Sexy nervous. Turned-on nervous. Excited and charged. I needed some release and wished I had somebody who could do some thangs to my nookie.

Instead, I thought about the trip I was about to take with Knowledge.

This was gonna be my first time spending some *real* time with him, and I looked forward to riding down to Brooklyn and finding out what he was all about. Something about that mothersucker just moved me. Hurricane, with all his endless weight lifting and probably some steroids too, was three times buffer, but there was something strong about Knowledge that I liked. He gave off a vibe that was just as powerful as Hurricane's but with none of that poser-ass bullshit attached.

Just thinking about him had me wet and horny, and if it wasn't almost time to leave, my fingers would have been all up in my panties getting me a quick one.

Riding the train with Knowledge was unreal. His gear was expensive without being outrageous. He was comfortable with himself and wasn't out to impress nobody, so you know I was highly impressed.

We were sitting in a two-seater on the number 4 train going downtown, and all kinds of feelings rushed through me. People was looking at us like we were a couple and I didn't mind at all. For the first time in a long time I was out and about like a regular chick. I felt young again. Free. Wasn't nobody watching me and nobody was telling me what to do. Just being up under Knowledge had me more aware of me. The underground sounds and smells had me hyped. The movement of the train rocked me with excitement. My thigh rubbing up against Knowledge's hard leg sparked a fire in my coochie and left me trembling inside. We were speeding through the tunnel and the noise was up, up, up. "So," I hollered in his ear, pressing my titty against his arm, "how long you been working for Hurricane?"

He leaned over and put his lips next to my ear, and a shiver hit me so hard I almost moaned. "Four years."

I crossed my legs and nodded. "So you like it then, huh?"

He shrugged, his dark brown eyes giving up absolutely nothing. "It's a job. It's what I get paid to do."

I cut my eyes at him. His voice was kinda cold, but ice ain't what I saw in his eyes. I'd felt him checking me out while we waited for the train. His eyeballs had been roaming all over me like loose marbles.

The train stopped at Ninety-sixth Street and I kept right on fishing. "You a real lawyer? You look kinda young to me. How's a brother like you get into a grind like that?"

He actually looked at me. "What? Only old white men are supposed to be attorneys? I got into law for the same reason most people do. Cheese. Green-boys. Money."

"Well"—I shrugged right back at him—"I used to do shit just for the money, and it almost got me killed. Now I do what I do because I got a goal. Because I got someplace in life I wanna be."

The train lurched and he turned to me. "What makes you think I don't?"

I hunched my shoulders and crossed my legs again. "I don't know. You one of Hurricane's top lieutenants, how much higher can you go? I figure most of y'all are just happy to be a part of all his hype, you know? In his mix. Satisfied with where you are."

I musta hit a nerve somewhere because ol' Knowledge bust out with the longest sentence I'd ever heard him speak. "Check this out, miss lady. Ain't nobody trapped under Hurricane's roof except you. You see anybody else living up in the middle with that niggah? All the rest of us are getting paid to be there.

And I'm getting laced the most. Now, if you *ain't* doing this shit for the money, then I sure feel for you 'cause that means your young ass is really stuck."

"I'm working too!" I shot back. "Since you the one keeping the books you oughtta know just how much bank Scandalous! is bringing in. Hurricane ain't in the business of giving away free albums, you know. I'm getting paid too," I lied, "but unlike the rest of y'all gaming niggrows out at the mansion, I got a solid career going. One that's gonna take me big places and set me and my sister up for life."

He gave me a long, bored look. Then he said quietly, "Cool. But just like I see what's coming through them doors, you ought to know I can count what's going out too. Ain't nobody getting paid from Scandalous! except Hurricane. You might wanna tell that dumb shit to somebody who don't know no better."

I guess that was supposed to be a shutdown. He pulled a book out of his back pocket and put his eyes on it. I folded my arms across my titties and stared straight ahead.

◊ ◊ ◊

The words swam all over the pages of his book as Knowledge pretended to read. She was pissed off, and deep inside he was highly amused. He'd just checked her hard and put two little angry red spots on Candy's light brown cheeks. She couldn't think of nothing to come back at him with, so she sat there steaming mad with her sexy-ass self, her arms crossed and her body swaying with the rhythm of the train.

She might not have had a plan, but at least she had a goal, Knowledge thought with approval. That meant she was smart enough to look at the House of Homicide as a temporary pit stop. Hurricane's label was hot, but it wasn't the only one out there. Besides, with all the grimy shit Hurricane was into, his shit could get flipped without warning. Every dirty empire in the world had had its rise and its fall, and if Hurricane kept fucking around with those guns and those Italians he could end up on his ass looking up at the sky someday.

The train pulled into the Atlantic Avenue station, and Knowledge closed his book and put it back in his pocket. He tapped Candy on the thigh, then stood up and reached for the overhead handle. Candy got up and faced away from him, even though the door was the opposite way. He laughed inside. The only reason she had an attitude was because he'd put a mirror in her face and showed her the truth. Knowledge knew how much the truth could hurt. He lived with that kind of pain every day.

They took the number 3 train to Nevins Street, then got off and started walking. The photo shoot was in a studio off of Hanson Place, and as Knowledge led Candy through the streets of Brooklyn he pretended to ignore her but was, in reality, stealing small glances at her as she flowed at his side. Men and women stared at her as they walked down the street, and despite himself he had the urge to grab her hand and pull her closer to him.

Knowledge knew the two brothers doing the shoot and had done some legal work for them a few times over the years. They greeted him like he was royalty. The elevator leading up to the studio was past tiny, and it was impossible for them not to touch each other. He noticed that Candy preferred to back up against him than to touch the two men who were strangers, and he was cool with that. Better the devil that you know than the one that you don't.

Knowledge was impressed with the interior of the studio and he could tell Candy was too. It was a small operation and mostly contracted for hip-hop magazines, but the brothers, Bilal and Jamil, were professionals and had all kinds of camera equipment and lighting set up. He waited while an older woman whisked Candy away to touch up her makeup, and when she came back in the room dressed in a pair of sexy white cotton pants and a simple crisscross white shirt, he couldn't take his eyes off of her.

He stayed out of the way, dick on the ready, leaning against a wall and enjoying the scene. Bilal showed Candy where the main light was, then directed her to her posing spot and started giving instructions. Even with his amateur eye, Knowledge could tell she had it. The girl was as hot in front of a camera as she was on the stage.

He had to admit it. Her package was puffed and it was kicking up the heat in him too. She had it all—body, looks, class. The back pockets was phatty and she was pure eye candy in the front. This girl could be large, he thought, wanting her as she turned and posed and basically made love to the camera. Looking the way she looked, and with a voice like hers, she could be bigger than any female artist out there. That is, Knowledge checked himself, if she could survive the fact that she was fucking with a sadistic killer who had her whole world on lock.

◇ ◇ ◇

Bilal and Jamil had been snapping pictures for hours, but Knowledge didn't mind. He could have watched this girl all day. She'd changed clothes about five times, and each time she rolled out in a different outfit it was sexier than the last one had been. They had just finished taking a short break, and Candy was back on her posing spot. Bilal got off two pictures, and then everything went dark.

"Whassup!" Jamil joked. "Somebody musta forgot to pay the light bill."

Knowledge glanced at his watch and saw that it was just after four. It was still light outside, but the studio had been artificially darkened, and it was hard to see anything much until Jamil pulled up the shades and let some sunlight in.

Knowledge stayed in his spot against the wall as Candy sat down in a director's chair. Bilal went to check the fuse box as his brother went to the door and glanced out into the hall.

"It's dark out here too," Jamil called out. "All the lights are out."

Knowledge went over to the window and looked down on the busy street below. It only took him a moment to figure shit out. "It's a blackout, man," he told Bilal, who had walked back in with a fuse in his hand. "The traffic light outside is gone, and people are pouring outside and standing in the street."

Candy joined Knowledge at his window while Bilal and his brother shared the other one. He moved over slightly for her, but still their shoulders and arms touched. Instantly his dick got hard. He could smell her perfume and whatever it was she had used in her hair.

"Shit!" Bilal cursed. "We got a tight deadline on this layout."

His brother shrugged. "We'll just have to use what we got then, 'cause if the lights are gone then this shit's a wrap."

Chapter 20

Crossing That Bridge

We walked down Fulton toward Atlantic Avenue and I couldn't believe how crowded the streets were. Everybody and they niggah was out here looking for a way to make it home, wherever that was. Cell phones were knocked out. The trains were shut down, and traffic was so backed up cars could hardly move. Finding a taxi was nothing but a pipe dream, so I followed Knowledge down the street as we flowed right along with everybody else.

"So what's the plan?" I asked, strutting beside him. I'd worn a pair of two-hundred-dollar sandals to the photo shoot, and I was glad those days of sporting cheap-ass jellies were long over.

"We walk," he said, but he didn't say it rough. He looked over at me. "You cool with that? I mean, we could hang out here in Brooklyn and wait until something happens, but it looks like that might take awhile."

I glanced around. It was the middle of August and the crowd was getting thicker by the minute as people dashed out of their hot-ass offices and onto the city streets. "Yeah," I said, hoping I sounded like a soldier. "I'm cool with that."

We followed the masses down the streets and toward the Brooklyn Bridge. The mood was high, and even under the circumstances New Yorkers were feeling each other and being nicer than usual. Especially for Brooklyn. The vibe was contagious though, and I decided right then and there I wasn't walking all the way across no bridge and back into Manhattan with no niggrow who had a funky attitude or gave me the silent treatment.

"So," I said, strolling easily. I had started to take all my shine off and stick it in my purse, but I felt safe walking with Knowledge, like couldn't nothing happen to me. "Did you dig that shoot or what?" I was waiting for him to say something smart so I could bust on him. His eyes had been on me more than the camera had, and if I stared into them hard enough I could probably find every single picture they took.

He nodded. "I thought it was hot. Tight. Da bomb. You really did your thang up there, Candy. You've got a lot of talent."

I started grinning like crazy, happy to get his approval although I didn't know why. We made a little more small talk as we walked. I told him one of my favorite singers was Aaron Neville, and he laughed and said he loved him some Aaron too and had all his cuts. We talked a while more, then ducked into one of those combination ice-cream shops that also sold chicken wings and french fries and probably some weed out the back too.

The owners were cool, and since it was so hot and they

didn't know how long the power would be out, they made our ice cream a freebie. I got a strawberry cone and Knowledge got him one scoop of vanilla in a cup.

"Vanilla, huh?" I said, slobbing my ice cream down and licking it from all angles. "So is that what you into?"

He looked at me with a slick grin. "When it comes down to my ice cream, yeah. Outside of that, I'm a chocolate man. Although I can go for a little strawberry every once in a while too."

I took a nibble from the edge of my cone, then held it up and sucked some of the melting ice cream from the tip at the bottom. "Umph." I grunted. He'd danced his ass all around my question and still left me wondering.

"What about you?" he asked, nodding toward my cone. "You got something against that cone, or you get down like that all the time?"

I laughed, then held still as he used his napkin to wipe some ice cream off my chin. "I don't know what you're talking about," I whispered, flirting my ass off. "I always eat my ice cream this way."

He dipped his spoon into his cup and ate a mouthful of ice cream, then said, "If that's the truth, then I bet there are a whole lot of hustlers and knuckleheads out there who'd like to be that cone."

I looked over at him and said softly, "I'm not interested in hustlers or knuckleheads, Knowledge. I'm into real men."

He nodded and ate some more ice cream. "Cool, Candy," he said. "That's good to know."

◆ ◆ ◆

By the time we got to the Brooklyn Bridge it looked like half of Manhattan was already there. It was still hot as hell, probably around ninety degrees, and rush hour had just begun. It looked like thousands of people were already on the bridge. Some were leaving Manhattan, and others were trying to get in.

I looked out at all that water so far down below and got scared to step one foot on that bridge. "I feel dizzy," I said. "I can drive over a bridge, but walking over one is something different 'cause I'm scared of heights."

Knowledge gave me a strange look, then held out his hand. "I feel you. I really do. But we ain't gotta live on this baby. Just cross over her. Act like you're walking down a regular street. Just don't look down."

He held my hand and helped me climb over a barrier to the bridge's walkway, and we joined the crowd that was trying to get back into the city. There were so many people that I didn't look down and I didn't even stress. Knowledge made me walk on the inside of him so I didn't have an excuse to look down anyway.

I couldn't help feeling like this blackout had happened right on time, 'cause I was starting to enjoy the hell out of myself on this walk. I knew there were probably a ton of people stuck in elevators and some in the tunnels of the crowded subways, and I felt for them. But for real though. I was aboveground and hanging out with a fine-ass man who had enough electricity flowing through my body to light the whole damn city back up.

And Knowledge was looser too. He was ten times more relaxed than he'd been on the way down here, and I was happy about that. I'd been wondering what he was about for the longest, and it made me even more curious when nobody, even nosey-ass Fatima, could tell me much about him. All they knew was that he was real big in Hurricane's game. That he was a shot-caller, an investment baller who handled Hurricane's empire and who stayed away from bitches and bullshit like they were the virus.

The bridge was longer than I thought it was, but that was cool. We talked the whole way, and by the time we reached downtown Manhattan I knew some things about Knowledge and he knew a few things about me too.

"Did you like Saint Louis?" I asked. He'd said that's where he was living before he came to Harlem when he was thirteen.

He shook his head. "East Saint Louis. It's a small town across the river in Illinois, and it's not big like Saint Louis. But, no. I hated it. We were poor as hell and life was hard. My mother got killed there, and when my grandmother sent for me to come to Harlem I never looked back."

I nodded. That's how I felt about L.A. After losing Mama there, I'd probably never even think about going back again.

"My feet hurt," I said softly. I leaned against a car and bent over to unstrap my sandals.

"What are you doing?" Knowledge said real quick. "Don't take off your shoes out here. There's glass and shit in the street, Candy. It's better to keep your shoes on."

"But my feet hurt," I whined. Right about now I didn't care how much these shoes cost. My feet were swollen and the straps were cutting into my skin. I wanted them off.

"Okay, okay," he said, holding up his hand. "I'll tell you what. I got a crib on Seventy-ninth Street. Right off of Broadway. Let's cut through Canal Street and over to the West Side.

We'll hit my crib and I'll give you a pair of slippers. If the power ain't back on by then, I'll put you on my back and carry you the rest of the way to Harlem."

"You for real?"

He nodded. "Yeah. Let's stop at my joint. I'll be a gentleman and you'll be safe. I promise."

I took that promise and tossed it over my head. *I'd* be safe from *him*? I laughed inside. He shoulda been praying his fine ass would be safe from me.

◆ ◆ ◆

I followed him to his building and we weren't even in his apartment good before I knew Knowledge was large. The neighborhood he lived in was funky and live and swarming with all kinds of high-rolling people. His building had one of those doormen who wore a real uniform, and there were fresh flowers and all kinds of pretty plants in the foyer. I figured Knowledge was probably paying just as much to live in a crib in this neighborhood as Hurricane was paying for the spread he had out on Long Island.

The building was tall, and my feet were so swollen I didn't think I could walk up too many stairs.

"You can make it. I only live on the second floor," Knowledge explained. "Our apartment got set on fire when I was ten, and I had to jump out the window. Heights don't scare me, but I don't trust them either. Anything higher than the second or third floor is usually too high for me."

"You jumped out a window? Uh-uh," I said. "I couldn't have done that. I told you heights freak me out."

He shrugged. "Those flames eating up the skin on my back

gave me a lot of motivation. These days if I'm not on the ground I try to make sure I have a plan B backing me up."

My feet were past swollen. Pain had crept all up my calves, and even my back was throbbing.

"This is where I rest," he said, unlocking a door that was a few steps down from the staircase. I stepped inside first and was surprised to find semi-cool air waiting for me.

"Ahh," I sighed gratefully. "It's cool in here."

Knowledge closed the door behind me, and I saw we were in a loft.

"Yeah," he said. "I keep the air conditioner on even when I'm gone. It stayed pretty cool in here since everything was closed up and the blinds were down."

He pointed at the soft suede couch and invited me to sit down, then went over to the window and pulled up the blinds to let in the last bit of daylight.

"You want something to drink?" he asked.

I shook my head. There had been boo coo vendors out there hustling cold water. They had their coolers set up and had scrounged up some ice from somewhere and were selling regular-sized bottles of water for five dollars each, and guess what? People were so hot and thirsty they were paying that shit! I know Knowledge did. He'd gotten us two bottles each, and now it was time for me to let at least one of them back out.

"Can I use your bathroom?"

He pointed me down the hall and I went in the bathroom and did what I had to do. While I was in there I admired the surroundings. He had good taste and everything about his place was perfect. I wondered if he had hired an interior designer to hook him up or if he'd done it all himself. Nah, I decided after a minute. He'd hired somebody. This shit was just too laid. It was even tighter than Hurricane's mansion, although on a much smaller scale.

I looked in his linen closet and got a thick towel, then washed my hands with the warm water from the tap. When I got back to the living room Knowledge was lighting candles. A whole shitload of them, and the flickering of the flames and the near blackness that was seeping in from outside capped off the whole atmosphere.

I sat back and closed my eyes for a second, and the next thing I knew he was lifting my sore feet into his hands.

"Here," he said, lowering them into a pail of warm, soapy water. "It's not as hot as it could be because the hot water tank is off, but it's not too bad."

I pushed my toes down under that water and I could have hollered it felt so good. But then it got even better. Staring into my eyes, Knowledge got down on his knees and plunged his hands under the soapy water. He started massaging my toes gently. Rubbing them with his fingers and bringing them back to life.

He was even nicer to the rest of my foot. His hands were easy but relaxing as he worked the pain and tension out of my feet and left them feeling light and tingly. I moaned out loud as his wet hands crept up my calves. Sliding over my skin and cupping my muscles with tenderness. He took care of my ankles, my shins, even my knees, and by the time the water started getting cold, everything on me was fire-hot.

I closed my eyes as Knowledge lifted my right foot from the bucket and dried it with a soft towel. Then he lowered it gently to the floor and dried my left foot. But this time he didn't put my foot down. Instead, I felt moist heat on my big toe as he sucked it between his chocolate lips and licked it like it was something sweet.

I moaned as his tongue flickered and darted between each of my toes, sending tiny chills up to my crotch. He licked the entire bottom of my foot, then kissed it like it had a cherry on the top before setting it down on the towel and touching my thigh.

"You wanna take a shower?"

I nodded because I damn sure couldn't talk. A shower would be right on time 'cause after all that good old toe sucking I wanted to see what else old Knowledge could do with his tongue.

"Cool. Everything you need should be in the bathroom. There's not a whole lot of warm water left, but it should be enough to make you feel good."

I nodded again. I already felt so good I wanted to melt. No man had ever sucked my toes before. I didn't even know that shit could feel so good! I took a candle and hobbled back down the hall to the bathroom, my feet aching and feeling delicious at the same time.

I stripped out of my sweaty clothes and folded them before stepping into the shower. It was one of those big old jammies with frosted doors and a bench inside. Even in the candlelight I could see how expensive the fixtures were. Boo had laid out some cash for this nest.

I turned on the hot water tap and stood under the flow. The water was still pretty warm, but I definitely didn't need to add any cold to the mix. I let the jets stream over my hair, then poured some of his shampoo over my head and rubbed it around. I had just washed my face and rinsed out my hair and was soaping up my body when I heard the bathroom door open.

I didn't say a word as I saw him enter holding a candle of his own.

I watched him set it down on a shelf and take off his clothes. He stood out there naked for a good minute, and I knew he was thinking hard on what he was about to do. Finally he stepped closer to the shower door and opened it to our naked bodies.

We couldn't take our eyes off each other. I stared at his perfect build. Muscled all the hell up, but naturally. When my eyes dropped down to his manhood I had to reach for the walls to keep myself from falling.

"Goddamn," I said, staring at that thick, and thank-God *long* black dick. "What took you so long?"

He chuckled and stepped inside with me. "I'm here now, baby. I'm here now."

◐ ◐ ◐

Knowledge took his sweet time with me.

He soaped my body and got to know me, and I gasped as he rubbed bubbles all over my round breasts. He turned me around slowly and took a few moments to admire my ass in silence. "Damn," he said under his breath. His dick was pressed against my thigh as he used the cloth to drip bubbles down my back. "You sweet for real, baby girl."

He licked my earlobes and sucked the back of my neck as the candles made orange shapes on the walls and I moaned into the darkness and pressed my hand to my slit. Juice leaked from me immediately, and I reached back and offered him my fingers, which he licked one by one. "I been wanting this," he whispered between licks, "so damn bad."

I turned around and kissed him, tasting myself in his mouth, and he slid two fingers inside of me as he sucked gently on my tongue. Then he left my lips and bent slightly. He got to licking on my breasts like they were lollipops. My pussy was on fire. I grabbed his dick and started stroking him, faster and faster. He took it as long as he could, then he moved my hands and cupped my ass, guiding the head of his dick to my opening and sliding himself up in me with one good long stroke. He pushed as deep as he could go, like he wanted it to come out of my throat, as if he knew that was just what I needed. There was still some of him left outside of me and I tried my best to use my muscles to suck it in.

I reached between our bodies and grabbed the base of his dick. I was amazed at that inch or so that just wouldn't fit inside of me. I was almost in shock. My pussy was filled to the brim and I wanted it to stay that way forever. I vibrated all over that dick. Clenched its thickness with my walls. Savored the sensation as it slammed all the way to the very back of my pussy.

Knowledge reached for my titties and squeezed them. "Strawberry," he panted, taking my left nipple between his lips and biting it gently. It was rosy and swollen, reaching out toward him. "I changed my mind. My favorite flavor is strawberry."

I was busy humping and grinding. Getting fucked thoroughly and taking advantage of it. The more he stroked and bit down on my nipple, the hotter and wetter my pussy got. "Don't stop," I panted rapidly. His tongue circled my nipples and made my whole body tremble. "Oh . . . ," I whimpered, grabbing hold of the towel bar. Tears were coming out my eyes he was fucking me so good. "Oh . . ." I threw my head back and moaned. And then my whole body fell loose. Every muscle in me spasmed and shook as I screamed and then came, pussy squirting, bouncing up and down on those nine thick inches and yanking that towel bar down from the wall.

"I'm not gonna come," he whispered, and pulled out of me. I came back to reality and felt a little guilty. I'd gotten down with him without any protection, which I knew wasn't smart at all. Good thing he had major dick control. If he'da gotten me pregnant I woulda never been able to blame it on Hurricane. The only way that niggah could put a baby far enough up in somebody's pussy was with a slingshot and some supersperm.

We dried off sharing one towel. Knowledge carried the candles and took me into his room and pulled back the covers on the bed. His area was simple but nice. The furniture was expensive and solid, but there wasn't no whole lot of shit in there just for show. The best thing was, there were no goddamn animals up in his crib, and I smiled to myself as I slid under the sheets and enjoyed the remnants of the thumping he'd put on my pussy.

We lay there talking and kissing under the candlelight, and I realized that this was the very first time I'd lain in a bed with a man and just cuddled. Knowledge held me in his strong arms and it felt so good I didn't know how to act. I couldn't believe how much tenderness was in his hands when he touched me. His fingers were strong and hard-core, but unlike Hurricane's there was no pain in them. No punching, no pinching, no punishment. There was nothing but love in my boo's hands.

I made sure there was love in my hands, too. I touched his back and felt his burned skin, and I wanted to kiss every inch of it away. I liked what Knowledge was doing for me. He was giving up tenderness. Straight tenderness. That was something that Hurricane had never learned. How to be tender with a woman.

I fell asleep with him holding me, and when I opened my eyes again, the candles were still lit but now the radio was playing. That let me know the power was back on, and so did the smell of something cooking that was in the air. I sat up on the side of the bed and tried to figure out what to do. Should I get my wrinkled, funky clothes out the bathroom and style them, or should I walk into the kitchen butt naked and surprise him?

Before I could decide, Knowledge was back. He was carrying a tray, which he set down on the bed beside me.

"Hungry?" he asked. "I ran downstairs and got some grub while you were sleeping."

I grinned as I looked at the spread. This mug had done made a sistah a fried baloney sandwich on Wonder bread. I lifted the bread and saw he'd put mustard on it and the meat was even split in the middle to keep it from bubbling up.

"Boy!" I laughed and punched his arm. "What you know about a fried baloney sammich?"

He bit into his and shrugged. "I used to fix them all the time when I was little. Shit, we was so poor, baloney was like steak to us. We ate it every day."

I thought back over my life with Mama. We'd been poor too. I knew hunger like the back of my hand. Wet cornflakes had been my steak.

I found myself sharing that part of my life with Knowledge. Even the parts that were most painful to me. Running drug money, Caramel's shooting, and Mama's death. It was like I'd held so much of it so deeply inside of me that it came unstuck from my heart and just poured out my mouth. My words were heavy with guilt and Knowledge picked up on that.

"Don't walk around feeling bad about the past, Candy," he said, holding my hand. "It'll only hold you back. The best you can do is concentrate on your future. When life fell apart for me, I chased down my future until I caught it. You can do the same thing, baby girl."

I touched the stump of his missing finger.

"Is that how you got this? Chasing down your future?"

He frowned and shook his head slowly. "Nah, baby girl. I lost my finger running away from my past."

"Tell me," I said softly, praying that he would trust me as much as I trusted him. "Tell me what happened to you."

He looked at me and sighed, and then he did.

◊ ◊ ◊

Knowledge talked for half an hour. When he was quiet I sat there with my little mind completely blown. More than ever I felt for Caramel. Like Knowledge, she'd witnessed her own mother's murder, and that had to be one of the worst things that could happen to a kid.

"How old were you when your mother got killed?" I asked.

"Thirteen," he said. "I was a little guy back then. A real runt. It used to piss my father off that as big as he was, I couldn't seem to grow."

I thought about that dick. "Well you sure big enough now. What about the other kids in your family? Who took care of them after your mother died?"

"I was an only child," he said. "Or at least I thought I was. When my father went on trial I found out that he had another family. I didn't know anything about them until his other son got up on that stand and testified about what a good father he was. That lying motherfucker helped him get life instead of the death penalty. Later I found out that my pops had an older daughter too."

"So you have an older brother and a sister? Do you ever see them?"

He nodded and picked up the leftover corner of my sandwich and put it in his mouth. "Yeah. I see 'em all the time. Now no more questions, girl. The trains are probably running and I need to get you back to Harlem before your niggah gets back and gets crazy."

Fuck Hurricane, I thought. After that dick-down I'd just gotten and the way I was being treated, I didn't even want to hear his name. Plus, I wasn't stupid. Thanks to Vonnie I knew the baller rules. Knowledge was still holding on to his nut, and I wasn't vacating his crib until that W was over in my column.

I pushed him down on the bed and crawled on top of him.

"Don't start nothing," he warned, laughing.

I ignored that noise. That dick was rock-hard and telling a whole nother story.

He slid his palms over my naked booty and I reached back and guided his right hand to my mouth. I was totally feeling him as I kissed his nub, then took it between my lips and licked and sucked it with mad attraction. I bobbed all over that thang.

I swirled my tongue over it and slobbed it down with hot, wet kisses.

And when I was done giving it the proper attention it deserved, I slid down lower and pressed my titties to his thighs, and showed the same kind of love to his long black dick.

Chapter 21

Candy Lickin'

We didn't leave Knowledge's apartment for another hour, and while I'd gotten mine and had my fun, the reality of what we'd done was slowly creeping up on me. Still, I didn't regret spending a moment with Knowledge Graham. Matter of fact, I wished I could have stayed up in that phat-ass apartment with him forever. Just me and him. But the truth was, I belonged to Hurricane Jackson. I was his bitch, bought and paid for, and if he even thought I was thinking on some outside dick, he could make me disappear, just like that.

Hurricane had taken away my cell phone not long after I moved in with him, so I asked Knowledge if I could borrow his. Hurricane had told me he'd be gone until the next morning, so wasn't no need in calling him.

"I need to call Vonnie," I explained, "and make sure my sister has been okay through this blackout."

I dialed Vonnie's cell, and the minute she answered I knew

exactly what kinda mood she was in. "What?" was her funky little greeting.

"Hey, Vonnie," I said. "This is Candy."

"I know who you are," she snapped, sounding nasty and half drunk. "What I *don't* know is why some niggah named Percy J. Graham came up on my caller ID."

"Oh." I laughed. "That's Knowledge. He let me use his cell phone."

Vonnie laughed back, but that shit had razor blades all in it. "Knowledge, huh? That stiff motherfucker. What else he letting you use?"

"Vonnie, please," I snapped. "Go 'head with all that mess you talking. I called because I wanted to check on Caramel. The power went out when I was at my photo shoot so I wanted to see how she did up there in the dark."

She really laughed then. "You wanna know how your sister did today? I'd say she did pretty good. Hell, you could even say she hit the jackpot considering the fact that the bitch been playing strip poker all day, and she's walking around with her shirt off and her titties sticking out right now."

I gave Vonnie the click. She was a jealous witch, and if I hadn't hung up I knew I would have said something foul that woulda created more drama between us.

To make things worse, Vonnie cold busted me and Knowledge coming out of Studio D about a week later. Hurricane was working as usual out of Studio C, and Jadeah had sent me downstairs to take him a Jamaican beef patty.

"I ain't hungry," he brushed me off when I offered it to him. He was playing a few beats and a few bars over and over again, going back and forth between an eighty-channel mixing console and an electric keyboard, up in his own world.

I set it on his desk anyway. "Jadeah said you would say that. She said for me to leave it down here regardless."

He kept right on doing what he was doing, rolling his fingers as he tried to get a harmony just the way he wanted it. I walked out of the studio and ran dead into Knowledge. He had a stack of papers in his hand and I stopped him.

"He's busy," I warned him. "And evil as hell too."

Knowledge listened to Hurricane on the keyboard for a moment, then grinned. "I wanna get busy too then," he said, pulling me up to him. I resisted for a hot second then pressed myself tightly against him. His dick jumped right up in his pants and we both laughed, covering our mouths even though we couldn't be heard over the music.

"For real," he whispered, kissing my face and neck. "I wanna get busy, baby."

He pulled me close and sucked my bottom lip into his mouth. His tongue tasted sweet as I opened my lips and let him in.

Knowledge eased his hand down inside of my shirt, rubbing my nipple and squeezing my titty until I moaned. Hurricane was right on the other side of the door. He banged that keyboard, playing his melody over and over again. Knowledge's mouth stayed glued to mine. He was tonguing me so deep I got dizzy in that little hallway.

He pulled his hand from my shirt and slid it between my legs, feeling my pussy through my clothes and rubbing it until my clit swelled up. I moaned again and started grinding against him like a fiend.

"Damn," he moaned into my mouth. "I can't get enough

of this shit," he said, and went back to stroking my nipples through my shirt.

"We gotta stop . . . ," I said softly. "We can't do this here."

Knowledge just grunted, cupping my whole titty and pushing his dick into my belly.

"Stop . . . ," I said weakly, pushing him away. "He's in his studio. We can't . . ."

"Yeah we can," he said, his tongue fucking me in the mouth. He backed me down the hallway and into Studio D. We moved inside still kissing, and Knowledge pinned me against the wall as he pulled my shirt up and started licking my breasts until my nipples were on fire. He made me feel so good I was tempted to cry out, but I clenched my teeth and moaned instead.

"What's your thang, Candy, huh?" Knowledge whispered. "Tell me what you like the best, baby."

I was trembling as I showed him. Cupping his face and pushing his head down lower. Lower. Down past my belly.

He laughed, but then he stood back up! "Yeah. I like that shit too," he said. And then he shocked the hell outta me by whispering a little freestyle rap in my ear.

> Can I lick that candy girl?
> Come let me taste
> that sticky part of your world
> Lemme lick that candy
> Lick it till
> U sweat
> Make that sweetness overheat
> Get it as hot as it gets.

He nibbled on my neck and swirled his tongue in my ear as he whispered his rap so thick and hot and nasty-like, my pussy got to quivering to his beat.

> I'll lick that candy
> the way ya niggah don't
> Tongue it down just right
> Like he can't and/or won't
> Make u feel
> A licking thrill
> Spread them lips
> Lemme get a steal
> I'm your candy licker
>
> Put some honey on it
> make you cum on my tongue
> Or lick it straight up
> Say what u want and it's done
> I'm your candy licker, I wanna lick that flicker
> Lick it up and lick it down
> Ain't no shame,
> Bend over, turn it around
> Lemme be your candy licker

By now my panties were hot and slick because my pussy was percolating with warm pudding. Knowledge was gripping my ass and sucking hard on my collarbone, whispering in my ear as he pinned me against the wall and humped that dick on me.

I wanna be the one
Who licks that candy
till u cum
all night
I got what it takes to lick that kitty right
Your man got pride, let him claim that shit
I'm lickin his candy tonight/ face all up in it
'Cause ain't no shame to it
25 hours a day/8 days a week,
366 I'll make that puddy leak
I'm your candy licker . . .

Yeah, I thought with my pussy quivering and thumping. *Be my candy licker. Lick this sweet candy till it melts, baby!*

I felt for his dick and couldn't believe it was so hard. He helped me unbuckle his belt and then we both worked on my pants. Knowledge dropped to his knees and slid one of my legs out and threw it over his shoulder, then he buried his face in my candy, licking it so good my knees trembled. I teased my fingers in his hair as his whole head rotated between my legs. He spread my pussy lips open with his fingers so he could lick it out better, moving his tongue faster and faster and faster and pinching my swollen, aching clit between his lips.

I was trying so hard not to let go. I leaned against that wall and fought the tornado that was trying to tear through my pussy, and then Knowledge tapped my ass and whispered, "Don't put no cut on it, baby. Just bring it."

I came twice. Back-to-back. My swollen pussy squirted warm cum and pulsated with the most intense orgasm I'd ever felt.

And then Knowledge stood up and slid that thang up inside my guts as deep as it would go. He was squeezing my ass and I was moaning out his name. Telling him how good he felt. Telling him how good he made me feel. Fuck whoever was right next door! Knowledge got him some up against that wall! While half-a-dick Hurricane was in his studio banging on that keyboard, his boy was right next door banging out my ass.

Hurricane was still trying to get his melody as we crept past his office grinning and satisfied. Knowledge was palming my ass and I was wiping a smear of lipstick off his mouth when Vonnie came around the corner and busted us.

"What y'all been doing?" she asked suspiciously as I tried to play things off.

"Eating beef patties," I lied real quick. "I was trying to get a piece of crust off his lip."

"Crust, huh?" Vonnie said, staring at Knowledge with doubt all over her face.

Knowledge winked at me, then licked his lips and adjusted his stack of papers as he walked up the stairs.

Vonnie glared at me and I couldn't resist the urge to straighten out my shirt. "I didn't see no crust on that niggah's face, Candy. Looked to me like some straight skull jumping was going on. You sure it was a beef patty he was eating? You sure that shit wasn't no pussy patty?"

I threw my hands up and sighed. "Vonnie, please. It was a goddamn beef patty, okay? There's another one in there on Hurricane's desk if you hungry."

◆ ◆ ◆

But there was no shaking Vonnie off. That heffah was like a bloodhound sniffing around at something stank. She started acting real shitty toward me and of course I knew why.

Caramel.

I had mad love for Vonzelle, I really did. But no matter how much history me and Vonnie shared, it didn't mean a damn thing when it came down to my sister.

Every time I turned around Vonnie was saying something foul about Caramel, and it seemed to me like her main goal was to try to get me to respond for my sister. Vonnie must didn't know that me and Caramel had much more than history vibing between us. We had blood and DNA, and if Vonzelle kept at it I was gonna have to let her know how much thicker my blood was than her mud.

"Look at them young bitches," Vonnie had complained one night in October during a private party at the House. It was Joog's birthday and Hurricane had opened the doors to the House of Homicide and invited every professional athlete, successful recording star, and high-rolling rapper on the East Coast. Me, Vonnie, Dom, and Fatima were the only females upstairs in Hurricane's booth. We were leaning over the rail watching Caramel and Asia down in the pit, doing their best to impress a couple of athlete ballers by shaking as much ass as possible. Caramel was straight killing a white Versace dress that she had probably boosted, and Asia had poured herself into a pair of bright red shorts that looked like they were choking her coochie to death.

"Them little hoes don't know they titties from they tailbone," Vonnie bitched, talking loud and making sure I heard her. "Asia got so much hair under her fuckin' arms it's braidable, and Caramel . . . I hope you taught your little sister something about birth control, Candy, 'cause that ass is gonna be knocked in about a minute."

Dom got mad and told her to leave that crack alone, but I just ignored Vonnie. I knew she didn't like my sister and I was cool with it. But the way she was handling herself was all wrong. Almost like she was daring me to say something about it so she could run and tell Hurricane what she had seen happening between me and Knowledge that day.

"Damn," Dom laughed. "I just thought of something. Let that girl get pregnant. Quadir and Caramel would make a pretty-ass baby, that's for real."

Vonnie broke. "Who said anything about Quadir? The way that skank bitch is getting run through she probably wouldn't know whose baby it was. Don't be wishing that baby daddy shit on my Quadir!"

Dom bust out laughing again. "Oh, so that's why your ass is so damn salty. You got a problem seeing Quadir with Caramel? Shit, there's more than one overrated entertainment baller in the house. Go scrounge you up another one, Vonzelle."

"Tell that bitch to go find her another one! Qua was eating my pussy before she even got here!"

"Well," I laughed too as I looked down into the pit. "He must wanna eat at another restaurant 'cause he's halfway up Caramel's ass right now."

"Don't get smart, Candy," Vonnie warned me. "Taking that bitch's side. Caramel don't know the shit I know, remember? Matter fact, how's Knowledge doing today?"

Dom and Fatima both had their eyeballs down my throat.

"First of all, Vonnie," I said, getting kinda quiet, "you ain't gone call my sister too many more bitches right in my face. And second"—now my finger was pointing because guilt can make you act like that—"Knowledge who? Oh, that would be the investment baller who wouldn't eat a piece of your rotten punanee, right? If you wanna know something about him you need to ask him. What do I know about how he's doing? I'm the laced-up bitch that you dying to be. I sleep with Hurricane Jackson every night. Remember?"

Chapter 22

Dirty Hustlin'

Knowledge jogged down the narrow flight of stairs leading from his office. It was early afternoon and the House of Homicide was quiet. He walked down the hall and past the steel door where Hurricane kept his small stash of recreational drugs. Business had been good, and Hurricane's territory had expanded rapidly over the last couple of years, forcing him to move his main drug distribution center further downtown into a large warehouse that employed over fifty people.

Knowledge passed the empty gambling room and the VIP Lounge, then walked down the bridgelike archway that stretched over the pit, then headed downstairs to Studio C. He had just reviewed a stack of contracts and needed Hurricane's signature for their execution. He hadn't gotten this far in life without a thorough understanding of the game, and Knowledge knew his boss ran a dirty shop when it came to his contracts.

Every one of Hurricane's artists was getting dicked in the ass when it came to their royalty points. Urban albums were the modern-day cotton—a cash crop that fattened the pockets of sharks like Hurricane and those moneygrubbing white boys up at Interscope, but left the field hands straight broke. As an attorney, Knowledge felt it was his responsibility to make sure Hurricane's artists had every opportunity to seek outside consultation before they signed with him. He'd even gone as far as to insert a clause where they had to acknowledge either accepting or declining that opportunity, and so far not one of them had bitten the bait. Time after time he had stood by shaking his head as their eager asses waived their right to seek an independent attorney and concurred with the contract terms just as they were. He didn't understand it. It was like going to your foot doctor and agreeing to get open-heart surgery without consulting a heart surgeon.

Downstairs, he passed by Studios A and B where most of Homicide Hitz' recording was done. He rounded the corner to Studio C and stopped in his tracks outside the open door.

Hurricane was in his office, but he wasn't alone.

Butt-ass naked and straddling an office chair backward was Asia. Her eyes were closed and her face was squinched up in pain. Behind her was Hurricane, on his knees and gripping her by the waist as he fucked her from the back with a bottle of Cristal, sweating bullets as he pushed it deep up inside her fifteen-year-old pussy.

Knowledge grabbed hold of his rage and forced it down. He took a few hard breaths until he got it to a place where he could manage it, then he nigger-knocked on the open door like he wanted to tear that fucker off the hinges.

"Whattup?" He held out his hands, gesturing with the stack

of contracts. "I thought we were gonna take care of *business* today?"

Asia almost jumped through the ceiling as Hurricane slid the wet bottle out of her pussy and set it down next to him on the floor.

"Whattup?" Hurricane said, breathing hard as he climbed to his feet.

Poor Asia didn't know what to do. She couldn't even look at Knowledge as she backed away from the chair and scrambled over to Hurricane's desk to get her clothes. She didn't have enough hands to cover everything that was exposed, so she pressed her arm over her breasts and reached back and spread her fingers over her plump ass.

Knowledge turned away to give her a little respect as she tried to get dressed.

Hurricane didn't seem pressed at all as he sat down at his desk. "Put the rest of your shit on outside," he told the young girl when she took too long jumping into her clothes. With his head still turned, Knowledge heard Hurricane smack her on the ass before sending the half-naked teenager scurrying out of his office.

"Aaight," Hurricane said real business-like, holding out his hand for the contracts. "What you got for me?"

It took everything Knowledge had in him not to slam his boss to the ground and stick that bottle of Cristal down his throat. Hurricane was buff and strong, but big niggahs fell the hardest, and Knowledge knew how to take a niggah down with one strike. Right then he made a decision. Shit had to to handled. There was no other way.

"Contracts," he said, swallowing what was in him. It didn't make sense to confront a niggah like Hurricane and argue over what he felt naturally entitled to. If it wasn't Asia it would have been some other hot young girl with a big ass and an empty head. They waited outside the House on a daily basis, and any one of them would have been happy to sit down on Hurricane's Cristal.

"We need to get these executed real quick," Knowledge said, his voice completely normal. "I'll get 'em notarized this afternoon and call the artists in to pick up their copies early next week."

Knowledge felt Hurricane searching. His boss was looking for a flicker of what Knowledge felt on the inside, but Knowledge was a born poker player. Nothing showed on his face, absolutely nothing. He'd perfected that technique in the courtroom.

After the contracts were signed Knowledge helped himself to a cold beer from Hurricane's small refrigerator. He kicked back in his usual chair and listened to a few samples his boss was thinking about using. He laughed and talked shit and did all the things he normally did when he was chilling in Studio C with his boss. But in the back of his mind Knowledge was already out. His brain was on whir, working numbers and calculating the net worth of all their underground accounts. Millions. At his fingertips. He laughed at something Hurricane said, but turned back to the fridge when he saw his boss reach for some dap. *Nah, no dap,* he told himself, passing Hurricane a cold beer instead. His whole body felt charged. Energized and ready to do battle. Yeah, shit was fittin' to get tallied. It was time to start shaking trees and moving money, because the scent of Asia's pussy was still in the air and Brother Hurricane was just too dirty to touch.

◆ ◆ ◆

"I need a favor," Hurricane said a few weeks later. "It's a big one, but I think you can handle it."

Knowledge leaned back in his chair with the phone in his hand and gazed out the window. Hurricane calling him up for a favor wasn't unusual. He'd given a lot of his artists and a few of his boys the hookup over the years. Some he'd helped out of tax jams. Others he'd created dummy corporations for in order to account for their illegal income.

"Whassup?" he asked. Knowledge was always cautious. He was a deep thinker and he never committed to anything until he knew exactly what he was facing.

"One of the big bosses out in L.A. is in a little trouble. Tax evasion. Racketeering. You know. All that legal shit hotshots like you know how to handle so well."

Knowledge sat up in his chair. "Who is it?"

Hurricane paused. "Paddy," he said, then spoke again when he heard Knowledge whistle in amazement. "Yeah, it's just that major."

Knowledge whistled again. This shit *was* major. Paddy Gabriano had gotten stung? That meant the feds were getting pretty slick. They'd roped in the big daddy.

"When?" he asked.

Hurricane paused again. "In three days. I know it's short notice, but Paddy got mad and fired his lead man. His number two guy just got hit with a bunch of his own charges, and my boy Nicky called looking for some powerful ammo. He knows you're the best, so I told him I'd send you."

Knowledge's brain went on whir. In seconds he'd completed a risk assessment and calculated his odds. "Cool," he said, standing up and holding the cordless phone against his shoulder. He brushed off his Versace suit and walked over to his picture window and picked up the small water bottle on the sill. "Anything else?" he asked, raising the window just high enough to mist the flowers that were already completely out of bloom.

"Yeah," Hurricane said. "This is big, ak. Real big. You pull this shit off and your pockets gonna explode. The family is picking up the tab and they know it's gonna be a heavy one. But I ain't gotta tell you that the rules work both ways. You fuck it up and the charge'll be on you."

Knowledge grinned. No matter what, the black man was always underestimated. Especially by other black men. He was used to it though, and unlike some, he welcomed it. Knowledge knew what the fuck he knew, and he would master this trial like a champion chess match. Fuck that pot of money waiting at the end, though. He had plenty of money. He had other payment plans for the Gabrianos, and if things worked out the way he lined them up, this was one case he'd be defending pro bono.

◌ ◌ ◌

Three days wasn't a lot of time, so Knowledge moved fast.

He figured on being out West for at least three weeks, maybe even a month, and a lot could happen in that time. As he went about preparing for his trip he realized that this was the first time he'd made such a major move with a woman in mind. No longer was he alone and existing independently of everyone else. He had somebody else to consider now, and of course Candy's safety would come into play when he made his moves.

The day before he left Knowledge checked to make sure everything was in order in his files and that all sensitive items and documents were locked away in his safe. He went to the bank and made a withdrawal, then ran the other errands on his list, checking them off in his mind as he completed them.

One of the last things he did for the day was get Jadeah on the phone.

"Hey," he said when she answered. "I need a favor, and if you don't wanna do it, you don't have to."

Jadeah was down even before she knew what he was asking for. "Knowledge, you know I love you like a baby brother. Just tell me what you need."

"I got a package I might need you to deliver for me. You don't have to do nothing, but if anybody ever asks for it, give it to them."

Jadeah sounded unsure. "Who's it for?"

"I can't say."

"Well then how am I supposed to know if I'm giving your shit to the right person?"

Knowledge thought for a moment. "Give it to the person who asks for it. If the right person ever needs it, you'll know."

Chapter 23

Diamonds and Hearts

Knowledge was ready for me when I got to his loft on Monday night. Hurricane had gone to watch a football game at his friend's bar up in the Bronx, and Knowledge had slid me some cab fare to get downtown and promised to make sure I was back at the House before Hurricane and his crew got back.

He had a hot bath waiting for me when I walked through the door, and I followed him into the bathroom and held still while he undressed me under the flicker of about ten lit candles. I knew he was leaving for L.A. the next morning and I didn't feel good about that shit at all.

"But I'm gonna miss you, boo," I had complained a few days earlier when he told me he had to go to L.A. for a trial. I was laying on his white fur bedspread making snow angels in the design. I'd jumped on the train and snuck downtown to his loft at lunchtime so we could get us a little quickie. "I thought you were handling contracts and investment stuff now. Why you gotta go back to court?"

Knowledge had held my hand in his lap and explained. "I'm

a trial attorney first and foremost, baby. What I do for Hurricane is only a small part of what I *can* do. They need somebody like me out in L.A. right now, and if things go the way I plan to make sure they go, well, life is gonna change for both of us." And then he made me laugh by suggesting we play a little game. He wanted me to let him put a blindfold on me and stick anything he wanted in my mouth.

"Okay," he said, "I promise I won't put no boogers or cockroaches on your tongue, but anything else goes." The first thing he made me chew was some sweet crushed pineapple. I liked that. Next he tickled my tongue with a marshmallow, then made me lick a bitter lemon. I didn't like that! "All right, I want you to take a bite of this Greek apple, okay?" That boy had me bite into a goddamn onion! He also fed me a cold slice of mango, then he licked the juice right off my chin. The last thing he did was pour warm honey all over my back. It was so erotic! I had moaned and squirmed as that stickiness dripped from my skin, knowing damn well he was gonna lick it off real good for me.

And now I stood in front of him watching the candles flicker as he sat on the closed toilet and ran some warm water in the sink. I felt his eyes admiring my naked body, and I wondered what was going on when he reached out and rubbed a handful of foaming soap into the curly red hair of my coochie.

"A shampoo?" I laughed. "You giving me a shampoo down there?" This was another first because nobody other than Mama had ever washed my coochie before.

Knowledge shushed me and pressed his lips to my stomach and started tonguing my navel down. I grabbed his head and started moaning but he pulled away and broke the contact. He knew what I wanted. If that soap wasn't all over my mound I would have been pushing his face between my legs as fast as I could.

He used both hands and worked up a bunch of lather in my pubic hair. I obeyed him when he nudged my legs open, shivering as he slid his fingers along the sides of my outer lips, soaping me until every strand of my red hair was white. Then he looked up with total seriousness in his eyes and asked, "Trust me?"

The second I nodded yes, he pulled out a razor.

I jumped my ass back, ready to fight. Hell, I even looked around the bathroom real quick trying to find my own damn weapon. "What you doing, Knowledge?"

He laughed. "C'mere, girl. I'm not gonna hurt you. I just need to know if you really trust me."

I put my hands on my hips and stared him down. I was thinking, trying to decide whether I trusted him like that. I'd learned a lot from Hurricane, and I was no longer about jumping off into anything and everything just because a man said so.

Knowledge couldn't take his eyes off me as I stood there butt naked with nothing but foam covering my pussy. I couldn't wait to feel this man all up in my belly, but first I needed to decide if he was really in my heart.

"Yeah," I finally admitted. "I trust you, Knowledge. You the only man I've ever felt totally sure about in my whole damn life. Okay, I said trust you. Now what the fuck you plan on doing with that razor?"

He smiled and reached for my hip, pulling me closer.

"I'm just gonna entertain you a little bit before I leave," he said softly. "But you have to trust me. You gotta promise you won't look down."

I promised, and Knowledge lifted the razor and pressed it to my triangle. I held perfectly still and didn't even flinch when I felt that blade touch me. He only worked on me for five minutes or so, but the way he acted it was the most important five minutes of our relationship.

"Check it out," he said, handing me a small mirror after he'd rinsed me off and wiped my wet mound with a soft cloth. "If you don't like it, you can tell me. I'll understand."

I took the mirror.

All I could do was laugh as I examined my coochie. "Boy no you didn't. No you did *not* shave a little diamond on my coochie!"

"Yeah I did," he said. " 'Cause that's what you are. My diamond."

I laughed as he kissed my stomach and swirled his tongue around in my navel again.

"Now me," I said, pushing his face away. "You got some skills, but lemme show you what a sistah can do."

I took that razor and went to work. When I was done I had turned his diamond into a heart, then I made him stand up so I could shave one on him too.

"There," I said. "Now you can take a piece of me with you."

Knowledge looked at those two tight-ass hearts I'd hooked up in our pubic hair and nodded like he was impressed.

"Damn, Miss Candy. You the one with all the skills. I'm gonna take my heart with me when I roll out to Cali, but you need to go ahead and shave yours off real quick. Let Hurricane see that shit and . . ." His eyes got dark. "Just shave it off, Candy."

I shrugged. I slept naked sometimes, but I wasn't stuttin' Hurricane's ass.

"I will," I went ahead and promised him, just to take that look out his eyes.

"Now check this," Knowledge said, pulling me into his lap. "I'm leaving you with a little something too," he said. His hot dick was throbbing against my inner thighs, and as I got busy kissing his neck and tonguing his ears, he gripped my ass cheeks and eased me down on his thickness and slammed me up and down on it until I just about melted.

◈ ◈ ◈

Late that night I was back at the mansion sleeping like a baby, mouth dead open and legs cocked wide, when something woke me up. It was dark in the room except for a large candle flickering on Cane's nightstand, and fear was already kicking my ass by the time I opened my eyes.

Predator was growling and straddling me on the bed. I felt his stank, hot breath on my face and turned my head, squinching my face up as a long string of nasty slobber dripped off his tongue and hit my nose.

"Don't scream," Hurricane said. "You know he don't like loud bitches."

Hurricane was sitting at the bottom of the bed, and at the sound of his voice Predator growled deeper. His teeth were showing and his mouth was right next to my throat. All I had to grab hold of was the silk sheets, and I balled those shits up in my hands and closed my eyes again, too scared to even cry.

"Did they have arts and crafts at that computer school you was going to when you was out in L.A.?"

"Please, Cane . . . ," I cried softly. Predator had his paw on my chest, holding me down. His nails pressed hard into my skin. "Please get him off me."

I heard him sigh like his patience was thin.

"I'ma ask you again, Candy. Did you take arts and crafts and learn computers at the same time too?"

I was shaking so bad I had to pee. I licked my lips and managed to whisper, "No. I-I-I didn't take no arts and . . . and crafts. Please get this fuckin' dog off me, Cane!"

"So no arts and crafts?"

"No," I whimpered. Predator was licking the side of my face and sticking his long, nasty-ass tongue all in my ear. "No. Please, Cane. Please."

"You sure? I mean, you didn't take none of them design classes while you was there, did you? Oh, you musta went to barber school, then, huh? Was it barber school or beauty school, Candy?"

I laid there naked and shivering in sweat I was so damn scared. I was disgusted, too, 'cause Predator was lapping at my hair, the side of my face, and trying to get to the back of my neck.

"I said," Hurricane whispered with ice in his voice, "did you take your ass to barber school, Candy?"

"No."

"Then how'd your pussy get shaved so tight?"

The heart. Back when I'd first come to the mansion I'd shaved my pussy bald because I thought it was erotic. Hurricane had hated it. He said it looked nasty. "What's up with that bald pussy?" he'd wanted to know. "Let your hair grow back and cover that big-ass clit up!"

I froze for a hot second, but then my lie kicked into gear. "I shaved it like that myself, Cane! I know you said to let my hair grow back but I sweat when I'm onstage and it itches me so bad it drives me crazy. I know you don't like it bare, but I thought you'd dig it this way. I was just playing around trying something different 'cause it was bothering me . . . that's all!"

I muttered that whole lie out the side of my mouth because Predator was still licking my grill and I wasn't trying to base hard enough to piss him off.

"Oh, so you want something different, huh?" Hurricane snapped his fingers twice and Predator jumped off the bed and trotted down the steps. He went up on the other side, then stopped at the door and sat down. "Then let's do something different, Candy."

That niggah made me turn over on my stomach and hold still while he tied my wrists and ankles to the canopy posts. I was buck naked and my legs were stretched wide open.

"You got a nice phat ass," Hurricane said as he straddled me on his knees like he was taking a horseback ride. "Problem is, I ain't too sure you know who the fuck it belongs to." I almost hollered as he sat his buff, heavy ass down on my back.

"You might not a' took arts and crafts where you went to school, Miss Candy. But I did. Lemme see can I do your back just as good as you did your snatch."

I felt him reach to the right, and a moment later I saw the flame flickering and felt a scorching pain on my upper back. My head swiveled damn near all the way around as I arched my back and let out the first long scream.

"Shut up!" Hurricane hissed between his clenched teeth. I stared at the candle he was holding over my back. "It's your fault I gotta treat your ass this way!"

I was still screaming when he called the dog again.

"Predator, up!"

The dog trotted back up to the bed and seconds later a cold, wet nose was touching me. Predator was sniffing my butt.

I shut right the hell up then, but I didn't stay quiet long. Not even that nasty dog could make me keep still as Hurricane dipped that candle over me and poured that burning wax down my back.

I must have screamed for an hour, and if Sissy or Teema or any of them house heffahs heard me, they sure as hell didn't come to find out what was wrong. I was just glad that Knowledge had already bounced because he would have killed Hurricane for doing some shit like this to me. I moaned and begged and tried to get away, but I was locked in the middle of the house with a maniac who owned my body and my life.

And you can best believe he broadcasted that fact to the entire world when he escorted me to the Stoned Soul Awards the next night too. He made me wear a sexy white dress that he'd bought for me at the last minute. It was cut high in the front, but dipped all the way down to my ass in the back.

My whole entire back was exposed for every damn body in the world to see, and I was so ashamed that it felt like thousands were taking notice. I was so glad Dom and Vonzelle weren't there to see me 'cause there was no way I could have explained it. Deep inside I wanted to cry, but I refused to go out like that. Instead, I stood right next to that niggah and smiled and posed as the cameras snapped and flashed. At least the night air was good to me, though. It helped soothe those thick black blisters that spelled out the four-letter word that stretched from my left shoulder bone all the way to my right.

The blisters that spelled CANE.

◇ ◇ ◇

Things had really changed for me since Hurricane broke up the Scandalous! trio. Dominica didn't stay mad for long because she knew it was Hurricane who'd been scheming to cut her and Vonnie out of the picture and not me. Even still, she was frustrated and fried about the whole situation and if there was a way she could have put some shit on Hurricane's ass she would have.

But Vonnie was still straight tripping. She blamed me for everything, even though Dom tried over and over again to put her down on my situation.

"I keep telling you Candy ain't calling no shots with that fool, Vonnie. He's using her ass the same way he uses everybody else, so quit with all that noisy drama. That's why us females ain't got no wins now. We too busy jumpin' on each other instead of concentrating on correcting all the low-down ballers of the world."

The last two singles on our album were due to be released in a few weeks so we were still performing together and stuff, but always under Hurricane's eye. Now that he had me going solo he played me extra sticky, putting words in my mouth during interviews and tapings and keeping me up under him so he could control my every move.

Dominica was getting fed up with the industry and all the backstabbing, throat-cutting bullshit that went along with it, and she decided to go back to school once our last single was released. "Maybe you should think about doing something with computers, Candy," she told me one rainy afternoon as we rehearsed for a show at the MCI Center in D.C. "This music shit ain't everything, you know, and with that sheisty-ass contract Cane gave us we might never see no real money. Hell, with a nut like him flipping out every other day your solo album ain't guaranteed anyway."

Dominica just didn't know. I was chained to Hurricane. His name might as well have been branded on my ass just like it was on my back. I had never told her or Vonnie about getting thrown into that trunk by Nicky's men or how Hurricane had paid off Mama's debt and kept those Italians from killing me. No, straight from that ass-kicking in L.A., Hurricane had whisked me right into his mansion and set me up in the middle, and I'd been so beat down and hurt with grief that when he said I needed to keep my mouth closed and forget that whole kidnapping drama, that's just what I did.

"I don't know, Dom," I told her. "I think I'ma have to go 'head and ride this one out."

It was cool that Dominica had a plan B, but Vonnie's shit was wide open. I was starting to worry about her. I was scared she was becoming an industry ho. All of us had been desperate to get in the door, and now that Vonnie had gotten a lick of what fame was like she wanted to cram the whole thing down her throat. I knew she would have given anything to be with

Hurricane. Plus, she was too bent on that niggah Quadir, with his no-good ass. Yeah, he was live on the mic coming out of Cabrini Green projects in Chicago and all, and he'd been around on the rap scene performing in underground clubs and on bootleg CDs for a long time and got a lot of respect from the up-and-coming rappers. And yep, I'd even admit that he wrote some mad lyrics and had good control of the stage, and they say he used to roll with Tupac real heavy before Pac blew up and got all famous. But for Vonnie to let him cause all this drama between her and Caramel and have it mess up the love she used to have for me? I just didn't get that. I could understand how Vonnie wouldn't wanna give up the bling or get off the stage, but damn. She was stuck on grabbing hold of a rich baller like that was her ticket out of the ghetto for life.

Case in point. Two nights later I was sitting in my usual spot in Hurricane's booth. Mad niggahs was crammed in swinging on his dick, just the way Hurricane liked them. Quadir was sitting on my left holding Predator on his leash when Vonnie walked up.

"Hey, Cane," she said, slinging her devastating hips and wearing a Donna Karan jean skirt to death. She had on a sleeveless white belly shirt and her nipples were poking through like pencil erasers. "We still gonna talk about that contract tonight, right?"

I glanced at Hurricane and saw his nostrils jump. He had been evil all day because fate had cheated him out of his satisfaction. Every now and then some young head in the projects got swole and thought he could do a better job of running Harlem than Hurricane was doing. This kid named Sharif had called himself organizing a cell to stick up Tonk's warehouse, and when Hurricane got wind of it he told his boys to take Sharif out, but first he wanted them to fuck him up so bad he would be an example for every other thug who thought his line was weak.

But fate had gotten the jump on Sharif before Cane's boys could get to him. The fool was crossing 125th Street and got hit by a car and killed, and Hurricane was so mad that him and his boys rolled up at Sharif's wake, dumped his body out of his casket, and shot his dead ass up right there in front of his whole family.

I had overheard Snake and Das saying that Hurricane was so damn mad that even after they shot up the body he was stomping and kicking Sharif's frozen ass all over that funeral home and they had to pull his crazy behind out of there before the cops came. And now Vonnie was begging for another contract after he had already told her she couldn't sing for shit.

"Sexy Vonzelle," he said, eyeing her firm body. "You want another record deal, huh?" He leaned across me and whispered something to Quadir, who laughed, then stood up and wrapped the dog's leash tight around his hand. "All right," Hurricane said. "I'll think about giving you one. But gone in the lounge and take care of Predator first, then we'll see what we can do."

Them niggahs bust out laughing as Vonnie followed Quadir and Predator into one of the empty lounges. I thought he had misspoke and meant for Vonnie to take care of Quadir, but then Hurricane started laughing the loudest. "Shit," he said, and took a sip of his drink. "Predator my dawg. He likes pussy too."

I couldn't believe it when Quadir came back with the dog about fifteen minutes later. I was looking around to see where

Vonnie was when Quadir slid in and sat beside me laughing. "That's one wild bitch, man," he told Hurricane, shaking his head. "Predator's 'bout wore out. Doggie-style is her favorite position." Niggahs roared.

"That's fucked up!" I yelled, and jumped to my feet ready to go looking for my girl. Hurricane grabbed my arm and dug his fingers in. "What's fucked up, Candy? What? You going somewhere?"

I looked down at his big hand on my arm and remembered what kind of fool I was dealing with. The blisters on my back had almost stopped oozing and I was still trying to keep the burnt skin from sticking to my clothes. I hurried up and corrected myself real quick. "Nothing, Cane. I just gotta use the bathroom real bad."

He nodded, flaring his nose and drilling me with his eyes. "Oh yeah? You gotta pee? Cool." He tapped Quadir and motioned for him to pass me the dog's leash. "Take Predator in the bathroom with you. And while you in there, find a clean cloth and wipe off his dick."

◊ ◊ ◊

Hurricane drank all damn night, and by the time we got back to Long Island he was mean and juiced out. All during the drive he kept eyeing me with hard looks, but I kept my eyes toward the window and sat there cursing him out in my head. He was leaving the next day for Miami to accept a *Source* Award for Producer of the Year, and I was glad he'd be gone for a few days because I needed a break. When we got back to the mansion I jumped out of the whip before he could open his door and went straight to the middle of the house without stopping. I was in the bathroom peeing when the lock exploded and King Kong kicked the door straight in.

"What was so fucked up about tonight, Candy?" He was standing there wobbling on his feet, and I coulda sworn his left eye was trying to swing down toward the floor the same way Jadeah's did.

"Huh?" I said, drawing a blank.

"Bitch, don't sit there shitting and looking stupid. Tell me what you said was so fucked up tonight about your friend and my dog."

I saw what was coming and I'd barely managed to jump up and pull my pants up before he was all over me. I tucked my chin to my chest and balled up, covering my head with my hands.

"What was so fucked up, Candy?" he screamed, his muscles flexing as he threw powerful uppercuts and deadly blows. For a drunk man he was pretty good at beating my ass and talking shit at the same time. I rolled over and kept my head low, giving him my arm and the side of my leg as a target.

He snatched a towel bar clean off the wall and started swinging it. "What's fucked up?" he raged, cracking me anywhere he could get me. "*This* is fucked up! No, *this* is fucked up! Nah, this is how you *get* fucked up! This is how I *fuck* your ass up!"

I crawled all up under the sink trying to get away from him. He dragged me out by my hair and I slid and spun around and around on my butt like a top. "You talk a lot of shit for a dead bitch," Cane growled. He grabbed the toilet bowl plunger and mushed that nasty thing down over my face. I slapped it away and kicked up at him with both feet, my heels striking his hard stomach and the metal buckle on his belt.

Before I knew it that muscled-up maniac was beating the hell out of me with that toilet bowl plunger. He swung that baby like it was a short bat, and only when my screams became unbearable and he got sweating tired did he snatch my pants down and jig me with it. And then all I could do was scream even louder.

The next morning I felt like I'd been in a car accident.

I looked like it too. My uterus hurt and there was almost no place on my body that wasn't purple and blue. Even the Gabriano boys hadn't kicked my ass this bad, and if I didn't know how crazy Hurricane was before, I sure knew now.

Hurricane had an early flight and he made me get my sore ass out the bed and ride with Quadir to take him to the airport. Afterward Quadir dropped me off at the House, and as I sat in the front office waiting for Jadeah to show up I broke down and cried.

This wasn't how I was supposed to be living. Where was my musical star? I was young and fine and had talent. Wasn't no man supposed to be abusing me like this and making me miserable every day. I missed Mama and all the fun me and Caramel used to have with her. I missed hanging out with my friends. I missed chilling in my own place and being my own person. I missed Knowledge and wondered if he was really coming back. I even missed Nicky Gabriano and the way he used to give me advice, like he cared about me.

True, if I was still out there muling my face would probably be on a mugshot instead of on the cover of a hot CD. My voice would not be all over the radio or my face all up in magazines. Mama would still be alive, and Caramel wouldn't be walking around doing all the crazy shit she was doing. But Hurricane had gotten ahold of my young ass, and now there were so many strings binding me to him that I just couldn't break free.

When Jadeah stepped in the office and saw my face she was hot. She took one look at my swollen nose, busted lip, and black eye and went the fuck off.

"That motherfucker!" she fumed. "I can't believe he did you like this!" She took her glasses off to get a better look at me. I looked back at her surprised. This was the first time she'd ever said anything against her brother. Tears was even in her eyes.

"Girl he busted your ass. I'm just sorry, Candy. Sorry because I know you a cool person and sorry because he's my brother. Junius is starting to act just like our nasty-ass father. That motherfucker had hand problems too. He got life for killing his woman, and Junius swore to God he would never hit a female."

I started crying again. "Well he fuckin' lied."

Jadeah went into the kitchen area and came out with a bottle of frozen water. She wrapped it in a paper towel and helped me press it lightly to my lip.

"I know you probably don't like me, Candy, because I'm always down for my brother."

I didn't say nothing 'cause she was right. She excused the crazy things he did when there was no excuse for them.

"But he wasn't always like this, Candy. The Ju I used to know was a good kid. He used to look out for me and my mother. Ju told my father that if he ever touched me or put his hands on our mother again, he would beat his ass into the ground. And as young as he was, he did it. He beat the shit out of Pug and put a gun to that niggah's head, and only my mother's tears stopped him from pulling that trigger. My father left after that. He had been sneaking around with this other female that he ended up killing. But as much as Ju hated Daddy, he spoke up for him at his trial. I never did understand that shit, but I let it go. Ju was good to me and my mother. He took care of us."

"Well what the hell changed him then?"

She frowned and shook her head. "I think it was his operation."

"What?"

"His operation. He had it when he was fifteen. The doctor said he had to get circumcised, but I think they fucked it up and it did something to his manhood."

If my lip wasn't so swollen that shit would have been on the floor.

That niggah was an amputee! He had got his dick chopped off!

"A bunch of other people had had the same shit happen to their sons at that same hospital. They petitioned to get circumcisions banned in the whole state and even tried to get my mother to join a class-action suit and sue the hospital, but Mama said for what? The damage was already done and my brother had already changed," Jadeah said, sitting down with a frown. "He got real mean and just didn't care no more. He dropped all his little honeys and started lifting weights and bulking up. You would've thought he was training for the Olympics or something. The only thing Ju was into was getting his body up. And then he found music."

I listened to Jadeah talk about Hurricane and part of me understood. Just like I was down for Caramel, she was down for her brother too. That fucked-up circumcision explained a whole lot of things about Hurricane, but it didn't mean I had to stop living my life and dreaming my dreams just because somebody had slipped and cut off almost all his dick! That wasn't my fault!

Jadeah called Quadir in the security office and told him to go get the whip and take me back out to Long Island.

"Go home and rest, Candy. Fuck writing. Fuck rehearsing. Ju's gonna be gone for four whole days. While he's out there taking care of his business and getting his props, you go home and take care of yourself."

I hugged Jadeah and waited for Quadir to bring the Jag around front so I could take her advice. I had four days to myself and I was gonna use them too. The first thing I planned to do was get my sore ass in that big old bed and stay in it for two days straight, and when I got back to the mansion that's exactly what I did.

◊ ◊ ◊

Five days later we were stepping out to an awards dinner sponsored by Urban Artists on the Rise. Hurricane had rented a stretch Hummer, and if I wasn't still so bruised and sore from his ass-kicking the energy would have been live. Scandalous! had been chosen to receive one of the top awards. Me, Dominica, and Vonzelle were being presented with a plaque for our musical success and we were amped and excited.

The stretch limo was stuffed with bodies. Most of them were flunkies, members of Hurricane's entourage that he kept around to make himself look big on nights like this. Me, I was still swollen. Swollen and sore. Hurricane had called for Jadeah to hook up my makeup, but hiding my big fat lip and twice-dotted eye was way beyond her skills.

"Here." He tossed me a pair of sunglasses before we left the House. "Put these motherfuckers on and make sure you don't take 'em off."

Joog was riding in the front seat of the limo, and I was sitting between Dom and Vonnie in the next row. Hurricane, Long Jon, and Peaches were sitting across from us, and the backseats were packed deep with rap artists and hoods from the block. Caramel was right back there with them too. Sitting her ass in some niggah's lap.

Blunts were getting smoked, lines were being snorted, and the whip was filled up with beer and liquor. Hurricane was throwing a party on wheels, and everybody except me was up and happy as we drove through the city.

I sat there cursing the driver out under my breath. Every pothole or bump he hit sent pain screaming through my bruised body. Vonnie was sitting on my left. As usual, she was getting stupid high, hitting line after white line. Powder was dusted all over her nose.

"She 'bout had enough," I muttered to Dominica.

Dom laughed, but it was one of them mad laughs. "Vonzelle ain't nothing but a vacuum cleaner." Then she crossed her arms and nodded at me. "And you ain't nothing but a punching bag. A banged-up piece of red meat."

"Dom, please," I said, waving my hand even though doing that shit hurt. "I ain't nobody's meat."

She reached over and snatched off my glasses. I tried to hide my black eye real quick, but she grabbed my hands. "What the fuck you call this then, Candy, huh? You a piece of meat when your niggah *treats* you like a piece of fuckin' meat!"

"Ooooh, girl!" Peaches hollered, looking at my eye. "He fucked you *up*!"

Suddenly it got real quiet in the car, and I knew that shit was dangerous.

But Dom didn't care. She turned to Peaches and talked big shit. "Holla girl! What kinda real man gotta put his foot up his girl's ass to control her?"

"Dom, stop," I whispered.

"No, no, no. I ain't stopping shit, Candy. A man is supposed to give up the *dick,* not the foot. This shit needs to be said, and somebody gotta have enough heart to say it."

Peaches's coo-coo ass laughed. "Not me!"

"Dom, it's cool," I said. "C'mon, chill. It's cool."

"See, that's your biggest problem, Candy. You and Vonnie are willing to do *anything* and accept *anything* just to be down with all this shit. You out here cutting records and getting your ass cut at the same time! I don't give a fuck how much money some three-hump chump got. If he beats his wifey, then he ain't no real man."

Then she fucked around and threw salt on it.

"In the goddamn bedroom or out."

Hurricane didn't say a word. First he turned and gave me a killer look like I had betrayed him. A look that said I musta been running my mouth and talking shit about his little-ass dick. Then he leaned back and signaled to Long Jon, and the next thing I knew the limo was pulling over to the curb and niggahs was dragging Dominica out. They was throwing man-blows at her too. My girl was screaming and reaching for Vonnie and me. I was screaming too, crying and trying to hold on to her. Vonnie was fighting both of us off, trying to stay her ass up in the whip.

Dominica hit the concrete and dragged me with her. I landed halfway on top of her and skinned both my knees on the pavement. My dress had ripped halfway down the back and my coat was still in the car. Joog slammed the door closed and the limo sped off, leaving me and Dom laying in the middle of the cold street.

Dom got up first, then helped me.

We were somewhere on the Lower East Side of Manhattan, near the projects where Dom used to live when she was in foster care. She made me take off my jewelry and let her put it in her pocket. We walked around the corner in the cold to the train station, arguing all the way.

"Fuck that, Candy," she just kept saying as she wiped blood off her busted lip. "Don't go back to his ass. Ain't no contract or no career worth all this. Get Caramel away from that maniac and come to my place. Ya'll can both stay in Brooklyn with me."

Then she got mad because I wouldn't agree. "Just watch, Candy. That motherfucker is gonna *kill* you."

I turned on her. "Dom, I can't just up and leave like that! It's not just about the contract neither. Hurricane got my life in his hands. Remember, I lost my mother behind this shit. I gotta make it work. Plus, I got Caramel to think about too. When the time is right for me to leave, believe me, I'll know it."

I was cold and my teeth was chattering. Dom still had on her coat. She helped me hobble my aching bones down the stairs to the train station, fussing me out in English and in Spanish. We looked real stupid sneaking on the train in designer dresses and heels, but we did it. I went under the turnstile first, and Dom was right behind me. Dom screamed when I bent over, and I whirled around to face her.

"WHAT THE FUCK HAPPENED TO YOUR BACK?!"

I couldn't even speak. I just didn't know how to explain.

The guy in the token booth looked up at us and went right back to reading his newspaper.

"It's a long story," I said finally.

Dom put her finger under my chin and made me raise my head to look at her, and I saw so much pain in her eyes.

"C'mon," she said, hugging me first, then pulling me toward the downtown side of the tracks. "I don't give a fuck what you say, Candy. I love you, but your head ain't on straight, girl. That means you staying in Brooklyn tonight."

The downtown A train was coming and we rushed down the steps. A Saturday-night crowd was waiting on the platform. I was freezing and wishing my coat had made it out of the limo with me. I couldn't wait for the train to come so I could get next to some heat. We stood on the edge of the platform and looked down the track into the black hole of the tunnel, and I was thankful to see headlights in the distance and hoped we could both get seats.

Dom was still running hot. She didn't even care about my black eye no more. Now she couldn't stop ranting about my back. She said it looked like one of those Greek brands that college boys in fraternities sported on their arms. She was steady talking shit about Hurricane and how I needed to leave him. She told me I needed to get Caramel out of that mansion and hide out in a homeless shelter until I could get back on my feet. She could get a list of them, she said, and she was sure there were some for battered women in secret locations with security and all that to protect beat-up women and their kids.

It seemed like one second she was standing next to me with her hand on her hip, making noise and laying out a plan for my escape, and the next second was a blur. The A train whooshed by and Dom was gone.

Somebody screamed.

People at the far end of the platform started hollering as the train squealed to a stop.

For a moment I truly didn't know what had happened. I looked toward the front of the train where everybody was pointing. A man who had been waiting stood stock-still. He looked like somebody had splashed him with a whole bucket of blood. Two transit cops came running, one fat, the other one skinny. A white lady pointed and screamed, "Her head! Her head!" and that's when I saw Dom's shoe. It was a red Luichiny pump. It had been knocked off her foot and was laying on the platform about fifteen feet in front me.

I sank down to my knees. "No," I whispered, clutching my stomach as the conductor got off the middle of the train and ran toward the front. People were hauling ass down the platform to see what had happened. The skinny little transit cop was leaning over next to a bench vomiting. I watched him stagger and sit down as even more people rushed past him. It was gonna take more than just his partner to hold back that crowd.

"No," I whispered again, reality trying to sink in on me

while I tried my best to keep it away. And then somebody was grabbing me by the arm, yanking me to my feet. I panicked. The uptown train was coming in on the opposite track and I just knew my ass was gonna go flying off the platform next.

"Yo, Candy," Omar said, hauling me up, looking crazy as fuck. He was one of them niggahs who had just punched us out of the limo. I stared up at him, scared shitless and shaking harder than I ever had in my life. My eyes darted around looking for help or someplace to run, but his fingers clamped down on my arm and dug in until it hurt. "Let's dip, ma. Hurricane want'chu."

◆ ◆ ◆

Omar yanked me out of that train station, hemmed up by the collar. The commotion was unreal, and transit cops and travelers were so busy running downstairs to the platform to see what had happened that not one person seemed to notice that my ass was being jacked or stopped to ask me if I was okay.

He jerked me up and dragged me up the steps and out of the underground station. Before we were outside good the winter air was cutting my ass in four different directions. Omar was so tall he had me walking on my tippy toes. I focused on keeping my balance and feeling the icy cold penetrate my body, trying my best to push that last crazy image of Dom from my mind.

Omar pulled me around a corner, and the second I saw Hurricane coming toward me I knew he had lost his mind and there was no point in trying to run. He was walking down the middle of the street holding a huge black gun in his hand. He was swinging his arm naturally, like carrying his shit out in the open like that was the normal thing to do.

He stepped up on me and swung hard, knocking the shit out of me with that gun.

My head wrenched to the left, and I staggered and lost one of my shoes.

At first the side of my face flashed real hot, then it went numb. Blood trickled from my cheek and hit my bare shoulder.

"Please!" I tried to scream, but I couldn't feel my lips. "I didn't tell her!" Hurricane bashed me upside the head with the gun again. Over and over and over. I fell against a car and tried to cover my head. He snatched a fistful of my hair and slammed my face down on the hood. He whipped me with that pistol in pure silence. New Yorkers walked past us and looked over for a quick second, then kept it right on moving. Minding their business and staying the fuck out of Hurricane's.

By the time he was finished whipping my ass I had crawled all over the hood of that car. It was a light blue Mercury whoopty and it was smeared with my blood. Hurricane was breathing hard, but I was barely breathing at all. My throat wouldn't even open up so I could get enough air. Hurricane wiped his mouth with the back of his bloody gun hand and spoke in a deadly whisper.

"Trifling bitch," he told me. "Your ass is MINE. No matter how far you run, I will find your black ass and stomp it all the way in. I could push you off a roof and wouldn't nobody give a fuck. You could drown in a motherfuckin' swimming pool, and won't nobody come looking for you. You could disappear down that street gutter right fuckin' now, and wouldn't nobody say a word. You mine, Candy, and can't nobody save you. Believe that."

As bad as I was bleeding he made me climb my ass back in

that limo full of niggahs and ride with them to the banquet. They was all partying and conversating like nothing had even happened. I had never been more hurt in my life. I could barely see out my eyes, but I busted Vonnie grinning when she saw how fucked up I was. I was gonna snatch that fuckin' smile off her face when I told her Dominica was dead, but when I tried to scoot closer so I could tell her, she held up her hand and hollered, "Eeew! Watch it 'fore you get that blood on my fuckin' dress!" Then she hopped her ass over on the other seat and snuggled up next to Hurricane. I turned around toward Caramel, but she just kept partying and wouldn't even look at me.

By the time we pulled up outside the awards center I was sitting there shivering and holding two handfuls of warm, sticky blood. More was seeping through my fingers and had dripped down into my lap.

Hurricane got out the limo with his crew and told Butter to ride with me back to the mansion and to make sure I stayed my black ass there.

"Yo, Cane. You'on't want me to run her by Harlem hospital real quick or nuthin', do you? I mean, it look like shawty here could use a needle and a lil' thread."

Hurricane shook his head. "Fuck a hospital. That ain't nothing but a little scratch. Take that bitch straight back to the house and let Teema or one of them pour some alcohol over it and put a Band-Aid on that shit."

Vonnie glanced back at me as she was climbing out the whip behind him. Her sneaky ass was shooting bullets at me from the slits of her eyes. "Hurricane . . . ," she sang in a little girl's voice. "Guess what I saw that crab doing one time, Hurricane."

She threw me a slick little grin. "Wait till I tell you who Candy was getting live with. . . ."

I held myself together all the way back to Long Island, but the minute Fatima opened the door and saw me holding my bloody face she screamed so loud that I started crying too.

"GirlwhatthefuckhappenedtoyourgoddamnFACE??"

I cried through my hands but wouldn't move my fingers so she could see.

"Oh, shit, Candy," she moaned, dragging me toward a guest bathroom by my arm. "Girl, you gotta let me see it. You gotta let me help you!" She stopped near an intercom in the hall and pushed the TALK button. "Sicily! Candy is hurt real bad. Get your ass down to the hall bathroom right fuckin' *now*!"

All I could do was cry as Teema peeled my fingers away from my face. It wasn't numb no more, and as soon as I let go, it felt like my whole cheek fell open.

"Ooooh," Teema moaned. Sissy peeked over her shoulder and the look in their eyes scared me so bad I swore right then that I'd never again look in the mirror.

"What the hell happened?" Sissy wanted to know.

I sniffled and clenched my teeth, trying to talk without moving my face. "Hurricane beat me."

"Well what the fuck did he beat you *with*?"

More tears fell from my eyes. "His gun."

Sissy shook her head and I saw tears in her eyes too. "That shit needs stitches, Teema. We need to get her to the hospital."

I thought about Dominica and waved my hand, no. "He . . . he said no hospital. I can't leave the house." I was so scared my mouth was dry. Right now Vonnie was probably telling Hurricane she'd seen me and Knowledge messing around outside of Studio D. Vonnie wasn't nothing but a shark on a hunt, and tonight she had smelled blood. If she thought telling on me would get her where she wanted to be with Hurricane, she'd sell my ass out in a hot second.

If Teema and Sissy had acted shitty and cutthroat to me in the past, I had to forget about it for the present. Right now they were there for me. Concerned about me and feeling for me in my fucked-up situation. I sat on the toilet and closed my eyes and let their hands go to work. They were gentle and soft as they washed my face with warm water and used Q-tips to put some Neosporin on my wound, then closed it the best they could by using a whole box of Steri-Strips.

When they were done my face was burning but at least it wasn't hanging open anymore. I had to hold a tissue right underneath my right eye to catch my tears, or else the bandage they put on woulda been pure soaked. As Sissy and Teema threw away the bloody gauze and Q-tips, I dropped the big bomb on them.

"Dominica is dead," I said quietly.

Teema grabbed my shoulder. "Bitch, stop playing."

I wished I was.

I told them how Dom had based on Hurricane in the whip, calling him out about my black eye, and how Omar and all them had punched her straight out of the limo and I fell out with her. How one minute she was standing there screaming on me on the platform, and the next minute she was a blur flying in front of the train.

"Omar pushed her," I whispered.

Sissy grabbed her chest when I said his name. "That junkie-ass fiend. You lucky he didn't push your ass too. Dominica musta been crazy though, talking to Cane like that. Why the fuck didn't y'all run?"

I looked down at the floor. Run? Run where? My situation was what it was. No matter where I ran, some damn body was gonna hunt me down like a dog and make my ass sorry I even tried.

Chapter 24

Working That Magic

Out in L.A., things had gone very well for both Knowledge Graham and Paddy Gabriano. The case had been well publicized, and prior to Knowledge's arrival, most people felt Paddy Gabriano had already been tried and convicted in the media.

For any other attorney, taking over in the middle of such a high-profile trial would have been terrifying and almost impossible. But on the morning of his first day in the courtroom Knowledge had introduced himself to the prosecuting counsels with a twinkle in his eye. One of their lead attorneys had taken one look at the well-dressed, handsome attorney from New York City and recognized him instantly. He'd thrown his hands up and run his fingers through his hair in frustration. With the Johnnie Cochran of tax law on the scene, the prosecution's case was about to be sliced to shreds.

Court TV canceled its scheduled programming and sent a team to cover every minute of the case. Reporters flocked to the courthouse in such large numbers that seating was limited and they could only be admitted by drawing a ticket from a random lottery.

Knowledge's mind went on whir and stayed there for weeks. He navigated, examined, and exploited every possible tax code and RICO law on the books. He knew them all intimately and used them to slice into the weakening prosecution like they were sharp weapons. He attacked and cross-examined their witnesses relentlessly, forcing them to trip over their words and recant their sworn statements and leaving them dazed and confused as they hobbled off the witness stand.

On Knowledge's fifteenth day in the courtroom, the case went to the jury. Deliberations lasted all of four hours. The courtroom was jammed with reporters and spectators as the members of the jury filed into their box. Knowledge looked around the courtroom and noted the slump in the district attorney's shoulders. *Good,* he thought, because losing this case was not an option for him. Knowledge understood the stakes involved. If he lost in this courtroom, he lost it all.

As the jury foreman stood before the judge and prepared to read the charges and their resulting verdicts, the entire courtroom went silent. Knowledge sat there too cool, neither exhibiting nor experiencing the slightest bit of stress.

"On the charge of racketeering, we the jury, find the defendant . . . not guilty.

"On the charge of federal tax evasion, we the jury, find the defendant . . . not guilty. . . ."

By the time the foreman was finished, Paolino "Paddy" Gabriano had been found not guilty on all charges. His team of defense attorneys was ecstatic, smiling and congratulating one another with claps on the back. The aging man reached over and hugged Knowledge close to his breast.

"I'm amazed, but you done good, son," he said. "My arms will forever embrace you. Whatever you want. It's yours."

Knowledge's expression never changed. There was no amount of money he would have taken for this defense. The fact that he'd won the case was all the leverage he needed. He could call Candy and go back to New York now because he'd done exactly what he'd set out to do. He'd walked into that courtroom under the arm of a conniving, sadistic Harlem kingpin, and walked out Mob-loved and Mob-protected. In the eyes of the Gabrianos, he was ten times more valuable than Hurricane.

◊ ◊ ◊

Knowledge pulled into the parking garage of the five-star hotel where he'd been staying since he'd come to L.A. As usual, he skipped valet parking and eased his rented Benz into a parking stall on the lower level of the garage.

He had specifically requested a second-floor suite, and he mentally calculated his next few moves as he walked toward the stairwell. He'd just had lunch with Paddy Gabriano, who had almost laughed when Knowledge revealed his asking price for defending him at trial.

"You sure you're up for that?" The old man had spread his hands. "You already have the family's protection for the rest of your life. Wouldn't you like a yacht? Some gold buillon? How about we front you a nice little hotel in Vegas?"

Knowledge had shaken his head. He'd made his request, and now all he needed was Paddy's word. That would be enough for him.

"Okay," Paddy conceded as he sniffed an Italian cigar. He stuck out his tongue and licked the length of it before biting the tip and sparking the end. "Hurricane goes down, then. He's becoming a pain in my ass anyway . . . screwing around with shipments, lifting arms from my trucks." He nodded and puffed on his cigar. "Oh yeah. I know all about that. I've known he was skimming ever since he cracked into the first crate. Guns have a way of showing up in odd places, you know. No offense, Percy, but I've never met a nigger who wouldn't hang himself if he was holding a long enough piece of rope."

Knowledge just stared at the old man.

Paddy sat back in his chair. "Business can't suffer behind this, you know."

"Yeah," Knowledge said. "I'll be on top of it. Things'll be hot for a minute. Maybe a week. But your customers are loyal, Mr. Gabriano. Demand is always high. Your cut's gonna be fatter than ever once the supply starts flowing again."

Paddy nodded. "And this girl?"

Knowledge's face hardened. "Nothing about her is negotiable."

Paddy puffed his cigar. The young man sitting before him had smarts *and* balls, and he liked that. The family could use a few guys like him, and if Percy had been born Italian instead of black he could have had a lucrative career as a mobster. It was a good thing he'd won the trial, though, Paddy mused. He'd had a triggerman trailing him the entire time, and if the verdict had come back guilty this talented young man would have been dead by now. "Fine," he finally agreed. "She's yours. You have my word."

Knowledge shook his head again. "No, Mr. Gabriano. She does not belong to me. She owns her own life. She's free."

The old man shrugged. "Fine. However you want it. She's free."

○ ○ ○

As he walked toward the stairwell Knowledge reviewed the next phase of his plan. There were several tasks on his agenda that had to be dealt with before he caught a flight heading east, and if he slipped up with his timing in the slightest he knew Candy could be dead before he could make it back to Harlem. He was sliding his key card through the stairwell's entry lock when the door was pulled opened and he was snatched inside.

"Stay easy," the gunman warned. Knowledge recognized him from the courtroom. He had "Mob killer" written all over him. He'd sat in the section reserved for the family of the defendant, and Knowledge had known exactly why he was there. What he didn't know was why the thugsta on the ground was there with him. Slumped in the corner with a bullet hole in his forehead and a trickle of blood flowing down the middle of his face.

Knowledge stared as the gunman waved his silencer-equipped Glock at the thug in the corner. "He's been on you for days," the mobster said, and Knowledge understood. He'd known about this Italian man. The Gabriano man. If the wrong verdict had come back it would have been him slumped over in the corner with a bullet in his head instead of this thug.

But the thug gangsta on the ground . . . Knowledge studied the corpse. Its gear and its style. This kid was all East Coast. Straight out of Harlem. Hurricane-sanctioned and Hurricane-sent. Knowledge took it all in, and shit got as clear as spring-water. If he'da lost the trial, the Mob would've hit him. But if he'd won . . . then it was supposed to be Hurricane's man right here who snuffed him out.

Knowledge nodded at the Italian hit man, then stepped past the dead body and headed up the stairs. He knew exactly what to do when there was heat on his back. He'd have to call the hotel desk and extend his stay. He'd also have to call Jadeah and make sure Candy was cool. He'd need at least a few more days to do everything that needed to be done. Hitting Hurricane where it hurt had always been part of his plan. But after today, wiping him out—no, totally annihilating his ass would be a more accurate term.

That courtroom glare was back in Knowledge's eye, and his brain clicked into whir. The first order of business was to see about Candy. Then he'd have to find an obscure little Internet café or maybe a public library. He'd need uninterrupted time and just a little privacy to access all of Hurricane's accounts. He thought about the financial nooks and crannies where his boss's funds had been stashed, and began adding a twist to his original plan. There were hundreds of accounts he'd have to consider. Some he'd bulk up and leave a trail that the feds couldn't possibly miss. Others he'd tap into and divert offshore under a few dummy names. Whatever he did, at the end of the day it would all bear out the same. Knowledge Graham and those he rolled with were going to be set. And Hurricane Jackson, that half-ass pimp and niggah out of pocket, would be all out of money. And more important, he'd be all out of time.

Chapter 25

Lights, Camera, Action!

Grief was kicking my ass.

First Mama and now Dominica.

I don't remember taking off my torn dress or crawling up the stairs and climbing into Hurricane's bed. I do remember having a nightmare about Dominica and crying out loud during the night. Dom had been my one true friend. The only somebody I could count on to love me no matter what, even more than my own sister did. That thing hurt me, I ain't gone lie. Knowing Dominica had never hurt anyone in her life and that I'd never see her again was like a knife in my heart. Ripping all the way through my back.

Sometime in the night I heard the bedroom door slam. My heart thumped and I was instantly on alert, even with my eyes closed. Somebody laughed and tripped over a shoe or something, and then Hurricane was hollering my name. "Candy!" Just the sound of that niggah's footsteps put fear in my heart. "Get up outta my fuckin' bed, Candy."

I pushed the covers off and sat up, hoping that big-ass bandage covering half my face would make him feel a little sympathy for me.

Not even.

"There's two kinds of bitches I can't tolerate, Candy," Hurricane explained after I had climbed out the bed and was standing in front of him in my panties and nightgown. "Bitches who talk too fuckin' much and bitches who ain't got no gratitude."

I stood there shaking so bad my damn knees kept kissing. I didn't know if he was gonna hit me again or find something to rape me with. I caught myself hoping it would be a rape because I didn't have it in me to take another ass-whipping tonight.

"Take my shit off," he commanded. "Strip outta that two-hundred-dollar tease-towel, and give up that thong too."

I didn't know where he was going, but I knew where I'd end up. Humiliated. Humiliated and in some kind of pain. That was Hurricane's MO. It was the only thing his twisted ass could do with a woman.

With my stuff on the floor, I stood in front of him naked and waiting.

"Get out my house," he said. It came out so low I wasn't sure I had heard him right. I knew good and damn well I hadn't heard him right.

"Huh?"

He said it again. "The front door, Candy. You don't appreciate the shit you got going here with me, then roll, baby. You let that stupid-ass jawn talk shit about your man. You lucky you ain't go down with her. I bet that bitch ain't tell you she sucked my dick, did she? Nah, I bet she ain't tell you that."

I knew that was a lie. Tears swelled in me again, and at that moment if somebody had'a passed a sistah a gun, I would have killed Hurricane on the spot. There was no way that Dom had sucked Hurricane's little baby dick. First of all, she was my friend, and second of all, Hurricane was too ashamed to let somebody like Dom see his half-a-joint. Forget about sucking it.

"What about my sister?"

He grinned and looked toward the lounge area. Caramel was slumped on the couch with her knees up, wearing one of my silk gowns. She looked high as hell, but at least she had enough pity on me to take the gown off and toss it my way. "I'm staying right here," she drawled like she was coming up out of a nod. "You don't do . . . shit for me, Candy. Roll bitch . . . roll."

"Caramel . . . ," I begged slipping the gown over my head. "Mellie, please. Come go with me," I cried.

And that's when he hit me.

That maniac snatched me so fast I lost my breath. My chest hurt so deep I coughed and moaned, but then I started fighting. Hurricane was yanking me toward the door by my arm, but I wasn't leaving my sister.

I grabbed that fucker with both hands and snatched a bunch of hairs off his chest. His eyes got little and he slammed his fist into my face, and the next thing I knew I was on the floor and that niggah had me by the gown, dragging me out the room and down that long-ass hall, out of the middle.

"Caramel!" I fought and screamed, my arms and legs waving in the air like a damn crab, the skin on my back tearing and burning as he dragged me along the cold floor. "CARAMEL, HELP!"

My silk gown was up around my neck, and now it slid right

over my head and left me butt-ass naked again. That didn't bother Cane. He flung that five-hundred-dollar bad boy on the floor like it was a toilet bowl rag, then grabbed me by the hair and turned back around and started pulling me outta there caveman-style.

My scalp was on fire. I tried to use my feet to scoot backward. I needed to keep up with him to put some slack in my hair because my head felt like a cannon had hit it. That niggah looked back at me and just got meaner. He started pulling me in a swivel motion, slinging me from side to side, wall to wall as I begged him to let go of my hair. The only sounds in the whole house were his grunts and my screams. By the time he got me to the foyer I was slobbering in pain and I just knew I was bald.

I was praying out loud for somebody to come and get this niggah off of me when Hurricane opened that front door and rolled me out like I was an old carpet. The ground was so cold and wet I forgot my pain and fear. I was trying to get on my feet when I heard the door slam behind me.

I straightened up and clutched myself, standing under the awning and crying as I looked out at what was now my world. It had started snowing and everything was white. I had nowhere to go and nobody I could call. The nearest neighbor was at least a mile away, and I knew I'd never make it without something on my feet. The wind blew a mist of soft snow over me and I shivered like I'd been hit with ice water. With my arms crossed over my titties, I dragged the doormat with me and squatted down to huddle in the corner near the front door. At least my back and one side of my body was protected from the bite of the wind and my feet were up off the concrete. I closed my eyes and thought about all the cold nights I'd spent snuggling up with Caramel on a filthy mattress. Instead of learning from our shitty childhood she had turned her back on me like we wasn't blood, and none of the hard times we had gone through together even mattered. I thought about Mama, and how even when she thought she'd been schooling me and preparing me for the game of life, she hadn't taught me half of the things I needed to know the most. And you know I thought about Dominica. My girl. Fucking slaughtered. That thing hurt my heart so bad . . . so bad. I wouldn't let myself think about Knowledge. About that good thing in his heart that had me loving him so much. I couldn't let myself think about how deliciously he loved me back either.

I don't know how long I stayed there, squatting on the ground and shivering in the bitter cold. I didn't know how long I could last out there butt naked, the same way I had come in this world. I know I had stopped crying though. I was hurting too much for tears, and them shits were useless anyway.

I didn't even move when I heard the door creak open. My teeth were clicking together and ice was on the tip of my nose. Hurricane musta thought I would be banging down the door by now, but he had tormented me and tortured me enough. I'd stay my ass right here and freeze to death before I gave that motherfucker one more ounce of satisfaction.

"Candy!" I heard somebody call me, then Peaches peeped her head out the door. "Get your ass back in here, girl! All them niggahs 'sleep!"

Peaches had to help me stand up. My body was so cold and stiff I could barely feel my legs or my feet. "Here," she said, and threw a housecoat over my shoulders. I didn't even feel it on me as I dragged my frozen feet across the floor.

Peaches snuck me into her bedroom and put a pile of blankets on the bottom of her junky-ass closet. Long Jon was in the bed snoring, so she worked quietly and in the dark. Peaches dressed me just like I was a baby. She put me in a pink sweat suit and pulled a pair of thick tube socks on my feet, and I crawled my ass under the covers in that walk-in closet most gratefully. The last thing I remember seeing was Peaches closing the closet door, and then there was nothingness and I was out.

○ ○ ○

I couldn't tell you how many hours I slept in that closet. However many it was, it wasn't long enough. I woke up with my whole body banging, especially my cheek. I didn't even realize where I was until I rolled over and felt one of Long Jon's boots. My side was hurting. I was laying on a hanger, and I pulled it from under me and bent the hook part back until it was straight. Just in case.

I didn't hear any noise coming from the room and I was scared to open the door and let Long Jon find me. I had to pee, though, so I twisted the knob silently and pushed the door until there was a tiny crack.

"Come on out," Peaches said flatly. "Ain't nobody in here except me."

I limped out of the closet, too sore to stand up straight. Peaches was sitting cross-legged in the middle of her unmade bed.

"Can I use your bathroom?" I asked. My mouth was swollen

and tasted like old blood. Peaches nodded, and when I went inside, I didn't let myself look toward the mirror. I didn't even wanna see all the damage that had been done to me.

When I came out the bathroom Peaches was still sitting there.

"Thanks for letting me in last night," I said, "but I gotta go get my sister."

"Queen Asia is pregnant," Peaches stated flatly. "I'm about to be somebody's goddamn grandmother."

I thought about Caramel again and my whole body sagged. I felt real bad for Asia being pregnant, for real I did. But that was something she could take care of if she wanted to. Abortions were still legal and that was her option. But Caramel, on the other hand, could be in permanent trouble. At this very moment she was laying up with Hurricane, and no matter how dumb she was or how fucked up she'd been treating me, she was still my sister and I had to get her away from him.

"Do you know whose baby it is?" I asked. It was the only thing I could think of to say.

Peaches looked at me with death in her eyes. "Hurricane's."

"Nah." I shook my head. "I doubt it," I said, grabbing my hanger and moving toward the door. " 'Cause that niggah's dick don't even reach."

◊ ◊ ◊

I opened that door and got straight bum-rushed.

It felt like forty hands had snatched me, and I started swinging and stabbing with my hanger in every direction. That crazy bitch Peaches had set me up. At least that's what I thought at first. And then I saw her man Long Jon. He was standing against the wall laughing as they bent my ass down to the floor.

"You fittin' to get fucked!" he said as I tried to jig my hanger in some eyeballs. "And that niggah Knowledge?" He laughed again. "Don't worry about him. He ain't comin' back." I started scratching and spitting. Rolling and dipping. Doing whatever I could do to defend myself. I stabbed somebody in the arm with my hanger. He hollered and capped my face.

Then they stretched me out, and about four of Hurricane's flunkies held on to my feet. I was cursing and twisting, and it took a minute before I realized what they were trying to do. I was still wearing Peaches's sweat suit and they were trying to get my sleeve up.

I started scratching at their hands, and then that fat-necked Butter got me. He plopped his soft stank ass right down in my face, muffling my screams and cutting off my breath.

"Hold your stupid ass still," he said, with his funky nuts bending my wrist back until I moaned and dropped the hanger. "Gimme the shit," he told somebody, squeezing my arm. A second later I felt a sharp prick on the inside of my elbow, then a burning sensation. Don't ask me what happened after that because my ass went out.

◇ ◇ ◇

Time went by in crazy snatches.

Action!

Turn over! Open your legs! That's right. Get it girl.

Cameras. Hot lights. Thirsty.

My pussy got licked. I liked it.

So tired!

Hard nipples and niggahs laughing.

Predator on the bed. Asia. Caramel!

Don't wanna.

Shoot her again.

Action! XXX!

Hurricane. Cameras. Bright flashes.

Moaning. Licking.

Fucking.

Sucking.

Barking!

Crying. My asshole hurts.

Shoot her again. Give the bitch more this time.

Nipples hard. Damn. She's sucking them just right.

Ooooh, shit, yeah. I'm cumming!

Niggahs laughing.

Roll that video!

Her pussy stanks. My face is in it.

Hurricane. So thirsty.

Asia. Predator. She gone lose that baby.

Stop, Caramel! Don't be touching me like that!

Please, no more.

Cameras.

Hurricane. Shoot that bitch again.

Action!

Hot lights. Need more film.

Knowledge! Where you at?

Shoot that bitch again.

Pussy on fire! Yeah . . . fuck me, Poppa.

Shoot that bitch again.

Cut!

Darkness. Tired.

Darkness.

Darkness. . . .

◆ ◆ ◆

A bomb exploded inside my left nostril and I grabbed my whole face.

I couldn't focus my eyes, and darkness tried to settle down on me once more.

"Ow!" That niggah dug up in my nose again and it hurt so bad I rose straight up outta my fog. The inside of my nostril was throbbing. My eyes were wide open now. Blood was on his fingernail and running down my top lip.

We were in the video room at the House of Homicide. How I had gotten there, I couldn't tell you. I was laying facedown on a cot, naked and thirsty. Hurricane was chilling on a director's chair right next to me, and Caramel was sitting on the floor between his legs, wearing just a torn, dingy bra and resting her head in his lap.

"You're a natural, Candy," he said as I tried to sit up. "You got real skills in front of the camera, ma." He laughed and nodded toward a large movie screen on the right wall. I turned my head and there I was. Ass to the wind. Live and on the big screen. I put my head down on the bed and closed my eyes.

"Open your eyes," Hurricane said, mushing me with his whole hand. He pushed Caramel off of him and she grinned and thunked to the floor. Her eyes were open but she wasn't seeing much of nothing. For the very first time I saw the track marks on her arms.

Hurricane climbed on the bed and straddled me. He sat on my back and yanked my head back. "Keep them blue eyes open so you can see. You wanted to be a big star, right? Well, check out the screen 'cause there you go!" He laughed again. "All those magazine covers? Out! All them endorsements I had lined up for your silly ass? Out!"

He pulled on my hair and forced me to watch. Me. Asia. Caramel. Three buck-ass niggahs. A dick-sucking contest. Butter with his joint up my ass. Niggahs shooting all in my hair. Me doing Caramel. Caramel doing Asia. Asia doing the dog. I wanted to throw up and die.

"What you crying for, girl?" Hurricane teased. "Yeah, your singing career is over, but we still gone be making money, though. As fine as your ass is? This shit's gonna sell bigger than R. Kelly! See, a niggah like R. Kelly can lick the assholes of all the little girls he wants and still wake up a superstar. But a sweet little up-and-rising singer like you doing all them freaky thangs. . . . hell, ma. Even the dog got him some."

I didn't say a word. The images playing on the screen were saying enough.

"Now get your ass up and get dressed, Candy."

I didn't move. This was just another one of his games. That niggah wasn't letting me leave and I knew it.

"Get up, Candy. There go your gear." He pointed to Peaches's pink sweat suit laying on the floor. "Right over there. Get your shit on and hit the door. You on your own now, little girl, and don't look to that fuckin' Knowledge for no help 'cause his ass done been handled out in L.A. Matter fact, I just made me a phone call to some crazy Italians on the West Coast, and the next time them Mob motherfuckas roll up on you and throw you in a goddamn trunk, remember who got you out the first time. You lucky I don't toss your ass up in a trunk somewhere myself. Now go."

I pulled that sweat suit on me because I had made up my mind to stay alive. If Hurricane gave me a chance to walk out that door, I was walking. I'd come back for Caramel when I had some wins. I didn't see the socks that Peaches had put on me, but a pair of Asia's turned-over shoes were next to the bed and I hurried up and threw my feet in them.

"What about my sister?" I had to ask. Caramel had crawled her tail back up into Hurricane's lap and nodded off into la-la land.

Hurricane reached over and slapped my sister on her naked ass. "Oh, this jawn?" He laughed. "This me. I'm putting her fine red ass dead in the middle."

◆ ◆ ◆

I bust out the door and ran down the streets of Harlem until it felt like my chest would explode, and even then I didn't stop. I slowed down to a fast walk, trying to shake off the panic that was in me and clear my head so I could think.

I couldn't believe he'd let me out. Yeah, I'd left Caramel back there, but there wasn't a damn thing I could do for her in my condition. But as soon as I got me straight I would go back and help my sister.

Knowledge had told me that if I got in trouble while he was gone, to go to Jadeah. I wasn't sure I could trust her, but I trusted my man to the bone, and if he thought Jadeah was down, then I'd just have to take that chance.

I saw a Spanish store on the corner and went inside and

asked to use the phone. The man at the counter took one look at my busted up face and handed me his cell. I dialed the front office at the House of Homicide and Jadeah picked up on the second ring.

"Homicide Hitz, can I help you?"

"Yeah, Jadeah," I said, trying not to cry. "I really hope you can."

◈ ◈ ◈

She met me down on 125th Street. I told her to come to a braid salon, but I was hiding near a store that sold halal foods, just in case she flipped on me and sent some of Hurricane's boys instead. I watched her go into the braid place and say a few words to the Africans who worked there. Then she came out looking confused and started walking further up the street. I made myself wait until she had looked in almost every store on the block, and only when she went back into the braid shop for the second time and started arguing with the owner did I come out of my hiding spot.

"Jadeah," I called to her from the doorway. "I'm right here."

She whirled around. "Where were you?" Then she saw my bruises and the cut on my face, and her eyes changed. "Oh my God," she whispered. "Not again, Candy."

She pulled me by the arm and we went into a pizza shop. Who knew the last time I had eaten, and as soon as I smelled that hot pizza I started drooling. Jadeah went up to the counter and ordered us both a slice.

"I want two," I mumbled. "With pepperoni and extra cheese."

When she came back to the table with our order I took two bites of my slice and felt sick. "I can't remember the last time I had something in my stomach," I told her, and covered my mouth with a napkin.

"Don't rush it down," she said. "Drink some soda first and take your time."

Jadeah opened her shoulder bag and took out a rectangular package wrapped in aluminum foil. "Here," she said, passing it across the table to me. "Knowledge called a couple of times asking about you, but I kept telling him that you were cool, chilling at the mansion. I didn't know you were out here getting beat down and abused like this." She nodded at the package. "He left that with me. That man is power, Candy. I don't know what's in it, but I don't have no doubts that it was meant for you."

I held the package in my lap and unwrapped it. Inside I found a thick stack of twenty-dollar bills and two silver keys. I took ten twenties off the top and slid them across the table to Jadeah. "For helping me," I said.

"Uh-uh." She shook her head and slid them right back. "Don't insult me like that, Candy. I know my brother did this to you. He's a evil motherfucker and I know he's responsible for a lot of dirty shit. If there's anything I can do to help you, *anything*. Just let me know."

I thought for a moment, then looked up at her. "Anything?" She twisted her lips. *"Anything!"*

"All right, then," I said, leaning in close. "Check this out . . ."

Chapter 26

Getting Took Down

Knowledge had left me ten thousand dollars in twenty-dollar bills along with the keys to his loft. I tried to call him from Jadeah's cell phone, but his voice mail came on and I had to leave a message.

I left Jadeah on 125th Street. I took a taxi downtown to Knowledge's place and let myself in. The first thing I did was take a long, hot bath. I still couldn't look at my face in the mirror 'cause I was too scared of what I'd see. An hour later I got out of the tub and dried off, then found a T-shirt in a dresser drawer and crawled in the bed.

I stayed up in Knowledge's crib for three days, waiting. No matter what Hurricane had said, I knew my man was alive because I could feel him. I knew he had gotten my message, and I knew he'd come. I didn't turn on the television and I didn't turn on no radio either. I thought a lot. I ate tuna fish and corned beef hash. Ramen noodles and mac and cheese from the box. And I thought some more.

On the afternoon of the fourth day I heard a key turn in the lock. I'd been laying on the couch with my eyes closed, and before the lock could flip I screamed and was off that couch and on the floor, rolling straight up under that bad boy.

"Candy," Knowledge said, rushing into the room. He got down on his knees and pulled me from under the couch and held me in his arms. "It's okay, baby," he said softly. "I'm home. I got here as soon as I could, baby."

I covered my face with both hands, ashamed to let him see what had been done to me. Knowledge kissed my fingers and told me I was beautiful. He whispered this as he pulled my hands gently away from my face. He examined me, getting a good look at the wound that I still hadn't seen.

"I'm ugly," I said, trying to cover my face again.

He shook his head no. "No, you're still you, baby. You'll have a scar, yeah. But so what? We all got 'em. It doesn't have to change who you are."

I thought about that nasty triple X video, and my face started burning, hot with shame. If Knowledge found out about it he might never look at me the same. "My career is over," I said. "Hurricane buried it."

Knowledge shook his head again. "Uh-uh, Candy. We've both been through enough shit in life to know better than that. No shame, no shorts. Whatever happened at that House, baby leave it there. And anything you got one time, you can get it again. But if the career is really over, then let it be gone. Don't never hold on to nothing you can't let go of in a hurry."

I looked up at him, then pulled myself up off the floor. Jadeah had been right on point. Knowledge was power. I walked into the bathroom and faced myself in that mirror, and what I saw was even worse than what I had imagined. *But?* I thought to myself. *And?* Yeah, I was gonna have a real nasty scar, and no, it wasn't going away. But I also had a life. I had a man. And I had a sister. I wasn't going away either.

two days later . . .

Jadeah unlocked the side door and the heavy chain fell to the floor. "Hurry up," she said, pulling it closed behind us.

"Did you turn off the security cameras?" I asked her.

She shook her head. "I tried to shut the system down like you told me, Candy, but I'm not sure I pressed the right keys. Besides, I couldn't stay up in there long. Something crazy is going down that got everybody shook in here tonight."

Knowledge helped her push the chains back through the door handles and snap the heavy padlock back in place.

"Oh yeah?" he said quietly.

Jadeah rolled her eyes. "Hell yeah. The IRS called this afternoon and said they wanna do an emergency audit on all our books. And when I tried to make a withdrawal to take care of the payroll, all I got was dust. Zero dollars and zero cents. Every bank account Ju got is frozen. The bank said something about the record label being seized as assets for his tax liabilities."

Knowledge glanced at me and nodded, then grabbed my hand as we moved into the House.

The pit was live and people were getting down in it. The three of us ran up the back stairs and down the hall, and when Jadeah walked out and signaled that shit was clear, we jetted past the gambling room and VIP Lounge and into the stairwell that led to Knowledge's office.

I was scared as hell, but it made me feel good to know that Hurricane's ass was already handled. He just didn't know it. The feds were about to put him and his entire posse about forty feet up under somebody's jail. All we needed to do now was get the books from Knowledge's safe, then wait while Jadeah went down to the pit and lured Caramel upstairs. We wasn't going for none of Caramel's bullshit either. We'd knock her ass down and drag her out the door behind us if that's what it took, because one way or another my sister was leaving this place to-night.

Knowledge had tried to make me wait for him back at the loft while he came and got Caramel and his books, but you know I wasn't having none of that. First of all, Caramel wouldn'ta left the House with him just because he said so. He woulda had to kill her crazy ass first. And second, I didn't like to fight, but I wasn't nobody's punk neither. If my man was going down into the lion's den, then my ass would be fighting, kicking, and scratching right in there with him.

Jadeah musta done a real shitty job shutting down those cameras because Knowledge had just opened the safe when his door crashed in. Butter, with his cock-strong country ass, kicked that bad boy down on the first try, and if Knowledge hadn't knocked me out the way it would have flattened me to the ground.

I hit the floor hard with my man spread out on top of me, protecting what was his to the end. I heard about thirty clicks, and when I opened my eyes I was looking down the barrel of so many gats I just gave up and closed them again.

How they'd managed to sneak up that flight of stairs without making a sound beat me. But how me and Knowledge got back down those stairs wasn't hard to figure out. They dragged us down together, both of us scrappin' like prime roosters in a country cockfight.

Knowledge was handling his with Snake and Long Jon. Both of their wife-beating asses fought like pussies, and even though they had him two against one, my baby still had the wins.

Vince and Butter were on me. Butter was trying to pull me up by the hair, but I was locked on to his ankles like a prison bracelet. He bent over and punched me in the face, and I pulled his feet forward and made that chunky, corn-bread-eating nig-grow come down right along with me. He got me in a headlock and I politely reached up and stuck my finger straight up his nose. Before he knew it I was doing like Hurricane had done me, trying to poke a hole dead through that membrane between his nostrils. Tears fell out his eyes as I dug my nail tip all up in his sinuses.

Butter screamed and bucked just like a little bitch, sending us both toppling down the stairs head over feet. By the time we hit the bottom I was back on his ankles again, and no matter how hard he tried to kick me, I wouldn't let go.

We fought out to the vestibule, and Butter started kicking at the banister with his free leg. If he thought I had been holding on before, my ass was a part of him now. I saw what he was trying to do. Sling my ass through the banister slats and send me flying down into the pit.

It wasn't gonna happen. Not unless he broke his leg off so I could take it with me.

Hurricane was sitting in the red, crushed-velvet king's chair chewing on a toothpick and enjoying the show—and not the one that was going on down in the pit neither. I looked at him with terror in my eyes and he grilled me. I glanced over and saw Knowledge getting his. He was kickboxing them niggahs like somebody's ninja. I screamed for Knowledge to watch out when I saw Long Jon pick up an iron plant stand, but he didn't hear me. He was too deep in the battle.

Long Jon swung, and I saw blood shoot from the back of Knowledge's head as my baby went down. I was screaming and crying and trying to crawl over to him when Butter grabbed me by the back of my shirt and flung me toward the railing again.

I landed on my back, with my head hanging over the edge of the balcony. I grabbed hold of the slat to my right and it broke all the way off in my hand and fell down below. The one on my left held, but all I could do was stare up as Butter glared down at me with a sweaty face and a bloody nose.

"You trick-ass bitch," he said, then sniffed real deep and ccgg-chewed a clog of hot blood right in my face. "You looked a lot better from the back when I was tapping that ass."

Then Joog ran up the stairs hollering for Hurricane. "Yo, ak! The phones is ringing like crazy in your office, man! Sissy just called from the crib and shit done got hot!"

I glanced up and saw that niggah Joog looking so nervous he was licking his soup coolers like they had pussy-flavored lip gloss on them.

"She said the feds just rolled on the mansion! They got marshals in the crib tossing shit up and saying they gonna padlock every fuckin' door and window in the place before the night is over!"

Hurricane stood up, and for the first time ever I saw fear in his eyes.

His cell phone lit up in a thousand colors, and every eye up there swung toward his belt where it was clipped. He snatched it. "What? . . . Well where the fuck is Tonk? . . . Get the fuck outta here! I got mad protection against that kinda shit!" He breathed real hard. "All right, all right! Tell them mothafuckas to sit tight. I'll be down there in a minnit."

He knew what time it was. The cookie was starting to crumble and the House was about to fall.

Hurricane snapped his phone closed and spoke to his boys, but he was looking dead at Knowledge the whole time. "Tonk got knocked and the supply is bone-dry. Ain't a drop of dope on the streets, and the connects are singing to po-po like a bunch a little bitches."

Snake touched his gun. "Somebody fuckin' wit'chu, boss."

"Yeah," Hurricane said, cocking his .44 and aiming it dead at Knowledge. "It's this grimy motherfucka right here."

And then the sound coming out of the pit changed. Panic rose in the air and the music shut down as people screamed and hollered. Long Jon stepped over Knowledge and peered over the rail. "Oh, shit," he said. "Motherfuckers is down there wildin'."

With his gun still locked on my boo, Hurricane stood up to take a look, and I took my eyes off Butter for a second and turned my head to see too.

Vonnie and Caramel were in the pit throwing down.

Caramel swung a bottle and Vonnie went down.

"A knife!" somebody screamed. "That bitch got a knife!"

People screamed even louder as the crowd went crazy and strangers started swinging on each other as they got hit by stray blows. Long Jon's security team tried to swarm, but they got swallowed up when it got to be every-man-for-himself time and fools started throwing chairs and turning over tables too.

"They fighting!" I screamed up at Hurricane, hoping he cared even a little bit about my sister. "Vonnie stabbed Caramel! They down there fighting!"

Just then a cluster of flares shot up out of the pit. I rolled onto my stomach as they whizzed past my head. They spun through the air real fast, spitting out thick rolls of white smoke and dropping hot silver sparks on the crowd below as people screamed and tried to scatter. A second later another thick cluster shot up. More sparks fell back down into the pit, burning fighting dancers and sending mad niggahs charging toward the exits.

The screams coming from the crowd were agonizing, but security was still yelling over the mic trying to get a grip on the madness. "Chill, chill, chill!" they kept saying, but at that point wasn't no damn body listening. Smoke was clouding the air and it was getting hard to breathe. My nose started burning real bad, and when the next canister shot up Long Jon hollered, "Pepper spray!" And then some fool screamed, "Fire!" and niggahs broke out running in every direction.

"Motherfuck!" Hurricane cursed, and put one hand over his nose. He still had his gat locked on Knowledge, but his boys were looking shaky.

Omar coughed and covered his nose with the neck of his shirt just as Peaches came running up the steps. Hurricane was about to swing his gun on her but checked himself when he realized a red dot was lighting up his chest.

Peaches stepped toward him laughing her crazy ass off. She

held a laser-guided Glock in her hands and every motherfucker up there took notice.

"Who woke this pyscho bitch up?" Hurricane said, and tried to swing his gun her way. But Peaches had him. Still laughing, she squeezed the trigger three times. The first two shots struck Hurricane, one in the chest and the other in the arm. The third one caught Butter in the shoulder as he was bringing his gun up, and it slipped from his hand and fell to the floor.

Hurricane fell like a cut-down tree.

"Peaches, *no!*" Long Jon screamed, and rushed his girl, knocking her over like a bowling pin and covering her with his body. Niggahs was firing and coughing. Coughing and firing. I saw spurts of blood shoot up from Long Jon's back as bullets dotted his shirt. Peaches was laying under him with her arms out at the sides and neither one of them was moving.

Shit started rolling in a cloud of smoke.

I could hear the crowd breaking downstairs. Females crying and screaming and niggahs coughing and kicking at the chained exits as they tried to get the hell out. I woulda been screaming too, except the pepper spray was all in my eyes, stinging like crazy and burning up the lining of my throat.

I tried to get up and run and it felt like a herd of niggahs knocked me back down. Omar, Vince, Joog, Snake, Grip, Das, Quadir pulling Butter—all them hard niggahs had to breathe too, and they ran toward the stairs, one or two leaping over me, but most of them stepping dead on me as they tried to get to the doors and get outside.

And then Knowledge was getting up on his feet. Standing over Hurricane. My baby's head was busted in the back and blood was running down his neck and his shirt.

"Yeah!" he said, picking up Hurricane's .44 and aiming it down at him. I squinted through my eyes as Hurricane tried to wiggle backward like a caterpillar.

"Knowledge . . ." Hurricane panted and coughed, reaching up with his big, powerful hand. "Knowl—"

"Nah, motherfucker," my boo said, cocking that gun with a look on his face that I didn't even recognize. "It's Percy, big brother. Percy Graham Jackson, Jr.!" he said, and fired four times. Hurricane screamed like a bitch as blood spurted from his shattered knees. He sat up and tried to grab his legs, but fell back as Knowledge's last two rounds blew his head into a hot mess of blood and bone. Then Knowledge opened his mouth and spit dead in Hurricane's face. "That's for my mother, you trifling bitch!"

Another canister of pepper spray whizzed up past us and I closed my eyes as it exploded in the air. Thick smoke spiraled outward and choked me, and I thought about my sister hurt and scuffling down in that pit and I tried to draw strength for her. Fuck Hurricane. Knowledge had handled his problem. I still had to go get mine.

"Caramel," I whispered, pulling myself up on my hands and knees as I moved toward the stairs where the smoke was now the heaviest. I hung my head and moaned as my lungs heaved trying to get even a taste of fresh air. "CARAMEL!"

I crawled blind. My instincts wanted me to get up and run the other way, where it was a little bit clearer, but I kept feeling for those stairs because I had to get down into that pit. And then his hands were on me and I was being dragged backward.

"Easy, baby," he said, but I fought and wouldn't give in.

"Trust me, Candy," he begged, coughing himself. "Trust me, baby. Please." Then Knowledge held my hand and turned me around, leading me away from the stairs and back the way I had just come.

With my eyes squeezed tight, I held on to my boo and prayed. Not for me, but for my sister. As I crawled next to him my hand came down on something wet and mushy. When I realized what it was, I choked and almost threw up.

It was Hurricane. My whole hand had mashed through his bloody face. I started spazzing then. Freaking completely out. *Mama,* I wept, tears leaking from my closed eyes. I needed to breathe so bad my bladder let go. *Mama, I need you, Mama . . .*

And then Knowledge was lifting me to my feet. He cradled me in his strong arms and carried me right back up that little flight of stairs that led to his office.

"My sister!" I wailed as I fought against him, my face burning and wet with snot and tears. "MY *SISTER*!"

"Don't worry, baby."

"But the goddamn doors are chained, Knowledge! We trapped up in here!"

He touched my hair. "No, baby. No, we're not."

I shook my head and fought him even harder as he moved me toward the window.

"I ain't jumping, Knowledge! Please. I just can't!"

I felt his lips. They kissed my ear. "That's cool, Candy," he whispered, sliding the glass up and letting the sweet air in. " 'Cause you ain't got to."

Chapter 27

The Power of Knowledge

Knowledge finished scrambling the four eggs in the kitchen of his loft and turned on the television to the Channel 7 news. It had been almost a day and a half since he and Candy had made their escape, and coverage of the massive stampede at Harlem's House of Homicide was dominating the city's airwaves.

Forty-three partygoers are dead, and countless others are wounded. Firefighters, reporters, police officers, and hundreds of spectators swarmed the scene Saturday night when the House of Homicide, the nightclub and recording studio that became a favorite gathering spot of urban entertainment greats like 50 Cent, Nas, Thug-a-licious, and Jay-Z, erupted in a stampede that also claimed the life of record mogul and owner, Junius "Hurricane" Jackson.

Details are still sketchy, but early reports suggest the patrons were the victims of a smoky death trap when a fight broke out between two women on the dance floor commonly known as "the pit." According to eyewitnesses, a bottle was thrown as a weapon, and then a knife was brandished and a victim was repeatedly stabbed. House of Homicide security personnel reportedly attempted to quell the violence by setting off several flares as well as a number of canisters containing a mixture of Mace and pepper spray. As the toxic fumes were released into the air, the resulting panic was magnified by the fact that three of the nightclub's four exits were found to be chained and padlocked and had to be sledgehammered open to extricate the dead and injured.

No new information is available on the status of the hospitalized at this time, and police have not yet been successful at identifying the bodies of at least two young women whose remains still lay unclaimed. Lawsuits are expected to be filed, criminal charges may be pressed, and funerals must be arranged. The Reverends Jesse Jackson and Al Sharpton are expected to make a round of the morning news programs, along with some of the nightclub's survivors. At this time the House of Homicide sits cordoned off with yellow police tape as a makeshift memorial, complete with photos of the dead, candles, carnations, and colorful stuffed animals, all in memory of the young lives that were lost inside.

Knowledge carried the plate into his bedroom where Candy lay still beneath his fur blanket. It had been almost forty hours since she had spoken to him. Forty hours since she had eaten a bite of food, used the bathroom, or taken a sip of water. No matter what he said or did, he couldn't get through to her. She just lay in bed beside him with her eyes half open. Whimpering every now and then as if terrible images were playing out in her mind.

Knowledge put the plate on his night table and sat on the edge of the bed. He pulled her head into his lap, then put a little egg on the fork and pressed it to her lips. Her eyes continued to stare, and she did not respond. Setting the fork back on the plate, Knowledge stroked her hair and cradled her head as he gazed out the window at the New York City skyline.

He had accomplished a big part of his plan, but he still had some business to take care of. Violators who needed to be handled. Them niggahs were living on borrowed time, but only for a little while. The main thing on his mind right now was his Candy, and whether she could make it through all this with her body and mind intact.

Fiji, he said to himself as he pictured a place where he could take her to heal and get away from the madness of this city for a while. *Yeah,* he thought. Fiji, a bunch of tropical Melanesian islands where the natives were friendly and the sun always shined, and no one had ever heard of Hurricane Jackson or the House of Homicide. He reached over and retrieved his portable CD player from the other side of the bed. He plugged in both sets of headphones and put one over her ears and the other over his.

As he pressed PLAY, the smooth, silky voice of Aaron Neville filled both their ears. Knowledge sat there for the longest time. His hands in her hair. Just listening. He was praying too. *Come back to me, Candy. Come on back, baby girl.* An hour or more passed, and then he saw it. Her small reddish-brown hand moving against the whiteness of his blanket. Just one finger. Tapping to Aaron's one-of-a-kind melody.

She'll make it, Knowledge thought, nodding his head to the same beat and watching that one finger move. Yeah, he nodded, smiling to himself. *She's gonna make it.*

And at the end . . .

one year later

The production assistant touched my arm as I stood waiting offstage behind the curtains. "Three minutes," she said, gazing at me like my eyes held the secret combination to some music mogul's treasure chest. She was so black and pretty and her package was so tight she put me right in the mind of Vonnie.

I nodded at her as I did a few practice moves to loosen myself up. This was gonna be my first time back onstage, and I wanted to make sure I brought it right. I was wearing a white back-out shirt and a red-hot pair of JuicyOriginal booty-banging shorts, and despite everything I'd been through, the mic and that stage were calling the hell out of me and my body was ready to answer.

The joint was packed with standing room only. I wasn't playing Madison Square Garden yet, but I planned on getting there one day soon. My hair was laid, my body was stacked with vicious curves, and my vocals were stronger than ever. My fans had turned out expecting a hot show tonight, and I was damn sure gonna give them one.

Almost a year had passed since Knowledge had taken Hurricane and his House of Homicide down. A lot of Harlem diehards had collapsed when Hurricane's empire toppled, but that's how it goes in this game. Some of his boys plain rolled over, and others had gotten knocked by the feds and were doing serious time, but a whole new crew of hungry young heads had smelled an opportunity and crept up on the scene so fast it was unreal.

But the minute Knowledge took control of Harlem he let all that shit go. The drugs, the hoes, the gambling, the stickup kids, the money laundering. He let them niggahs from across town fight it out for control of the streets and kill each other off in the process. All he kept was the recording studio and the new label we co-owned, Power Productions. It was home to twenty new recording artists who were not only mad talented, but they also understood the runnings of the industry and how to win at this music game.

Sometimes as I listened to a hot mixtape or demo, or watched young artists perform on talent night I would catch myself wondering how far me, Dom, and Vonnie could have gone if we hadn't got hooked by a niggah like Hurricane. We probably coulda been the next TLC or Destiny's Child if we hadn't tried to choke ourselves on industry bling and then sold our souls to its number one devil. And don't think I'm just hatin' on a dead playa neither, 'cause I'm not. I'm not even hatin' on the game 'cause it's one that I love, and I know it can only trap you up if you drop your common sense and ignore the rules.

When I look back on my life, I see shit now that nobody could have even *tried* to show me back when I first got in this business. Eager young eyes can't see jack, which is why I had to lose almost everything I loved before I could understand what had always been right there in front of me.

And my sister? What can I say? The truth about Caramel really hurt. Everything about her hurts. Even if she had made it out of the pit alive that night, between the way we'd been raised and the kind of street life we had lived, that bullet she took and that dope Hurricane had her shooting up in her veins . . . my baby sister was just too fucked up for me to save by myself. I had tried my best to love my sister, but no matter how much I wanted to, I just couldn't change her fate.

So Mama, Caramel, Dom, Vonzelle, crazy Peaches, sweet Jadeah . . . all gone. For six whole months I stayed balled up in a knot. Trapped in a bubble of pain that wouldn't let me go. It was music and my man that eventually saved me 'cause they both was in my blood. I still have some pretty heavy moments even today. I mean, that shit still hurts me so bad that sometimes my bones ache with grief, but I can't let myself concentrate on what I lost. I gotta think about what I've found. I gotta do like Hurricane had said at one time. Keep my vision aimed steady on forward, 'cause if I don't, then it'll mean that all their lives got snatched for nothing, and I just couldn't live with that.

My three minutes were up. The music starting booming and the curtains slid back.

Cameras were flashing and the fans were screaming my name before I could get out on the stage good. I came out working it for them too. Rolling my hips and rocking them red shorts like I had sewn them myself. That shy little girl who used to sing into toilet tissue rolls was smiling and dancing and showing the world what a strong black woman was made of. *Hell yeah!* my moves and attitude screamed real loud. *Sistahs like me might*

*get knocked down, but check out how we get our asses the fuck
back up!*

"New York!" I hollered into the mic moving my hips like
I could feel the beat way down deep in the bottom of my
coochie. "How my people doin' out there tonight?"

The stampede at the House of Homicide had made national
news. Fans, ballers, artists, everybody in the music industry
knew the hell I'd been through. All the torture and the ass-
kickings, all that crazy abuse, that nasty-ass triple-X video, the
whole nine. They knew it all and they still respected me, and
now they were making noise, giving me mad love and even
madder energy.

"I said, how y'all *doin'* tonight?!"

Oh, and that video? Damn. New York can be a dangerous
place. Every niggah who was either on that tape fucking me or
had helped Butter and them drug me up and hold me down?
Gone. Dead. Handled. Vince, Omar, Snake . . . It was weird
how every last one of them got caught out there and ended up
dead. The newspapers was saying the killings looked like Mob
hits, but when I asked Knowledge what he thought about it a
hard look came across his face. "Fuck 'em. This is Harlem,
Candy. Violators either pay their dues or get planted."

The crowd was up, up, up. On their feet and making outrageous sounds as the love flowed through the air and rushed all
up on the stage to cover me. I looked front and center and saw
my boo. He was sitting up there looking fine as hell and wearing a proud smile on his face.

Knowledge was my niggah. My rock. My one and only
candy licker.

I knew my baby was a real man because he had used his love to set me free.

"Leave the past in the past," he had told me this morning as he slid his big dick up in me while we were in the shower. "I got your back, Candy," he whispered, kissing my neck and pounding my pussy real slow and deep from behind, just the way I liked it. "But more important, you got the talent and the skills. Remember," he said, pulling his snake out of me and turning me around to face him before dropping to his knees, "no shame, no shorts." He lifted my leg over his shoulder and got ready to do that thang that drove me wild. "It ain't over until you say it is."

Our shit was straight jelling on all fronts these days. Our personal thang was da bomb, and Knowledge wanted me to be his wife. Did you hear me? His wife. Not his damn wifey. There is a difference, you know.

Our business was growing large, contracts were legit, artists were schooled about the industry and making their rightful money. I thought about that production assistant who had led me out to the stage. I'd seen her before on talent night. I recognized that I'll-do-anything-to-be-a-big-star grin she had flashed me. I saw the way she had drooled just looking at that mic. Like it was a big fat silver dick she was dying to suck. Vonzelle the Second! I was gonna have to get with her after the show. Sit her down with some of them other young female artists I was mentoring and put her up on what was real.

The crowd was steady clapping and whistling. They was letting me know I was doing the right thing by saying fuck no to hiding my scars. Fuck all that guilt and shame. It was all out in the open and the crowd was welcoming me home. Telling me they respected me to the max for making a grand comeback from my many mistakes.

"I'm back!" I yelled out to my man Knowledge. "Baby, I'm back!" And then to the rest of the world, "DID YA'LL HEAR THAT SHIT? I'M BACK!!"

No shame, no shorts. The lights flashed and I turned around and dropped it like it was hot. Popping my spine and giving them a good look at my phat ass and that dead niggah's name that I still carried on my back. Then I turned back around and angled my face right at the main camera. *No shame, no shorts.* I pushed my red hair back behind my ear, making sure the cameras had a real clear shot as the stage lights shined their heat down on my zigzag scar. And then I smiled and broke out in my song and worked that whole stage just like Mama had taught me. Worked that shit until the house fell down.

About the Author

NOIRE is an author from the streets of New York whose hip-hop erotic stories pulsate with urban flavor. Visit the author's website at www.asknoire.com or e-mail the author at noire@asknoire.com.